JOEL A. ROBITAILLE

A DOG'S RELIGION

Anne Cowan,

Happy Birthday/Retirement!
Does that mean you're available
to babysit Jenna's child?

Joel Robitaille

Copyright © 2011 Joel A. Robitaille
All Rights Reserved.

ISBN: 146093217X
ISBN-13: 9781460932179

To Cali, with all my love

Special thanks to Dania Sheldon. Without your help I'd be in revision purgatory.

I also express my love and appreciation to my wife, Jenna, for her encouragement and willingness to listen to countless passages; and my father, Glenn, for offering his insightful criticism every stage of the way.

Thanks also to: Hélène Balvay, Desiree Bee, John Buie, Lisa Cameron, Lindsay Clayton, Andrea Cole, Greg Daniel, Cherie Jacobs, Dave Jacobs, Patricia Mannion, Mike Meyer, Matt Moherman, Bob Robitaille, Joshua Robitaille, Bruce Watson, and Digby Wolfe.

CHAPTER 1

Working at the animal shelter has afforded me two observations: a dog without a master has no religion; and there is no sin more punishable in this world than failure to find love.

The way I see it, two types of dogs ended up in my care—those who had been part of a family, only to find themselves outcasts, and those who didn't know any better. To me, the outcasts always seemed sadder. Every dog has a heart that can be broken, and I can't think of any spiritual benefit that comes from their suffering. Abandoned dogs aren't capable of introspection. They simply know they miss their family and want to go home again.

While there were plenty of low points involved with my job, the highs were witnessing the adoptions. In my thirty years of life, I've learned to look for miracles where connections are formed. A dog adopted by a family is a connection. I've watched it play out many times over, and I think there is something more transcendent at work than a family simply deciding that one dog is more attractive or friendlier than the others. There's a pervasive sense that it was "meant to be." Such interventions of fate have shown me that goodness will always find its way into the trenches.

Following an adoption, the initial relief I experienced would gradually succumb to what I can best describe as a happy, self-indulgent kind of grief. Because I became so attached to all our animals, there was an emotional "letting go" involved in every case. This disconnect was always at the forefront of my thoughts. Still, I decided early on that I would never let the end result discourage my emotional investment. There was no holding back.

Although dogs are my passion, Emily Arum was the great connection of my life. How two people like ourselves found each other is beyond explanation. The one person who seemed capable of understanding me had grown up in White Sands as well, only five grades behind. We were definitely an interesting contrast. While I'm tall and fair and wiry, with a slather of scrubby beard, Emily was my diminutive shadow—dark and short, with curves that gave her the appearance of being on the plumper side of slender. Her black, shoulder length hair was so polished that I often thought I detected tones of blue, purple, or burgundy, like my mind was playing tricks on me. Emily's most prominent feature, though, were her warm brown eyes, filled with caring and goodness and a loneliness I wasn't meant to understand.

This "unknowingness" is how I came to realize that Emily's essence was in her mystery. For most of our relationship we weren't a couple, and yet I felt like her husband. This vagueness between us left me continually aspiring to explore her from closer vantage points. She was too sly of a cat to tame, though, and so I found myself shouldering the responsibilities of marriage with only delusions of romance in exchange. We drifted on this way for some time . . . until the night we dared to disturb the strange complacency between us. At the time I didn't know it, but this was the "ripple" I had been counting on. And from this mere ripple emerged the crisis we needed to experience if we were ever to become something more.

* * * * *

It was an August evening, and after dinner we were out on the back deck drinking coffee. Off in the distance, the sky's orange and lavender hues had reached the peak of their intensity, with the clouds sinking below the tree line like an armada of ships going down in flames. Frogs, crickets and the gurgle of the small brook next to the house seemed like the only sounds for miles, although in reality the center of town was only a ten-minute walk away. The night felt like togetherness, yet I could sense by Emily's glances that something was bothering her. After looking forward all week to this quiet evening at home with her, the last thing I anticipated was an argument.

Finally, with a sigh, Emily gave up, rested her head on my shoulder and said softly in my ear, "Grant, honey, I accept or reject you based on the day."

Although her admission was pretty much bang on, I wasn't exactly pleased. Despite the initial disappointment, I recognized that something important was taking place. For the first time since moving in with me she was acknowledging our relationship. All it had taken was a careful bit of planning. Earlier that day, I had come home with two thick sirloins, which I seasoned and marinated for hours before cooking them slowly on the barbecue. I'd also picked up a bottle of her favorite wine to enjoy throughout the evening.

"Good thing it's an 'accept' type of day then," I replied, trying to be funny.

Emily glared at me. "You're not taking me seriously."

"That's not true. I was hoping the lines between us could become clearer and less complicated tonight."

"Is that what this has been all about?" Emily laughed, pointing at the wine and empty plates.

I nodded, knowing full well she read me like a book.

"For future reference," she advised with an ironic smile, "seduction should be smooth and subtle . . . enough so that a woman's unaware it's even taking place."

"I was hoping that tonight could be different," I explained, holding my ground.

Emily gave me a half-amused, half-exasperated look, then tactfully changed the subject. "My mother's been in contact with me again recently . . ."

"Really?" I asked, surprised. "Since when?"

"Look, don't be angry, but I ended up visiting my father in the hospital yesterday. We thought his heart was failing . . ."

"Why didn't you tell me? I would have gone with you."

"I'm sorry. I was feeling weird and needed to deal with it on my own."

"That's understandable."

"You know, I've been so angry with him for so long," she confessed, "but when I saw him there, as pathetic as he was, all I felt was love and pity . . ."

"He's going to be all right, though?"

"Yeah, it was a pretty massive heart-attack, but he's going to survive. It's funny, I've wished he was dead a million times over . . . and yet this weekend I discovered how much I care for him still."

"It's hard to know how you feel until you're in the situation."

"That's true," Emily agreed. "And another positive came from it as well. While we were in the waiting room, I used the opportunity to talk to Mom and work some things out. We also talked about you."

"What did she say?" I asked, feeling curious.

"She's not happy about us living together, and she's not impressed by your job."

"You realize your opinion's the only one that counts."

"That's the thing, I agree with her . . ."

"Oh," I said, rather taken back. "You never said anything before."

"Look, I know that you care about the animals, but it's killing you. From my perspective, you're not coping as well as you used to."

"So you two know-it-alls start planning my life?"

"Relax, Grant, nobody's planning anything. But would it hurt you to consider the implications of what you do? You do realize it affects me, too."

I thought about this for a second. "No, it never occurred to me, but it makes sense."

"It's tough on both of us, that's all. You're always preoccupied these days."

"I know I bring my work home with me. But for the first time, I'm doing something selfless . . . I'm putting the dogs' well-being before any personal consequences."

"Please don't mention the dogs," she said, visibly troubled.

"Why are you getting upset?"

Emily considered this for a moment. "I guess it disturbs me to think how reliant they are on a stranger seeing something in them that's worth loving."

"You realize I'm not just their advocate? I'm their friend as well. They all get to experience what it feels like to be cared for."

"But look what it's done to you. Maybe it's time to get a new job."

I couldn't believe what I was hearing.

"Would it make any difference if I promised to leave work at work?"

She shook her head in frustration and sighed deeply. I moved closer and put my arm around her.

"I feel like I can't talk to you anymore," she said sadly, pushing me away. "You want too much from me."

"Right now, all I want is for us to go upstairs together," I said, taking her by the hand, trying to be charming and make her laugh. "The night is young . . ."

"That's not funny," Emily said irritably, freeing her hand. "Besides, you're with that girl, remember?"

"I told you, I'm not seeing her anymore," I said. "Let's just go upstairs."

Emily's eyes seemed to ponder the possibility, if only for an instant—certainly not long enough for me to get my hopes up. Then she snapped back to her senses.

"It's a bit chilly," she observed, wrapping her arms around herself. The breeze had picked up as we were talking.

"I'm going in now. But please think about what I said this evening."

"As long as you do the same," I countered.

With that, she touched me gently on the cheek, gave me a concerned smile, and left me to my thoughts while the first stars of the evening appeared.

I stood there thinking about the situation, how Emily had insisted that I pursue romance outside of her and how conveniently she used this to keep me at arm's length. Her contention was that it was important to her that I find happiness with a woman truly deserving of someone like me and that our friendship was strong enough to endure. I resisted for months. When I finally did start dating another, she seemed to show more romantic interest in me again. This only proved that I wasn't "man enough" to lay it all on the line because of my reluctance to make an ultimatum. I wanted her to come to me of her own volition, and in my heart I was hopeful that one day she would do just this.

As it was, we shared a house together. She was a waitress in the evenings and I worked the night shift at the shelter. Although she had her own room, she felt more comfortable sharing my bed. Emily and I also had children together—of course, of the doggy variety, each a unique personality and a saved casualty from the shelter. When I first started my employment, I would spend my days lobbying for the life of each one. Each animal's life was so valuable to me that the price of failure could only be paid in spiritual coinage. But the only way to ensure that these rejects and strays left this world with a religion was by overseeing the process. Emily let me adopt three before I had to face the shadow side of my decision to work with homeless dogs. What I appreciated about my job was that it never got easier, and the emotional turmoil, I assure you, did not become dulled with experience. There is nothing "routine" about managing the clock on the amount of time a dog has to be chosen by a master.

*****

I went to work around seven every night. This shift was ideal for me because I liked to write in the early morning—about an hour or two before going to bed. Although I was accustomed to spending a few hours with Emily and the dogs before heading off to the shelter each day, I would occasionally get a drink with my good friend, Dan Tamer, on his night off instead. This was the case that early September evening—two old pals wetting their whistles at the local pub.

That night, about two or so weeks after my night off with Emily ended in unspectacular fashion, Tamer was doing his best to stick a pin in the balloon of my growing seriousness.

"I need you back, old man," Tamer said. "I need the more reckless Grant, the man who accepts my outrageous bets and goes out with me on the town—the guy who disputes everything about my lifestyle."

"I'm still here," I insisted.

"Well, I need your commentary to keep me honest. There's too much room these days to spread my wings."

"I thought working at the shelter would simplify things. If anything, I feel further removed from my beliefs than ever."

"That's why you'll never be happy like me. I keep things simple. When I need evidence of the divine, I look to a beautiful woman."

"Why am I not surprised?"

"I have my doubts about men," Tamer continued, "but women are definitely God-breathed: the hair, the eyes, the breasts, the hips, the feet . . ."

"The feet?" I laughed.

"You know what I'm talking about. When I find myself thinking too much, I know my soul's telling me it's time to make a new acquaintance."

Tamer had a strange faith with some "shazam" to it, and his personality, infectious enthusiasm, and natural charisma made others listen. He was immaculate in appearance to the very last detail, from his hair—frosted platinum and painstakingly spiked—to the colorful, crisp, collared shirts and gold chains, to the polished leather shoes that seemed to glisten with male ego and exquisite taste. He was very selective in his colognes, referring to them as pimp-juice, and he contended a man could succeed in life having every shortcoming minus one: a man, you see, had no excuse whatsoever for being inarticulate in the presence of females.

"Of course, I see what you're saying," I said, trying to look past Tamer to the figure approaching from behind. "I'd believe you more if your experiences with women didn't leave you so jaded."

Before he could respond, Megan joined us at the table. The room was starting to fill and the beer on tap was flowing. She looked distastefully at the Cokes we were drinking.

"You going to buy me a real drink, darling?" she said.

I slapped down a five-dollar bill.

"A small sum to satisfy my God-breathed evidence," I said as she snatched the bill from my fingers, shot me a confused look, and then wiggled her way past a wall of bodies to the counter.

When she returned, she had a pint of beer and a cigarette she had bummed off someone. "When I can't afford 'em, I'll take what I can get," she said, the whites of her hazel eyes pink from the stuff she'd smoked on her way over (a more justifiable expense). Yes, she was the girl I had been seeing off and on, and since I'd patched things up with her again, part of me suspected she was the reason Emily was in such a fuss. If I was supposed to be dating Emily's "ideal woman," how could this cute, plump little "disaster" (as Emily liked to refer to her) be the solution?

"I have a perfect dog at the shelter for you, Megan," I told her. "She's medium-sized, pretty blue eyes, house trained . . ."

"You know I don't want one of your stupid dogs. They smell, they get fleas, they require walks, and baths, and trips to the vet. Who would take on such responsibility without even getting paid for it?"

"Smart woman," said Tamer with a chuckle. "Such needy critters that suck time, attention, and emotion. The trade-off—it just isn't worth it . . ."

"I never asked for your input, Dan."

Megan looked thoughtful for a second, smoke hovering above her head. "But I do have a friend who works for a lab and may be able to take some animals off your hands—you know, when doomsday approaches."

"Are you serious?" I said in disgust, fighting the impulse to walk out the door.

"And who would your friend be?" asked Tamer, who viewed things in black and white terms and appreciated women with a similar outlook.

"She's out of your league," Megan snapped.

Tamer was insistent. "Set me up, would you? I'll bet my little black address book she'll eat red meat. Nothing sexier than a woman of conscience, right old man?"

"How about a woman of kindness?" I shot back. "But it doesn't matter. Your priorities have always been perfectly clear."

Tamer laughed at my honesty. "I'm just misunderstood, right Megan?"

"Don't expect me to back you up. You've insinuated your way through at least half a dozen acquaintances of mine. Besides, I don't know anybody who works in a lab."

"Then why'd you say so?" Tamer asked, looking puzzled.

"That was my way of communicating to thick-skulled Grant that I don't like being put on the spot. For the last time, I don't want a dog."

Tamer broke into a wide grin. "Looks like you've got yourself a woman with some spunk, old man. I know I wouldn't mess with her."

Megan glared at him.

"You have to be able to read between the lines," I said playfully, quite relieved that Megan was only trying to make a point. "That's her way of saying she needs some time to think about it."

No sooner did the words leave my lips when I felt the sting of a swift kick to the shin. I looked up to find a pair of no-nonsense hazel eyes burning a hole into me. Not above bribery, I passed her another five bucks.

After we wrapped things up at the pub, I walked Megan home. As usual, we never said much when we were alone together. But she would always take my arm as we walked along, and believe it or not, this was one of the things that kept my interest in her. I appreciated it as a gesture of possession.

Having dropped her off, I found my way to work. The new volunteer was waiting for me, his bicycle leaning against the building. He was a young kid, freshly out of high school, and considering being a veterinarian. He had a youthful face, with bright, dark eyes that were both pious and mischievous, and curly hair that the young ladies probably adored.

"Sorry I'm late," I said. "I'm Grant."

"Brent," he replied with the lifeless voice of his generation, extending his hand to me. But he did have the respectful confidence that I liked in a youth.

"I like your mop, Brent. You'll do fine here."

"Sure, I know it," he said, not quite genuine. I could tell he considered me old.

"Alright, kid, my routine is pretty much the same every day. We punch in, say hi to the dogs, put on some coffee, and then feed Otis."

"Otis?"

"I'll show you him, but first you need to punch in. We're tracking your hours here, even though they're voluntary. You never know, your experience here may help you get into a program. At the very least, it should help you make a decision as far as a career path involving animals goes."

"Cool."

After I showed him how to punch in, I led him to where we kept the dogs and then I introduced him to Otis.

"Is that an iguana?" he asked.

"Yeah, he was brought in one torrential night by a couple at the end of their rope."

"What?" he asked, looking confused.

"Forget it," I said. "The one aquarium has a python named Hector in it, and the other one, the smaller one, has two anoles, Pinecone and Mussolini."

"Can I feed them?" he asked.

"Sure," and I passed him a container of mealworms. Brent seemed pretty amused by the site of the lizards gobbling down their dinner.

"Where did they come from?" he asked, glancing away from the aquariums.

"People just brought them in and I didn't have the heart to turn them away. Are you ready to make coffee?"

Brent shrugged and then casually followed me to the break area. Once the coffee was brewing, I showed him my mailbox where the day supervisor, Kelly, had left a note for me. A new dog had been brought in that day and I was curious to have a look at him. After we each had poured a cup of coffee, I led Brent into back room beyond the kennel area, where we kept a pen for new residents. Dogs were whining and barking incessantly as we walked past. I could detect the words and tone of each individual animal echoing and reverberating in the hollowness of the bay. Many of these dogs had given their hearts over to me and it was hard to walk by without throwing a milkbone their way or giving them encouraging words.

Once we arrived, I got out my trusty pole and noose, and opened up the small pen to have a look at . . . I read the chart . . . Silver.

"Hey Silver," I said, looking in. Immediately, I knew there was no need to restrain this animal. In fact, I guessed this new resident wouldn't last a day without being adopted. Silver had all his shots; he was house trained, friendly, and simply a beautiful dog.

"What did you say his name is?" asked Brent, crouching to pet him.

"Silver," I repeated.

"Hi Silver. You're a good boy, aren't you?"

I could see that Brent had an instant connection with animals. This job was going to be a system shock for him.

"Why would anybody not want this dog?" he asked.

"The note says that his master brought him in because he decided to move the family to the city," I said, scanning the intake notes. "Didn't think the dog would have access to the outdoors anymore."

"It's unfair," Brent declared, for the first time admitting some feeling to his voice. "I mean, wasn't he part of the family?"

"He was probably an integral part of one as long as it was convenient."

I looked down into Silver's sad, brown eyes, patted him on the head, and then flipped him a milkbone.

"You're going to be fine," I reassured the young dog, then showed Brent how to use the scale and record various data.

When were done with him, Silver sniffed around for a bit and finally curled up at our feet. After instructing Brent on how to fill in the paperwork, I patted my leg to communicate to Silver that I wanted him to follow us. Then we brought him out to the main bay and put him in a larger receptacle.

I had Brent put in some fresh bedding and provide him with clean water. We both felt better when we had locked him up for the night with a familiar bone that his master had left him.

Once we had finished up with Silver, I checked the time. In about fifteen minutes we would let the dogs go outside before locking them up for the night; in the meantime we went back to the office and hung out for a while. I slipped a Metallica CD into the stereo and we leaned back in our chairs, munching potato chips.

"It's so hard to accept that a dog can be abandoned so easily," said Brent.

"Yeah, I know," I nodded. "On a nightly basis my job requires me to overlook my personal resistance so that I can fulfill the duties expected of me."

"Then why do you do it?"

"Because if I'm not doing it, who is? By taking on the responsibility myself, I know these dogs are cared for, but it's a reward that comes with plenty of sacrifice. If you stick around long enough, you'll know what I mean."

"I love animals," Brent began, "but the dogs here, they all have such a desperate desire for attention in their eyes. We can't possibly give them all the attention they deserve."

"Don't worry about Silver," I reassured him. "I wouldn't be surprised if he was adopted tomorrow."

"What about the others?" Brent demanded.

"Follow me," I said, and took him to see Porcupine—an older dog, gruff but loving, and not very attractive to visitors.

"See this fellow, Brent? Now this is a different situation. This dog has been in the shelter for about as much time as we can allow and he has never disappointed. Once in a while I even take this old veteran into my office while I work away, just to let him know his companionship is valued."

Brent was bent down, petting Porcupine, who soaked up the attention, panting away with a look that could have been a smile.

"The reality is that next week I'll arrive at the shelter, punch in, feed Otis, put on a pot of coffee, and then spend a few minutes with Porcupine before saying goodbye to him forever. That's the nature of my job. I tell you, Porcupine has five more years left in him, at least, yet his experience and survival have earned him an early departure from this world."

"But there has to be something we can do," Brent challenged.

"You could adopt him if you wanted."

"I can't," he admitted sadly.

"Then you can see how difficult it is."

After our break, we got back to work. I showed Brent how the cages were networked so that we could release the dogs into outside pens to enjoy the fresh air and perform their natural functions. It didn't take long for any of the dogs to learn the system, whereby a small trap door was opened behind them and then they'd walk directly into the outdoor confines. It took us thirty to forty-five minutes to take care of them all. While they were outside, we refilled their water dishes and did a quick clean up of their pens.

"Where did you learn how to mop?" I asked.

"What?" Brent looked confused.

"No, you first use a wet mop and slosh it everywhere, then squeeze it dry, then you can do a dry mop over it. That way you don't have to put so much muscle into it."

"Ok."

Of course, Brent still kept doing it his own way. I made a mental note of this.

When he got to the last cage, the first of the dogs started to come back in. We gave them all a bit of individual attention.

"So where are the cats?" Brent asked.

"They're in a room on the other side of the office," I explained, "but I don't have much to do with them. The day workers pretty much take care of them."

"My girlfriend said if there was a cute little kitten around that I could bring one home to her."

"How long have you been with her?"

"A year," Brent replied with almost a look of pride in his eyes, "but I'm a man of variety, you know what I mean?"

"Sure," I smirked. "You're admitting you're whipped."

"I'm not whipped! The girls I date are well aware of who wears the pants."

"And that's why you're already pestering me about a kitten? Why don't you show me that you're man enough for the job before you call on any favors?"

"Sure dude," he said dismissively, right before I hit him square in the head with a roll of paper towels.

"Make sure you clean the sink areas, too. You'll find cleaners in the cupboards below."

"Yes, sir," he mumbled on his way by me.

Once all the dogs were all locked in for the night, I took Brent over to a shelf and showed him the toys I had stashed there. I then introduced him to my family away from home.

"This is Crystal," I said, showing him a fast, medium sized dog that resembled a beagle with beautiful blue eyes.

She was a mixture of grays and browns and white and black, with a big bushy tail. "She's my baby girl, you know."

"She's stunning," Brent exclaimed. "Why is she still here?"

"See how her left ear is torn? That and the fact that she's pretty skittish with strangers. She'll howl at you if you try to touch her."

In fact, some days Crystal was crazy in love with me, while on others she acted as though she resented my company and was fearful.

"And this is my pal, Pete," I said, showing him a dog with no discernible ties to any breed—just plain brown with matted fur and exuberant, chocolate eyes. Pete may have been the most adoptable animal in the pound, and yet people shied away from him because he was so ugly by conventional standards.

"I like this guy," said Brent. "He has some character to him."

"Go ahead, you can say it: he's ugly. But I think he's a good ugly, and he's as faithful a friend as I've known."

Then I showed him the brute.

"This is Tory."

To say it plainly, Tory didn't like me. He was bulldoggish looking, with a pug face and obstructed breathing. I'm not sure what breeds flowed in his veins, but his lack of faith in humanity made him a hard dog to find a family for. It had taken weeks for me to gain a working trust with him, but it was clear that he loved the companionship of other dogs.

I watched Brent extend his hand then pull it back quickly.

"Watch yourself with him, he'll nip," I warned.

"You're not kidding."

"And finally, this is Lady."

"Hi Lady," said Brent, on his knees trying to coax the shy dog to him.

Lady was an interesting case. I've never seen a dog so taken by me. She was a big dog, perhaps with some collie in her, lots of bronze fur mixed with white; she had a prissy looking face with the ears set back and a long, pointed snout. She seemed to demand my approval before she'd make any decisions, and was fanatical about my attention and loyalty. Obsequious and quite affectionate when it came to me, she was suspicious of everyone else.

"If you stand out of the way, she'll join the others." Brent moved to the side and Lady slunk into the bay, keeping a watchful eye on him.

While the dogs were out snooping around, I pulled out a rawhide ring selected from my stash. They all started to whine and gather around me, their eyes glistening with expectation. I threw it across the room and they bounded after it with the signature enthusiasm of their species. The dogs observing from their pens were howling and carrying on and scratching against the wire caging as the spectacle played out before them. To ease Brent's concerns about "blatant favoritism," as he put it, I assured him they all had the chance to play in the open, on top of receiving regular exercise during the day.

It was when the dogs were wrestling with each other and trying to steal for themselves a satisfactory chew, obviously having a great time, that I thought I heard a thump. I looked up to see the man I refer to as the Inspector watching us through the glass window on the door looking into the bay. I quickly ushered the dogs into their pens and greeted my superior. He was an older man, tall and wiry, gray hair, gray eyes behind gray-rimmed spectacles, gray skin, in suit and tie, and I could tell he was unnerved by the "free-for-all" of fun he had just witnessed.

"Having a good night, I see," he said sarcastically, motioning for us to follow him to the office.

I offered him a coffee after we sat down but he declined. He frowned at me after looking over the reptiles, his eyes resting on the motionless Otis. "I thought you were going to find homes for these."

"I'm working on it," I replied. "They're not hurting anybody and the health board has no problem with them."

"Get rid them soon," he demanded.

"Yes, sir."

"This is the volunteer?"

"Yes, this is Brent. He seems to be doing quite well."

Brent looked very uncomfortable and I felt bad.

"How do you do?" said Brent, extending his hand.

The Inspector ignored it and asked him, "Do you think I should get cameras in the bay so that I can keep an eye on you guys?"

"Maybe you should," Brent replied, obviously uncomfortable, but too young to know that silence would have been the most appropriate answer.

At this point I was confident the old man had come in looking for someone to bully.

"Look, sir," I interjected, "I put in at least ten hours of my own time every week. I take my job very seriously."

"That may be so, but that doesn't give you free reign to break policy. These are not your pets and I will not tolerate you excusing yourself from the rules. You can never justify having dogs wandering about the bay, you hear me!"

"It won't happen again," I assured him.

"Grant, you're walking on thin ice. It's the straight and narrow here, no exceptions. I'll be leaving now."

It was like being in grade school again, surrendering my sense of autonomy before the rigid rules of the principal. I wondered whether the Inspector really cared about animals; maybe this was just some philanthropic activity providing him with tax relief. I needed this job, and not even a living embodiment of rigid steel was going to remove me from my vocation—especially after I had worked so hard to find my place.

Once we were sure the old man had departed, Brent and I shared a good laugh over this ridiculous figure before the boy left for the night himself. I'm sure he pedaled away on his bike with some unique experiences to digest. I then organized my desk, typed up my notes, and got out the leather notebook Emily had given me for Christmas. Often I'd use the couple of hours of downtime I had every night to journal about my day as well as jot down ideas for a book I was writing about a man trying to salvage his life after being responsible for a deadly car accident. Then I would do a bit more cleaning and fiddle around with some maintenance projects until Kelly arrived at seven.

That morning, I joined Kelly outside and talked with her while the sun crept above the horizon. She smoked and listened to me complain about spontaneous supervision during the night. Kelly was a hefty girl, kind, loving, and cheerful, but I got the sense she didn't really like me (until I arrived at the shelter, she pretty much ran the show). Still, there is not a doubt in my mind that when it came to loving animals she was my equal. She said she sympathized with my ordeal and promised to ease the Inspector's concerns about me the next time she had a chance. She asked me whether I was also able to record her notes on the cats, which I promised to do, and she agreed to work with Silver throughout the day.

My shift over, I walked home feeling drained and hoping I wouldn't have to discuss my evening with Emily before typing my notes, writing a bit more, and finally going to bed.

CHAPTER 2

Much of my decision-making in life has to do with my gut feeling. I always supposed the woman I married would just "feel" right, and that our claim to each other would be undeniable. At 30 years old and having spent the past two years so close to the woman I felt destined for, I began to think that maybe . . . just maybe . . . it was time to consider making concessions and compromises.

When I'm in a relationship that has become complex, I exist in a state of relationship anxiety, and my conscience reveals the tensions involved in proceeding further. You know what it's like—you feel it might not be healthy to go on, and yet the pain of severance is still being weighed against the potential benefits of terminating the relationship. Then once you do break it off, the mind will often rewrite the relationship so that you question your decision time and time again, even though you consciously know you were right to seek love elsewhere.

So, what if the person you love shows indisputable signs of returning your affection, but the proof has yet to demonstrate itself in the pudding? In reality, you're committed to a possibility, and a possibility left open remains merely that—a possibility. So your love life ends up mirroring that of an ascetic monk in the practice of desert spirituality, with only your religion to attend to. The danger is that if you don't actively seek some type of transformation, your days could become lost in the barren sands of relationship resentment.

If my feelings for Emily had been returned, I would have committed myself to her in a heartbeat. I loved her down to the fine details and I often internalized her suffering when I considered her fear of closeness and how shallow her expectations of life had become.

I guess that's why I chose to date Megan, who I very well knew was a figurative spitting in Emily's face. The funny thing is, there was a part of myself that could see me ending up with Megan. I'd be lying if I didn't admit that she had become a sliver of hope for an alternative future. But no matter how I arranged it all on the table, I never could have been comfortable with Megan caring for me the way Emily did. Emily was the only person I could truly be myself around, and maybe that's why I had no problem using Megan to break her resolve.

A specific example is when Megan slept over one weekend. I can admit that I wanted to get a reaction out of Emily. Part of me desired the type of satisfaction I would get if she showed any jealousy at all, while another part of me just wanted to test the waters. So I informed Emily of my intentions and then I made arrangements for her to stay at Tamer's place. Megan came over and we watched a movie and had some dinner. Then we spent the rest of the night upstairs.

When Emily arrived the next day, I was out taking the dogs for a walk. It was quite a scene when I returned. From what I can gather, Emily began making the bed and supposedly the fragrance of foreign perfume on the sheets really set her off. By the time I came home, she was storming around the house in the middle of some angry cleaning. After some choice words on her part, I decided there wasn't any sense in talking about it until she calmed down. I thought this would probably be a good time to visit Tamer while he was at work, so I carefully maneuvered my way around her—making sure to keep out of striking distance—and made my way to the car.

Something about this unusual display of emotion, though, made me reconsider my decision to leave. I walked back to the house and peered through the front window, to see Emily sitting on the couch with her face in her hands.

I found it unfair. She was the one who'd demanded that I date another—and yet when I respected her wishes, she saved her suffering and experienced it in isolation. Worse yet, she never came clean about the harm I was visiting upon her, instead choosing to juxtapose words like "accept" and "reject" in a way that left me wondering whether she was describing a very real ambivalence or using calculated language to keep me insecure and at a distance.

And yet I couldn't resent her for it. She had this appreciation for the natural world that she needed me to share, and, just as much, I think I needed to learn how to share it. That's why, regardless of the season, she'd have me take her on long drives down country roads to admire farmhouses set against ever-changing landscapes and vast exposures of sky. Or in the summer, she'd take me on hikes along trails in the wilderness to further expand my knowledge of exotic wildflowers: vervain, silverweed, saxifrage, and corydalis. And even in the evenings, she'd like us to take walks under the stars together because it gave her, in her words, a "deep feeling of pathos." So how could I resent her? She taught me to sentimentalize the moments we captured together on our way to an authentic platform for our friendship.

And here I was a spectator to her crying—something I had never witnessed in all my time with her. I didn't know how to respond. While considering an appropriate course of action, I felt this deep sympathy for her simmering near the top of my emotion, and yet confusion, anger, and resentment were bubbling up from the base. When these feelings were reduced and caramelized, the result was a serving of guilt that left my stomach churning. At this point, I was very tempted to go on as though I had never witnessed this uncomfortable portrait of Emily's vulnerability. I'm sure this would have been her preference as well. But then again, walking away would have meant living with the knowledge that I had surrendered my greatest opportunity thus far in our relationship to acquaint myself with the genuine article.

So, looking through the window at my hurting companion, I was left with little choice but to confront her. I took a deep breath and walked back through the front door. Emily didn't even bother trying to hide the fact that she had been crying.

She stared up at me and said with great composure, "Do you think you can love her?"

"I thought I could."

"I don't believe you, Grant."

"There's something different about her," I explained.

Emily laughed cynically.

"What's so funny?"

"You can try to deceive yourself, but not me. You know she's a temporary fix."

"That's probably true," I admitted.

"Then you're a jerk," Emily said plainly.

"That might even be an understatement."

Emily struggled for words before practically spitting out, "I find your . . . utter disregard for others' feelings to be . . . repugnant . . ."

"But I respect her!" I insisted.

"Well what about me?"

"Of course I do."

Emily had a look in her eyes that conveyed a desire to strike, but she calmed herself down. Then her disposition changed and I saw a glimpse of her vulnerability.

"Grant, do you feel closer to her than to me?" Her voice was sad and nervous.

I chose to be evasive. "Megan will allow herself to be intimate with me."

Emily paused for a second and then said in a regretful tone, "I wish I could make you understand . . . but it's hard to explain without sounding stupid . . ."

"Don't bother," I answered. "At this point I'm so sick of it that I don't care anymore."

Emily then became very serious—almost uncomfortably serious, considering we had never gone this deep with each other before.

"I'm not good with timing, but I'm going to throw caution to the wind and for once try to express my feelings as clearly as possible."

"You've never needed my permission," I reminded her.

Emily took a moment to form her thoughts, then said, "I want you to know that there's never been a time I didn't want us to be together."

I was taken completely by surprise and looked at her for some time in silence, trying to find the right words to say.

"Well, Grant?" Emily coaxed, trying to get a response.

"Are you serious?" I finally managed.

"Of course I mean it," she said convincingly, looking at me as though I was crazy. "I've always imagined us together."

"I . . . believe you," I reassured her, trying to slow everything down. "It's just that . . . that for all this time I've felt the exact same way . . ."

Emily sighed. Her eyes became moist, but they also looked angry. This reaction was outside of my expectation. I awaited an explanation but received none.

"What's wrong?" I finally asked, breaking the silence.

"Oh, I don't know," Emily said sarcastically. "Maybe it just raises questions."

"Like what?"

Emily shrugged. "I don't know, maybe it makes me ask myself why it is that I'm here. It makes me ask why it is that I trust you."

"What did I say?" I demanded.

Emily ignored me. "It makes me ask why it is you've never told me you love me."

I was speechless. Perhaps dumbfounded would be a better word.

"You sure have a hard time explaining yourself today," Emily sneered.

"I don't know, Emily. I don't know why I've never said it."

"Sure you do," she insisted. "Just tell me the truth, I'll understand."

"I—I'm not sure," I said, fumbling with my words. "When I felt like saying it, it seemed like I was going out on a limb."

"On a limb?"

"I don't know how else to explain it," I said, my mind reeling.

"Just try," she urged. "Or are you afraid to be honest with me?"

Then, in the midst of the pressure and confusion, the truth seemed to tumble out of me.

"Maybe I was just afraid you wouldn't say it back."

She considered this for a second and then nodded in understanding.

"I should have had more faith," I backpedaled, trying to comfort her. "It might have simplified everything between us."

Emily started playing with her hands, her gaze downcast. "I don't blame you . . ." Then she looked up into my eyes. "But do you know how often I prayed to hear those words? It would have made all the difference."

"I wanted to say them!"

"It's my issue, not yours," Emily said reassuringly. "I'm not blaming you. But why me? Why am I so scared all the time? Why can't I allow myself the same dreams as all other women?"

I put my arm around her then, but she only pushed me back. "Grant, stop! Stop right now! You're not listening to me."

I said nothing; there seemed to be very little I could say to bring her comfort.

"If only we could move far away," she whispered. "If only there was a way start all over again . . ."

A single tear formed in her eye, overflowed, and then slowly navigated the structure of her cheekbone, leaving a glossy streak along her face before beading on her chin and falling to the floor with an isolated patter. I felt its splash within me, over me, and under me—as if I were being baptized for the first time. At that point I began waking up to the allegory behind the dream, the subtext—the underlying truth implicit to the writing of our relationship. All of a sudden, I felt responsible for her hopelessness and wished that I could go back a year or two in time. Then I wouldn't have to live with the knowledge that we could have avoided this whole mess if I had voiced the feelings in my heart from the beginning.

As it was, I found that the moment between us that I had desired for all those months proved difficult to swallow. It was shocking. Given my feelings for Emily, it's easy to think that I would have declared my intentions to her on the spot. Believe me, I wanted to tell her that she meant everything to me. I wanted to reassure her that sharing her feelings with me was the right thing to do, but I felt awkward and uncomfortable from the sudden injection of seriousness between us. There was also a great deal of pressure in the recognition that we had encountered one of those shared moments in a relationship that tend to be called defining. Our relationship was at a crossroads no matter how we cut it, and there was a sense of no turning back.

With this in mind, and being possessed of little skills as a counselor or comforter, no better course of action came to mind than to kiss her.

Yes, I leaned right over, took in her my arms, and then kissed her with an insistence that left little room for negotiation. It took her a second to comprehend this decision before she added motion to the embrace, her eyes wide with surprise then slowly closing and yielding to acceptance. Although this gesture removed me from the discomfort of conversation, I spent the duration of the kiss wondering how my decision was going to change things between us.

I didn't wonder long.

Emily suddenly pushed me away. "What are you doing?"

"I thought this was what you wanted . . ." I explained, totally confused.

"No, Grant, haven't you been listening to me?"

"What is it then?"

"It's time you stop dangling my heart over the abyss," she replied angrily.

"What does that mean?" I asked, even more confused.

My lack of insight frustrated Emily beyond her means of restraint.

"Damn it!" she cried. "Don't you get it—I'm not one of your dogs!"

Before I could respond, she stormed out of the room and slammed the door behind her, shaking the whole house with the impact then scorching her tires as she tore down the street in a blur of color. Having watched her disappear, I sat down and tried to calm myself by repeatedly playing the discussion in my head. I just couldn't seem to get a handle on it, though. On the one hand, I wanted Emily to come to me of her own volition because I imagined that our togetherness was imminent, as if written in the stars. And yet when she'd made this first step, I felt a resistance within me.

The quiet house felt like judgment and no amount of mental rearranging could change what had occurred. Seeing that I couldn't solve this on my own, I gave up and decided to visit Dan Tamer.

Tamer ran a pizza joint in town, the only place he was easily accessible to all his friends. Fortunately for me, he savored my misadventures like a cold beer after a hard day of work. The truth is, it made me feel better to describe my misery and then hear him chuckle as though my problems were no more of a crisis than an itch. He could provide me with the laugh of context that I desperately needed, giving me the perspective to make crystal clear decisions apart from personal feelings.

When I walked into the restaurant, Brent, of all people, was sitting at one of the tables with his pals, apparently getting some food before work. The table in front of him looked like it had hosted feasting vultures. I told him to join me so that I could introduce him to the chef.

When we walked in the kitchen, I was greeted in familiar fashion.

"Old man," said Tamer, a big grin on his face.

"This is Brent," I said. "He's the new volunteer at the shelter."

"You don't look like a Brent," Tamer observed, looking the boy over. "We need to give you a real name."

"Brent's just fine," said the kid.

"No, no, trust me, we can help you out," Tamer urged, then turned to me. "He looks like a chicken, doesn't he? With that hair he looks like a chicken."

"Sort of."

Brent did not look impressed.

"Bet the ladies love you, don't they?" Tamer asked Brent, giving me a wink.

"I need my friends to peel them off me," Brent replied, flashing his arrogance.

"That's good," said Tamer. "We're going to raise you right."

"No we're not," I said.

"You want a job, kid?" Tamer asked, not afraid of putting a new acquaintance on the spot.

"A job?"

Tamer nodded. "Sure, come work for me. It's easy to see that I can instill some values in you. You have all the makings of a warrior. Wouldn't you say, old man?" He turned to me, grinning.

"No, he doesn't," I objected. "Tell him to go to hell, Brent."

"You know how I live vicariously through my warriors, Grant. It keeps me young." He swiveled back to Brent. "My pizza warriors go out into the world and do me proud. I'll show you how to live right. I've had an abundance of women in my life and with my guidance I promise that your lonely nights will be over."

"Enough, Dan," I said, trying to put my foot down.

"Seriously, come see me, Brent," said Tamer, ignoring me. "I need a new lad for prep."

"I need to talk to you," I interjected.

Tamer nodded. "What is it?"

"I—"

"Wait, Grant," Tamer interrupted, turning his attention back to Brent. "Don't you know when you've been dismissed, you sloppy little fool?"

"What?" the poor kid asked, almost looking frightened. If I hadn't known Tamer so well, I might have felt sorry for Brent.

"Listen, chicken, until you have an answer for me, get the hell out of my kitchen!"

"I was just leaving," Brent replied cockily, quickly regaining his composure. He even took the time to pour himself some pop from the fountain before giving us a sly grin and strolling out of the kitchen.

"I'll beat that spirit out him," Tamer mumbled, but looking happy at the prospect of a new addition to his staff. "So what's this all about?"

"It's about Emily."

"Go on," Tamer encouraged.

"She cracked today," I confessed.

"What do you mean?"

"She tried to guilt me into saying I love her."

Tamer started to laugh. "What can I tell you? Women are crazy. I keep telling you this and yet you ignore the evidence. So what did you do, throw it back in her face?"

"Not exactly."

"After what she's put you through, didn't you tell her to her go to hell?"

"No."

"Oh, you're a pathetic man . . . you spineless fool. Don't tell me you bought into the insanity?"

"I actually felt really guilty, Dan. You know how I am when it comes to Emily."

"I don't want to hear it," Tamer said in disgust. "You're so pathetic I can hardly look at you. You had a prime opportunity to take control and you squandered it."

"What do you mean?" I asked, starting to laugh. "I'm not that pathetic, am I?"

"Haven't you listened to a word I've said all these years? Women need black and white. They need the firm hand, not the permissive admirer, the pushover."

"Well, what would you have done in my position?"

"Don't make it about me, old man," said Tamer, shaking his head. "If we look at the facts, it's easy to see that up until this point you've been willing to sell out for a little you know what," and he made a triangle shape with his hands.

"Maybe," I said, considering the possibility. "I'm just not sure what to do now."

"Of course you're not," Tamer said with understanding in his voice. "You're at the crossroads, buddy. The only way to proceed is to know exactly what you want."

"It's difficult. If I settle for Megan, I know what I get and she's predictable. Emily, on the other hand, might never be a sure thing. Still, she could become the joy of my life. It's equally possible she'll be my absolute ruin, though."

"You know what I think, old man?"

"What?"

"I think you're shallow. Perhaps superficial would be a better word."

"How can you say that?"

"Easy. If Emily wasn't so attractive, would you really even be giving this any consideration?"

"It's not her beauty," I insisted.

"Oh, I beg to differ. I've known you for a long time, and you're superficial."

I couldn't help but smile. "I'm not going to argue with you, Tamer. But you haven't told me what you think, really."

"Well, what do you want to do?" he asked, glancing around the kitchen.

I thought about this for a second. "In all honesty, Emily hasn't convinced me that she's ready to be with me. She's only convinced me that she doesn't want me to be with Megan."

Tamer took a pizza out of the oven, sliced it up, and dished it off to one of his beautiful young waitresses to be transported to the dining room. Judging by the scowl on the girl's face, she didn't seem to appreciate me diverting her manager's attention.

"You know what I think?" said Tamer, looking very serious. "Save yourself. Disentangle yourself entirely from both of them. Maybe then you'll actually play more than two games of tennis with me a year."

"I just can't," I said. "I'm too old to cut my losses."

He shrugged. "Well then, play it for all its worth. Technically, you're dating Megan and Emily is just your roommate."

"You're right," I said, feeling relieved. "If I don't do anything, things will work themselves out on their own."

Tamer shook his head. "What a surprise. So much turmoil over a little bit of this," and he made the triangle shape again.

* * * * *

Brent was waiting for me when I got to work. I unlocked the door and we punched in together. I was beginning to enjoy having a *protégé*. It was a rainy night—not that this made a difference. The singular beauty of the shelter was that weather did not exist in that world within a world. Sunshine, rain, or snow, it never really mattered because you could never be aware of the outdoors once you entered the facility. It was like voluntarily condemning yourself to a harsh reality you would never consider otherwise. The rules were different, and you were very conscious of your spirit and the fragility of your physical existence—as well as your beliefs. The shelter was something you could never learn or understand from a book, no matter how detailed the description.

After Brent put the coffee on, he approached me while I was sitting at my desk.

"Was your friend Tamer serious today?" he ventured.

"Unfortunately, yes. He's been looking for a peasant to beat on for a few months now."

"Do you think I should take him up on his offer?"

I thought about this for a second and then gave the kid some context.

"If you work for Tamer, I want you to understand that you're getting a lot more than just a manager. It's more like you're being adopted into his family. But being a member of Tamer's family is a unique experience. He'll always be there for you, and yet he'll steer you wrong for the sport of it. He'll respect you personally, but he'll seize the opportunity to laugh at your missteps. You also might think twice about bringing your girlfriend around him because you'll find that he communicates with women on a level you could never comprehend."

"Really?"

"Women come from far and wide for his advice. They cry on his shoulder. They seek his approval. And yet it's amazing how much they respect and disrespect him at the same time. Tamer has a reputation, both good and bad, and it's hard for people to reconcile the sheer logic of his advice, which comes from a truly good nature, with the side of him that has earned him a dubious reputation."

"I want to work for this guy," Brent said with conviction. "I want to see how he lives his life, especially what's in his bag of tricks."

"Tamer has no magical bag of tricks. He just knows how to talk to women and make each one feel special. If he wasn't my friend, and my girlfriend was spending time with him, I know I would be concerned. Every man in town is aware of Dan Tamer and prays that his girlfriend never crosses Tamer's path."

"How can you guys be buddies, then? You seem so different in philosophy. It's amazing you get along."

"I would do anything for him. I've learned more about myself because of him than from anyone else I've known. I used to work side-by-side with him at the restaurant and it was an educational experience for both of us. And what's funny is that neither one of us has impacted each other's views in the least. Some would call that futility, but I think that it's through relating to each other that we find out what we truly believe. I know what I believe because of him, and he knows what he believes because of me."

"But keep my girlfriend from him?" Brent asked.

"If you know what's good for you."

When we started our clean up, I gave Brent a heads up that tonight was going to be difficult, the type of night that robs a person of something precious: namely, the ignorance of something transpiring behind the fabric of society that's unavoidable, and yet unconscionable according to humanity's concept of justice. Simply put, the hourglass on Porcupine's life was up. Brent, if he chose to stay, was going to gain insight into the canine reality of dwelling in a cash-tight world. There is a reason why people are much more upset when a dog gets killed in a movie than a movie star. We're desensitized to seeing a person die on the screen, but a dog in trouble screams to our soul for protection. The injustice is that a dog—the conceptual embodiment of innocence and loyalty—should never end up a casualty of human conflict. Their whole lives are like a suspended childhood; that's to say, very few dogs get to depend on their own devices.

Justice in the shelter meant administering injustice. The dogs we housed were definitely victims of human affairs, yet the consequence for failing to find a home remained theirs and theirs alone. There was nothing more we could do. We only had so much space and we only had so much funding.

My cell phone rang. It was Tamer.

"Hey, Grant, I got it. I got a name for that kid."

"We're talking about something serious here," I muttered, glancing at Brent.

"It'll only take a second," Tamer insisted.

"Go ahead then."

"Gizzer . . ." he said, then began to laugh.

"Gizzard?"

"No, Gizzer. Remember, that chicken we incubated and raised back in high school, with the ridiculous crown on its head?"

"OK," I nodded, starting to form a memory.

"Remember what happened when we went to eat it?"

"Yeah, he had so much personality that we couldn't do it, so we gave him his freedom and chose another instead."

"So what do you think?"

"I think you nailed it" I replied, grinning. "It suits him perfectly."

"Make sure Gizzer comes and sees me about the job."

"You got it, man."

I put my phone away.

"Who was that?" asked Brent.

"That was Tamer. He's come up with a name for you in the event that you work for him, but I think I'll adopt it myself."

"What?"

"Look, Gizzer, we need to get a move on. I still plan on having you out on time tonight."

"Gizzer?" he objected. "That's what you two geniuses came up with?"

"There's no sense in fighting it. Once Tamer decides these things, everyone pretty much follows his lead. Now let's get working."

When we entered Porcupine's pen, he was curled up in the corner sleeping soundly. Big, broad torso with pointy tufts of fur; ears with satellite maneuverability; wet, intricately-patterned nose; chestnut eyes; big paws with polished, black nails; whiskers upon whiskers; little upside-down "V" above each eye for eyebrows; raspberry tongue; red collar, one of the few items he considered his; thick, prideful tail. I patted my leg for him to walk alongside us. He seemed slow, cumbersome, as he followed us into the office and flopped down on the floor, and yet undoubtedly he was happy about the special attention. As I typed my notes, I drank some coffee while Brent stretched out on the floor beside him and stroked his soft ears.

I thought about what Emily had said. The connection seemed obvious. She was accusing me of putting her in that same situation as the dogs: either form a relationship or be extinguished. The question became, how could she not see my selfless motivation for working at the shelter? Or the home I provided her, for that matter? My life was not dedicated to observing dogs fail. The reality of my job—outside of my personal control—was that I could only provide dogs with hope for so long before I was forced to kill them. So what did she mean when she chose the word abyss? When you break it down, can't the abyss be considered the dark emptiness that's the backdrop for hope's silvery glimmer? Or does the abyss exist by virtue of hope's eternal presence?

"Grant," said Brent, disturbing my concentration. The boy was looking up at me from his sprawled position next to Porcupine.

"What is it?"

"I just can't believe there's nothing we can do," he said innocently.

In my throat I could feel the lump forming that I always get when the moment draws near. "At this point, kid, you always ask yourself whether you did everything you could to help this dog. But either way, the outcome is what it is."

"But I love him . . ."

"Give him this," I said, producing a chocolate bar I had in my pocket and flipping it to him.

Brent removed the wrapping and presented the chocolate to Porcupine. It was rewarding to see the flicker of excitement in the dog's eyes as he tried to make sense of this special gift. I then observed the joy the chocolate bar gave him, from the first sniff to the gentle manner in which he took it from

Brent's hand, to the way he lay down with it and broke it up between his paws before wolfing down every piece, still licking his chops well after it was gone. He clearly savored the experience. Whether chocolate was unhealthy for him or not made very little difference at the time.

When he was done, he looked at Brent and then to me as if expecting another.

"No more, boy," I said, showing him my empty hands.

Porcupine nuzzled me, insistent, then looked up expectantly, his tail wagging.

"It's time, Brent," I said. "Technically, you're not supposed to be part of this. But I'm leaving that up to you."

By the look on the kid's face, it was obvious he was conflicted, but he replied, "I feel it's something I need to experience."

"Alright. Let's be done with it then."

I reached down and lifted Porcupine up, then carried him in my arms as a shepherd carries a lamb. It had become my symbol to carry the animal on the last steps of the journey. Porcupine was heavy, but he didn't resist, and there was no struggle as we walked him through the bay, past his empty pen, past all the other dogs and into the room where death and resurrection were one and the same.

I put Porcupine on the surgical table and gathered the instruments that would end his life. He sat there panting, looking quite content and utterly trusting.

"Are you sure you're ok with this?" I asked Brent, who at this point looked absolutely sick.

"If I can't handle this, what kind of vet will I be?" Brent replied.

"Well, come over and here and pet him while I do this. Look in his eyes and tell him that he's a good boy and that you love him."

Brent obeyed me and began petting the old timer with trembling hands. In such cases, it feels like the dog understands what's going on because you project your own heartbreak into his situation. It's such a bizarre phenomenon because you believe the dog is sad about his fate and yet stoic about it at the same time.

When I walked over with the needle in my hand, Brent stopped me for a second. "It just occurred to me," he said. "There's no dog waiting to take his place."

"That's true, but there will be."

He looked confused. "Well, shouldn't we delay this at least until another dog gets brought in? I mean, can't we extend his time?"

"It's not about space," I explained. "And sadly, we could give him an indeterminate amount of time, but I know from experience that nobody's going to adopt him. Porcupine's not the adoptable type, and waiting around isn't going to change anything."

Brent nodded in understanding, but I wondered how a young mind could wrap itself around such a cruel fact of life. Before he could provide further objections, I worked the needle into Porcupine. The dog gave only a small yelp and then composed himself, panting away and still seeming to enjoy the unusual attention. I stroked his fur myself, and it wasn't long before the light disappeared from his kind, brown eyes.

As he passed away, I whispered in his ear, "I'll miss you, good friend. We'll see each other on the other side."

Porcupine's spirit departed quietly in our presence. Afterwards, I put a white sheet over him, showing him the same respect people afford each other. I would go through the disposal process by myself later that night.

Brent was quiet and had a blank, almost spaced-out expression. Without a word, he left the room and closed the door gently behind him. It was pretty easy to tell that he needed some breathing room. When I checked on him a few minutes later, he was gathering his cleaning supplies and I could see by his body language that it was still best to leave him alone.

Once I pushed my concern for him to the side, as always my grief for the animal came upon me in full force. I went to the bathroom and splashed some cold water on my face, but that didn't stop me from experiencing the mixture of retching and hot tears that always followed such an occasion. No matter how you looked at it, it was such a cheap, petty and unjust end to a life.

About an hour later, after I'd had a chance to compose myself, I approached Brent while he was cleaning a pen.

"Are you okay? Do you want to talk about it?" I asked.

"I'm alright," he insisted, but didn't make eye contact. "Just leave me alone."

It seemed fair to oblige him. For the rest of the night we did our own thing. We were both lost in our own thoughts and feelings, and it was hard to deny that an awkwardness had entered the picture that I had no real answers for anyway.

By the time his shift was done, I could see that Brent had more color in his face, and so I decided to approach him one last time while he was getting his stuff together to go home.

"This is about as bad as it gets," I said, trying to be reassuring.

"I've never felt such a pit in my stomach," he replied, struggling to find his voice. He still appeared kind of dopey and distracted.

"Nobody can be prepared for it, and you never become used to it."

When I said this, he looked at me thoughtfully for a second, like he was struggling to articulate an idea, and his eyes seemed to regain some of their lost intensity.

"The burden you mentioned," he began, "I think I know what you mean now . . ."

"Go on."

"Porcupine's life ended peacefully and without any fear, and yet afterwards we're left behind to shoulder the guilt."

Brent was starting to understand me. But only partly. For me, the sacrifice was the whole process, from start to finish. Every night I sacrificed my personal resistance so that my spiritual eye could catch a silvery glimmer of understanding in the empty black space.

"There's always a point where the burden is shifted," I explained. "When they're adopted, that's the ideal shift in responsibility. But if they have to be put down, the weight of responsibility is on us. When it comes down to it, everything we do here is for them—even when they fail to find a home . . ."

"But it's so unfair," Brent protested.

"It is unfair," I agreed, "and I can see how affected you are. But just because you're sensitive doesn't mean you can't be a good vet. It's a calling—a vocation, not a job—and if you can't show people that you care about their pets then you're meant to do something else."

"Being a vet is a different kind of burden, I realize that now."

"In what way?"

"I know that helping people part ways with their old and sick pets is part of the responsibility. I think I can handle that. But putting healthy dogs to sleep is extraordinarily painful—a knife through the heart. Porcupine didn't deserve this. No dog deserves this."

"Don't worry, kid, I won't ask you to participate again."

"Haven't you been listening? I want to help animals: the old, the sick, the abandoned."

"Well, if you can handle this, I'd say you're one step closer."

"I do have one question, though."

"What's that?"

"What do you do to cope when you go home afterwards? How do you find comfort?"

"I'll tell you, but you're going to laugh."

"I might not," Brent said, managing a weak smile.

"When it becomes too much for me to deal with, I consider this psychic on television who assures people their dogs' souls are immortal and will be reunited with their families."

"And you believe her?"

"I know she's right."

"How can you know for sure?"

"Because of how desperately I want it to be true."

* * * * *

Later that evening, I sat outside on the steps of the building. It wasn't raining anymore. The moon was out, grappling with a dark cloud. There was a breeze and I could see the bluish glow of televisions emanating from the windows of the houses along the block. There was a peaceful aura to the summer night. The opera of Dionysian crickets and Apollonian frogs could be heard faintly in the background, rhythm and lyrics. So I just happened to be outside when Emily showed up with a picnic basket of food. She plopped down beside me on the steps and there was no exchange of words between us for a few seconds.

"We need to talk about what happened today," she said at last, opening the basket and passing me a soda.

"I have nothing to say," I replied, feeling uncomfortable and nervous. "How was work tonight?"

"I made ok tips."

"That's good."

Another awkward pause followed.

"It was nice out tonight so I thought I would bring you some food," she explained.

"That was very nice of you," I replied, a little wary of my words after what had been said earlier.

We sat there for a few seconds while I went through the basket. There were a couple of sandwiches, some cookies, a yogurt, and a banana.

It wasn't long before Emily got to the real intention behind her visit.

"Grant, I was wondering, do you ever expect one thing from me and say another?"

I shrugged.

"Because I do have certain expectations of you that I don't have of any other person and I try to convince myself that you put me first. Sometimes I tell you to do things, and yet I wish and hope that you'll do otherwise."

I thought about this. "I'm sorry. I should have been a better listener all along. I know this now."

Emily nodded. "The day we first met on the bus to the Toronto Book Fair, you seemed to hang onto my every word. We talked some, and then you let me read a few pages of the book you were going to peddle. You humored me about some of my poems. What a wonderful day we had there together."

"Yeah, I had never met a woman who had read so many books."

"And then when we began dating, you would pick me up, we would go somewhere and talk about books and ideas; we'd get some food, go for walks. Then you'd drop me off at home and nervously give me a kiss goodbye at the doorstep. Never in my life did I think that I'd find myself a gentleman."

"I was something, but I'm not sure I was a gentleman."

"Don't kid yourself. I couldn't believe that there could be a man so caring, so capable of listening, so content with the affection I was prepared to give. You cared about animals more than any person I've known and you treated every person you met with great respect, right down to the children playing on the streets."

"So?" I said, taking a swig of pop.

"For a time, I didn't know I could be so happy in a relationship," she murmured. "At the same time, I was living in a state of dread. I knew it would have to end and I did everything to postpone that."

"I guess I sensed this."

"Since it was only a matter of time before I screwed things up, how could I expect such a relationship? You were deserving of something more. While I may not be that little girl who used to lock herself in the bathroom and find ways to bleed, I still have my problems. I'm selfish, though, and I've never been able to fully cut you loose. I've infected you, changed you for the worse. You're no longer the same person who used to show up at my doorstep and then kiss me goodnight. I'm so sorry, I—"

"Emily, our relationship is complex. There's a lot of gray. I never wanted to give you the impression that it was all or nothing. I didn't want to tack that type of guilt on you, nor did I want the responsibility."

Emily nodded.

"And now, because we've tampered with the core of our friendship, I don't see how things can change," I concluded.

"Look it, I came here to apologize and I've done that," Emily said sharply.

"What do you want of me?" I demanded. "I've respected your wishes; I share my home with you; I care for you as if you were my wife. I even let you drive the car all the time while I wear holes in my shoes. So what do you want of me?"

I was being uncharacteristically vocal and this clearly was unsettling her. After a pause to reclaim her composure, she said very plainly, "I want to get away . . . I want to go anywhere but here . . . I'm just so tired . . . I just want it to end . . ."

"Us, you mean?" I asked, feeling a bit queasy.

"Don't pretend you don't know what I'm talking about," Emily warned, her sad, angry eyes fixed on mine.

CHAPTER 3

Emily could have been assured that she was loved to the very last molecule. I was just unprepared to express my feelings for her on the steps that night. When I find myself struggling to calculate outcomes or implications, my instinct is to play it cautious. While I suspected she was trying to get a reaction out of me, this seemed insignificant in light of the deep concern she had aroused. At the same time, there was no disputing that her warning tapped into my biggest insecurity: that I didn't understand her. If this was her intention, it certainly worked. Never had I met such a closed book, such a mystery of a woman. If she was vocal about any of her struggles, it was about not being able to get along with anyone in her family, especially her mother; or she'd rehash the job she'd had in an office, which she was fired from when she couldn't distinguish constructive criticism from managerial persecution. She had no real female friends to speak of. And when she did manage to make friends, it was only temporary. In the end, she would eventually drive them away.

People who perceive they've been written off so many times will often fortify themselves against the possibility of disappointment by lowering their expectations of others. Our relationship proved to be no different. This left me wondering about the point a person reaches when conflict and emotional distance become more comfortable than love, and whether such a migration can be reversed. The fact was that for me to be of any benefit to her at all, I needed her to accept that I genuinely cared about her and to desire an outcome where friction no longer felt like such a safe haven.

We ended up living together by coincidence. When my uncle died, I received a bit of an inheritance. My uncle was a literary sort and believed that having a house paid for would allow me a greater opportunity to write. So I put this money down on a house and was able to work things out so that I had a very reasonable mortgage. When I first moved in, Emily and I were not seeing each other anymore, which made her appearance in my house all the more surprising.

One morning, I woke up and went downstairs to find Emily curled up on my couch.

"How did you get in here?"

Her eyes opened slowly and she looked up at me innocently, not in a hurry to offer me an explanation.

"What are you doing here?" I demanded.

"I needed to go somewhere where I felt safe," she explained.

"But you've never been in my house before," I said in dismay.

Emily didn't say anything, leaving things unspoken.

"Oh . . ." I said, realizing the implications.

"I don't want you to get any ideas about getting back together, but I need a place to stay."

"What happened?"

"I'm not welcome at home anymore," she admitted, her eyes downcast and secretive.

"I understand."

"Do you?"

"Look, you can stay as long as you like . . ."

Circumstances and compassion left me little choice but to open my door to her. And so began my experience of cohabiting with a woman. At first Emily exhibited such gratitude that it was almost embarrassing. My biggest complaint was that she'd disappear for days at a time with no explanation. But she was fun, easy to chill out with, and seemed intent on making me feel comfortable: preparing meals, tidying up, buying groceries.

As she felt more at home with me, she began to assert herself a little more. I'm still not sure how I woke up one day to find myself abiding by a cleaning schedule, eating dinner at the table, and spending my free time doing yard work, among many other projects I would never have taken on otherwise. For all practical purposes, I had become a married man.

At first I was satisfied with these circumstances, even happy, but then again, the relationship existed with no real vision of a future together. Days turned into weeks, and weeks to months and years, but the season became constant—a season composed of all seasons, with Emily the sun at the center. Because I was becoming so accustomed to having her actively involved in my life, my imagination was flooded by possible outcomes. Sometimes I fancied that she was a Dostoevskian heroine and that our unique circumstances afforded us an experience that was literary and meaningful—and yet pointing to tragedy; or I imagined that she was playing Regina to my Kierkegaard and that my true insight lay in my willingness to one day embrace the principle of conscientious abandonment; or I thought that we were like Leopold and Molly Bloom and that the odyssey of pain between us could be traversed with time, misadventure, and forgiveness. No matter how many times I played it out in my mind, though, I found it hard to believe that we'd truly end up together. Our togetherness seemed to belong more in a dream. But I could never downplay its significance. It was the dream that kept me convinced I was grasping for hope while wrestling with the very high price tag for my chosen profession.

Confused love cannot be solved intellectually, but has to be experienced and dealt with on an intuitive level that sorts itself out through feeling. In a way, my passion for Emily and God mirrored each other in the sense that both existed despite a huge lack of insight into the source of their flame. But when I contrasted them, I recognized that the physical and spiritual spoke volumes about each other—if only I could get a handle on what my feelings were telling me. This is how I came to believe that my experiences could be analogous to something deeper. It's difficult to explain, but somewhere along the line I came to ask myself the question, "What does my personal experience say about God?" In my journals, I refer to this as "analogy."

Even before I worked at the shelter I came to believe that an appropriate analogy carried through to a conclusion created its own rewards. I remember this clearly because Tamer and I were at a bar one time, shortly after Emily had ended our romantic relationship, and we were approached by a couple of attractive ladies. They sat down with us and had a few drinks. In typical fashion, we got to know each other's favorite beverages—this is always a good place to start in a bar—and as we felt more comfortable we talked about our individual interests. And then, as we got a little more alcohol in our systems, we loosened up and delved into such topics as political views and philosophy. Eventually it came out that I had been a seminarian and so we talked about God for the rest of the night. When it was time to leave, the girls gave us their phone numbers and Tamer and I began to walk back home together. Tamer asked me whether I preferred one girl over the other, because he was genuinely indifferent. He just thought it would be nice for us to get together once in a while with some intelligent, attractive women.

"I'm not interested," I told him.

"How could you not be?" he asked. "They enjoyed talking about God."

"I'm just not," I said and kept walking.

Tamer stopped me.

"You serious prick, are you honestly not interested in women?"

"Sorry, Dan, I'm just not interested in their type," I clarified, feeling like my judgment was being challenged.

"What type are you looking for, then?" he demanded.

"I'm looking for the type of woman that fits the analogy," I tried to explain, definitely with Emily on my mind.

"Analogy?" he demanded, almost ready to plow me.

"The analogy of a monogamous relationship. I want a woman who is just as willing to suffer for the one relationship as I am."

"You're driving me crazy," said Tamer. "Tell Emily how you feel in black and white terms and let the cards fall as they may."

"I can't do that."

"Why not?" he asked, looking totally baffled.

"It has to be her idea. She needs to come to me on her own."

At one point in his life, Tamer actually leaned toward monogamy himself. But he was burned on multiple occasions and experienced severe repercussions for his trust. There's no denying that Tamer had been dragged through the mud, but by his own admission, his addiction to flirting had always played a prominent role in pushing his significant others away. When it came to his cynicism, I tried to shock him back to his senses by using such words as "misogynist". Or I would try to appeal to his good nature and offer him some hope by saying that there were plenty of reliable, trustworthy women around if he weren't so lazy about the way he approached his search.

I recall one time we were talking about women and he was using Emily as his example. He was making a sporting effort to get me to admit that women were too irrational to get close to and that I was equally jaded myself.

"Women are not the problem," I argued. "We have to take responsibility for our relationship failures because nobody put a gun to our head and said we had to go out with these girls. Therefore, the failure is ours, and it's up to us to learn from it and be better prepared for the next time around."

Tamer shook his head. "Is it really our fault that we've been screwed? I mean, you say we have a choice in the women we date, but do we really? Look at your situation. Are you telling me that you felt you had a choice?"

I thought about this briefly. "No, it feels like my situation with Emily kind of fell in my lap somehow. It's like the tide came in and she was there."

"Exactly," he said. "You've proven my point. I just think you're happier if you avoid the hassles altogether and just enjoy your life, concentrate on yourself."

As a response to his disappointment, Tamer turned from the ideal of having a close relationship to the watered down satisfaction of drinking from a fast moving stream of countless watered downed relationships. In choosing this lifestyle, he often complained about feeling spread thin, but at the same time he enjoyed his freedom and the fact that his current situation could never leave him disappointed again. I couldn't decide whether giving up like this was a sign of weakness or the logical extension of his negative experiences. I often compared Emily's unwillingness to be open with me to the impenetrable shell that had formed over Tamer's heart. They would spend time together once in a while, and I was comfortable with this because I believed they shared a similar struggle. I also thought it was possible they could help each other restore the ability to trust themselves in relationships again. Besides, I long suspected the reason Emily talked to me about Tamer's challenges was to describe, albeit indirectly, her own feelings.

The day after Emily visited me at work, I finished showering to find her waiting for me in the bathroom. She passed me a towel and I began drying myself behind the curtain.

"Your manuscript got returned again," she said.

"I'll be engaged in revision for a lifetime," I muttered, showing no emotion.

"That's all right, we're accustomed to revising our circumstances."

"Are we?" I asked.

"I've been thinking about moving out. Mom wants me to move back and be around Dad. It might be better for both of us."

"For both of us or just for you?" I probed, stepping out of the shower with the towel around me.

She seemed thoughtful, sitting there using the toilet lid as a chair.

"Grant, your ideas have radically changed over the years. You're more mystical now—don't even try to deny it—and your values . . . they're not the same and I think you've become less sensitive as a result."

"I don't know want you want from me. You said that you want me to love you, but nothing has changed. What am I supposed to do?"

"I don't know what I want," Emily admitted. "I'm just so sick of revisiting this over and over. We need to do something."

"I agree. Things are surfacing now that we can't ignore."

Emily put her face in her hands and sighed deeply.

"Look, I don't want you to leave. I know this. But I can't elaborate right now."

She looked up at me and I could tell she might become emotional again if she wasn't careful. She controlled her voice. "I thought I was strong enough to suppress any notion of having expectations of others. It's not your faults that upset me, it's my weakness."

"So we'll talk later?" I asked.

"I want you to go to couples counseling with me," she said. "I've already talked to a local pastor about listening to our problems."

"Are you kidding me?"

Emily became defensive. "I just couldn't think of a better solution."

"Did you tell him we're not married?" I asked, somewhat astonished that she had gone to such lengths.

"I've talked to him some and he's agreed to see us as a couple. This is what it will take to make me stay."

* * * * *

White Sands is a tiny community built on the southeastern tip of Georgian Bay. As a child, I'd walk down to the docks around dusk and wait for the fishermen to come in with their catch from up the lakes. I was fascinated by these men—how they'd dock their boats and make for their trucks, carrying stringers of gigantic fish that had lurked in waters totally foreign to me: northern pikes and muskies, large and smallmouth bass, pickerel, and the occasional channel cat. Back to my earliest memories, this quiet bay had always stirred my spirit. Even today, spending time at the waterfront almost always evokes a certain sense of nostalgia, perhaps of childhood wonder, but it seems to go deeper than this—like the water itself holds memories of aboriginal heritage and explorers and military vessels. If you traveled north from Toronto, you would cross marshes and rivers, open farmland, and obscure little communities, all the while winding your way through back country to a town guarded by two angels blowing trumpets, known for its historic naval positioning, mental health facility, and now for its more recent contract to house some of the province's criminals.

This was my home, and yet it seemed to me that the distinct feel of the town—built on its French and English bilingualism; its devotion to Catholicism; its proximity to the reservation, Christian Island; the regular encounters with day patients in the streets; its love of good conversation in coffee shops and restaurants, neighborliness, hard work, and all levels of hockey; its fondness for coffee, spirits of any kind, cigarettes, and of course, a Giants Tomb-sized appreciation of the cannabis plant—was becoming secularized by the outside world. Where once stood woodland, open fields, and waterfront property, I now saw subdivisions, expansive housing, and insidious development.

Returning from university, it took me time to recognize the community that had grown without me. At first it was as if the people I had known throughout my lifetime existed as ghosts, while new inhabitants had taken their place, friendly but still unfamiliar and seemingly out of place. The most bizarre part is that many of the people I had grown up with still navigated the streets and frequented our restaurants and malls. I ran into them all of the time, and yet to me they were testaments to the White Sands of my past. It actually took me a while to decide whether or not I could belong to this community again.

Ultimately, it was the shelter that answered this question for me. I feel you're part of a community to the degree of your participation, and it was working with dogs that provided me with a renewed sense of connection to my childhood roots. Perhaps the sense of belonging came from knowing my dogs loved me as their surrogate master. Their love stemmed from their faith, and yet that faith was double-edged. I was all too aware that this same faith, responsible for that sense of meaning and purpose in my life, also proved to be the source for the greatest pain I had experienced in all of my days under the sun. It's no wonder I came to view my employment as both my cross and my reward.

I was reminded of the contradictory nature of my profession when I arrived at work to find a post that we were downsizing our population of dogs again. Funding wasn't as good this year, and we had taken in more dogs than we had the previous two years. The implications of the post were evident, being that two of my special dogs were already nearing the point where I'd have to actively petition for new homes or see them suffer the same fate as Porcupine. My immediate response was to question my strength, commitment, and resolve. When I arrived at the shelter in the evenings, I was greeted by gray, industrial-looking walls of brick and mortar. Every night I slowly eased from the world of verve and color on the outside of the confines into the murky workings of conscience. In itself, the shelter was possessed of no poetry. Its language was prosaic and uncompromising. It was the animals themselves that refused to be constrained by the neutral colors of their prison. As a family unit, a veritable pack, they were a litany of protest—each one of them a candle aglow in the hostile darkness.

Crystal was the light that evening, her blue eyes searching for a smile. She was the one in danger, and yet I projected her concern onto myself like she existed in that moment to exorcise my fear. I had to take her for a walk before I could even start my evening routine—a real walk outside of the confines. I told Gizzer (by this point he had accepted the name) to keep an eye on things and go about his regular tasks. A few minutes later I was outside with Crystal prancing contentedly beside me, so content, in fact, that she wasn't even straining the leash. The evening was muggy and I perspired heavily, and as I walked I found myself anticipating the coolness of the shelter and the ability to breathe again. We continued on, though, and there was a cinematic quality to our surroundings: televisions emanating blue through windows, frogs and crickets, and an indiscernible, black emptiness to a starless sky.

Crystal was very happy, her tail held high and swaying back and forth, her nose to the ground most of the time, painting a picture for her brain that I could never understand; I meanwhile was living through emotions she could never understand. And yet we walked together as a singular concept: a worshiper directly united with her religion. At that moment she had no idea about the truth of things, for we were on a walk and that was all that mattered to the young orphan. I was the one with the burden, trying to convince myself that she was sensitive to my grief.

Crystal was a wondrous creature to me. I tried to register in my mind the decree of fate surrounding all of life and why my individual character was endowed with a human mind and all the rights of being human—and Crystal, an individual character born into the life of a dog, possessed of almost no rights and whose continued existence was reliant on factors totally independent of her personal effort. In my mind, she had as much personality as anybody and the injustice seemed tremendous. A pity response is an affirmation of the interconnectedness of all life, and it has the capacity to precipitate the movement of the soul into the underground of emotion. Pity can lead the emotions to deep sadness and even despair when another's life circumstances are measured against one's own. But what's the reality and nature of pity? Am I reacting to my own devastating crisis through the projection of myself into another's situation, or do I sincerely care about the object of my pity? Initially, I had allowed Emily to move in with me out of pity, and yet my love for her certainly became a united existential response: body, soul, and mind. Perhaps my employment at the shelter followed the same pattern. My greatest fear was that I was selfishly motivated—and thus unfit to carry my cross.

As we walked along, the night took on a sultry quality. When I found a way to breathe in the warm air again without feeling like I was suffocating, my thoughts turned to the one escape that I could look forward to. Megan's apartment had no air conditioning and I recalled the effect of a warm summer night on her skin. With the right combination of humidity and physical exertion, Megan would get a light covering of sweat all over her body. Her eyes—they'd distribute just the right amount of tenderness and desire to make my daily struggles meaningful, if only for a little while. It was the actual act of providing pleasure to another that I found addictive. Certainly with Emily I had never had the opportunity, while each successful experience with Megan provided the transcendence, strength, and confidence to perform a job and maintain a lifestyle that I never would have chosen for myself.

Don't get me wrong—I cared very much for Megan. In some respects, I really had been trying to detach myself from Emily and cling to someone who I thought could wholeheartedly accept me. It's just that Megan had made it quite apparent that our relationship was secondary to her chronic dependence on something smokable and a little more organic. At first I mistook this cynical indulgence as a declaration of profound spirituality. And then, over time, it became quite obvious that there was more of my imagination in Megan than a proper interpretation of the cold, hard facts. But there was no denying that we had a physical connection, and so in her own way Megan was a very positive presence in my life. Still, in my experience, when you get your physical needs met on a continual basis by someone who you know isn't right for you, a lingering aftertaste of dissatisfaction develops that eventually sours everything.

It was for this reason that each visit left me depleted and fulfilled in equal measure, and yet I was willing to accept the guilt of this conflict in order to get my fix. Even though Emily had begged me to pursue other relationships, I often wondered at how it all came to down to a self-perpetuating lie. How could I bring myself to look Emily straight in the eyes when I desired so badly to tear her clothes off, take her in my arms, and then coax that womanly sigh out of her that satisfies every last ounce of the male disposition? And believe me, I took my frustration out on Megan, who didn't seem to mind. And so after work that evening, I walked over to Megan's.

By the time I got to her apartment, I had convinced myself that Emily was going to move out regardless and that it was time to give Megan the exclusive attention that she deserved.

When I slept with Megan, no doubt I loved her. But, once again, I found out that my experience under the sheets with her and my feelings for Emily had no separation. In the dark one relies on the other senses, and so the lie was invisible to me until exposed by the light of day. In this case, it was the morning sunshine flooding into the kitchen. Megan was walking around with her housecoat open, cooking me breakfast, repeatedly lighting her pipe. Emily would have killed me if she knew I was even near one of those things. She viewed them as a sign of the emotionally weak, which leads me to believe that she probably had a dependency herself at one point.

A few moments later I was sitting at the table, with Megan serving me breakfast: four eggs, all the bacon I could eat, whole grain toast, jams and jellies, orange juice, and coffee. The intensity of my hunger was only matched by the guilt I had begun to feel. Megan nibbled on a muffin and sipped some coffee across the table from me.

"The bitch is going to be pretty upset, I reckon," said Megan, looking scornful.

"I told you not to refer to her as that," I replied with my mouth full. "And it's too early to start with that southern voice you use when you're jealous."

"Why would I be jealous of your roommate?" she asked.

"Oh, I don't know, maybe it's because you throw a southern drawl in there when you speak of her. Let's just enjoy this breakfast before I go, if that's all right with you?"

"You're the one with the mood right now. I really don't care what she thinks; I just know she hates it when you show up in the middle of the morning."

"Fine, you're not jealous," I agreed.

"I'm not . . ." she reiterated, putting her muffin down and meeting my gaze.

"What's wrong?" I asked.

She stayed quiet for a few seconds, looking like she was mulling something over.

"Why are we together, Grant? I mean . . . you're right . . . I do feel jealous all of the time. I can't help but be jealous of her. Don't you understand that I'm not naturally a very jealous person?"

"I never said you were," I replied.

"I don't understand why I feel so possessive of you, though. It's not right. And yet it seems you're not possessive of me."

I just looked at her.

"Well are you?"

"I trust you," I replied.

"Maybe after dating for several months you'd find a way to reassure me that you give you a damn. But you haven't said it, and your actions speak nothing different. Which leaves me possessive of you without actually caring about you. You can see why I have this anxiety."

"It's hard for me, Megan. I find all of this uncomfortable."

"Well then, I'm going to ask you point blank: do you care about our relationship?"

"Of course I do," I said, but even I knew that my voice lacked conviction.

Megan took it in stride. "My whole life I've had a hard time saying no to guys. I'm not sure I have any boundaries when it comes to sex, and I have no idea where the physical ends and the emotional begins."

"Why are you telling me this?" I asked.

"Well, it's just that . . . that it's important to me that you like me, and given my inability to draw a line in the sand that I will not cross . . . and before I let myself love someone who could never love me . . . I suppose I'm saying that I won't allow myself to care for you in the same way other women might."

"Don't you trust me?" I asked, starting to feel a little sick. The conversation was becoming personal enough that it felt like infidelity to my feelings for Emily.

"The question is, *can* I trust you? I mean, are you going to tell me that my jealousy is imaginary and that there is truly a possibility that we could end up together for ever and ever?"

I just looked at her, speechless.

"That about answers it," she said. "I want you to know this, Grant. It's very important to me that you cared about me and valued our time together. Don't you understand? My very confidence as a woman rests in the fact that I did trust you with these things."

"I've appreciated everything, I promise," I said.

"Then how come I feel like a fool?"

"I never meant you to feel this way," I tried to reassure her.

"Everything with you is a lie, and yet it's not an offensive lie because you honestly care. You honestly care, but you don't know how to care honestly. I'm sick over what I have to do. I really do like you."

I was totally taken back by the confrontation. It seemed that every encounter I had with a woman proved to be a circumcision of the heart and this one would be no different. It was becoming apparent that the decision I had been considering was being taken out of my hands.

"What do you have to do?" I asked, already knowing the answer.

"Before I say, what is it about me that holds you back?" she asked.

"I don't know," I said.

"Tell me, Grant," she demanded.

"I don't trust you with yourself because of your addiction," I told her straight up.

"Then why did you date me? I never hid the fact."

"I thought you were deep and that you were spiritual."

"Spiritual," she laughed. "There's nothing about me that suggests spiritual. I don't even care about spirituality. I just want to survive each day."

"It's what I thought," I defended. "So what are we going to do?"

"I'll tell you what *I'm* going to do: I'm going to ask you not to come over anymore."

Megan's hazel eyes still had a glassiness to them from the stuff she smoked. They were sincere in that moment—so sad, perhaps still hoping that I'd object—and I thought her to be pretty in her natural environment. I had never considered her to be beautiful under any other circumstance.

"I am so sorry, Megan," I said, standing up. "When we met, I never thought it would come down to this, I promise."

"You should be sorry. If someone like you can be dishonest, where do I go from here? Who can I trust? What am I supposed to do now?"

"I promise you, I needed you."

"I believe that you needed me. But you never wanted me. Please just leave me alone before I become emotional."

"I'm sorry," I said again.

Megan nodded. "Whatever. I'm just sorry that we've wasted each other's time."

I leaned over to give her a hug, but she pushed out a palm and turned her head away, leaving me to depart in awkward silence. The last image I have from that morning's encounter was her leaning down to take another puff from her pipe. The last sound I remember was the flick of her lighter.

Walking home felt like a sickening digression. I put my personal loneliness before all else, and my need for comfort took me out of the realm of compassion and into a mode of survival. It was clear to me that in everything I did there was no consistency between thought and deed. And I did want to be the type of person who puts others first. But when it came to relationships, for whatever reason I would trick myself into thinking my motives were pure. Now, though, my eyes had been opened. The consequence of failing those I had come to love was unimaginable. Emily, the dogs—their safety was in my hands and I could never let them down like I had let Megan down.

The true price for my eventful evening was waiting at home for me. I just didn't know that yet.

CHAPTER 4

Megan provided me with an amazing gift that morning. She told me straight up that my values were confused. My lie was exposed. I was always in it for myself. And the worst part was that I couldn't help but reflect on Emily's words: "You can't fix yourself by protecting the innocent." This made me question everything. When I worked at the shelter, was I truly protecting the innocent, or was there some deep, dark part of my soul that needed to protect the innocent in order to manage my faith? And if this was my motivation with the dogs, did this same principle apply to my friendship with Emily? All of a sudden, I had to question my selfless actions in life because Megan proved I was capable of being highly selfishly motivated. So I walked home from Megan's apartment with the sun shining and the birds singing and my heart aching.

But this was only the start to my day. When I arrived home, I tried to sneak in quietly so that I could make it to my bedroom without being detected. Emily was waiting for me, though, on the alert. She didn't ask me to explain my lateness. Instead, she took my hand and led me to the bathroom upstairs.

"Take a shower," she said. "Then get dressed. You picked a real good morning to show up at this time."

"What's going on?" I asked.

Then the doorbell rang.

Emily exhaled in exasperation. "You don't have time now. Don't you remember? We talked about this."

The doorbell rang again.

"Get downstairs, Grant. We're going to have to do this with you looking the way you are. I can't believe you. At least change your shirt."

I quickly splashed some water on my face, then doused my hair. After drying myself with a facecloth, I changed my shirt.

Still clueless, I walked downstairs. A familiar figure was sitting in our living room chair: Pastor Daven.

My first impression of Daven had been gathered two years earlier. I had attended a Christmas vespers service one evening at the request of a friend, and I was taken in by Daven's character as a whole. He was probably about forty-five, and he had a voice that resounded with compassion, confidence, and most remarkably, a passion for the message he staked his life upon. He had the type of voice that made you feel secure before all the trials life has to offer—like there was nothing that could happen to you that couldn't be overcome. In appearance, he was a tall man with probably a strong athletic streak as he was growing up, dark eyes, dark hair. He had a square jaw that could stand resolute before all opponents, and no doubt his chin could also stand up to any violence cast against it. All things considered, I believe God put him in this world as an encourager and confidence builder to those around him, and all his features and attributes concurred to form this universal impression—both within and outside of congregational life.

"Grant, I'd like to introduce you to Pastor Daven," Emily said.

"Good to meet you," I said, extending my hand.

"Thank you for inviting me," Daven replied, shaking it firmly.

While Emily slipped away to get coffee, I sat on the couch and watched the pastor pull out a binder and pen from his briefcase. When I observed him write something at the top of the page, I wondered exactly how much time Emily had previously spent with this man. In that moment, I felt like Daven had penetrated my defenses and already planned to indict me in my own living room. It seemed, that day, that everything was going to come crashing down.

"Don't look so worried, Grant," he assured me. "I'm here to listen and advise you, as the situation demands. I'm not here to judge you."

Emily appeared with a tray of coffee and sat beside me on the couch.

Daven continued, "But my concern here is for Emily and her well-being. My associate pastor, Justin Fancy—I'm pretty sure you know him—expressed concern over this young woman and asked me to meet with her."

"You didn't tell me you had talked to Justin," I said to Emily.

"Not now," Emily replied, darting me a sharp look.

Daven reached into his briefcase and pulled out an old briar pipe, still redolent with the faint smell of tobacco. "I don't smoke it, but this used to be my mentor's pipe. It has become my way to invoke Wisdom's presence into my sessions. I hope you don't mind."

Emily and I smiled when he put the pipe his mouth. "Knock yourself out," I said.

He withdrew the pipe again, licked his lips, and grew serious. "Grant, this is one of the strangest cases I've encountered, and the delicacy of the matter leaves me little choice but to inquire into the core of this unusual lifestyle you two have fashioned for yourselves."

"Ok," I said, "ask away, but I can't guarantee you'll like the answers."

"Emily tells me that you work at an animal shelter, and yet you've had a theological education and have done some pastoral work yourself."

"That's true, I spent a year in ministry."

"Do you mind if I ask why you left?"

"In my experience, belief in God is a gift, not something that can be earned or acquired. I couldn't continue pastoring while waiting to be chosen."

"Ah," he said in understanding. "Have you tried praying?"

"I pray every day. I'm not above doing anything if it leads to conviction."

Daven looked at me quizzically and tapped his pipe. "Including your job?"

I nodded.

"From what I understand, your responsibilities at this shelter greatly disturb Emily."

"I agree, it's been a problem," I admitted. "But I've tried harder to leave work at work. She has no stomach for the role I play at the shelter, while I feel like I'm making a difference."

"Does that sum it up well, Emily?" Daven asked.

"Pretty much. But it's what he's capable of doing that's upsetting to me."

"All right, you two. Let me begin by explaining to you why I decided to counsel you as a married couple. While I don't support the idea of living together before marriage, I recognize that you're experiencing the same types of challenges. My hope is that our time together will help you consider going down that road."

"We appreciate you seeing us," I said. "And I'm on board—but I want you to understand something. To me, living together before marriage speaks a great deal about the human desire for commitment and nothing about character."

Daven smiled and stuck the pipe back in his mouth.

"He's trying to help us," Emily scolded, glaring at me accusingly. "He didn't come here to talk about your views."

"It's ok," Daven said reassuringly, now twirling the pipe around with his fingers. "Perhaps Grant would like to share his thoughts over a coffee someday."

"Yeah, maybe."

"Emily talked to me about how you two have lived together for several years without having relations. It's strange to me that I'm counseling a platonic couple who view themselves as married."

I looked at Emily sitting there beside me, withdrawn and pensive, then replied, "How do you know we view ourselves this way?"

"Emily told me that you were married in principle."

I looked at her for a second, but her gaze remained downcast. "I can see how we could view our relationship as a marriage. We have the same tensions and struggles. But we'd probably be married if Emily wasn't so prone to pushing me off on other women rather than dealing with her issue."

"That's not fair!" Emily exclaimed. Then she turned to the pastor. "I told him to date others because I thought I was no good for him."

"Emily has assured me that she has your best interest in mind," Daven said soothingly. "But you said something that intrigued me. You said Emily's 'issue.' What do you think her issue is?"

I looked at Emily and considered my words. "She's terrified of the vulnerability that comes with a committed relationship. I think her issue revolves around a shaky self-worth. My struggle is trying to get her to realize that she's the most valuable presence in my life."

Emily did not protest my explanation. Her eyes had the look of being criticized, with no desire to fight it.

"That proves what I'm saying," I said, pointing to Emily in her silence. "She doesn't get it."

Daven tapped his pipe on the table again and looked at Emily. "What is it that you want from all of this?" he asked her.

Emily remained frozen for a second, almost spaced out, and then she looked up at the pastor and said, "I don't want him to sleep with her anymore."

There was a silence in the room.

"I had a girlfriend because I didn't know what else to do," I explained. "I mean, what could I do? I could eternally wait for Emily to come around, or I could at least prospect for another opportunity so that I could find someone who could be close to me."

Daven seemed to consider this for a second. "But that's not the reason you dated another. What was your ulterior motive? You can be honest about it."

"I'm trying to be," I insisted.

"If I was in your position and I had your feelings for Emily, I know what my motive would be. You're not going to be struck down for admitting it."

I sat there for a second, stunned at the turn of events. Who could have predicted that I would have pie thrown in my face this early in the morning?

"Emily, I suppose I dated Megan because I knew she would get you incensed, ultimately making you jealous," I admitted.

"I understand that," said Emily sharply. "But you slept with her while loving me." Then she turned to Daven. "I don't know how I can reconcile this."

"Is she right, did you have relations with this Megan?" Daven asked.

"I don't have to answer that," I replied.

"I don't have to be here," Daven countered. "But I'm here for a purpose. Let's stay honest."

"I need closeness in my life, too," I protested, watching for Emily's reaction out of the corner of my eye. She showed no emotion.

Daven considered this for a second, lightly tapping his pipe again. "This is where you and I would diverge in our thinking. Emily has talked very little to me about her problems and she never told me about how you two relate. But I have to tell you, I see a big problem here and I can't see how a man of your background could feel very good about himself right now."

"You don't understand the situation," I snapped.

"No, I don't," Daven said calmly, "nor can I imagine any situation where the feelings you inspire in each other in light of your decisions would be acceptable."

I said nothing.

"Emily, maybe you should consider moving out and starting again. It's just easier. There's a lot of pain between you two. When you had me come over, I was under the impression that you two were a moral couple living together out of necessity. But this seems much messier."

"I understand that at first glance our relationship is complicated," I agreed. "You might even feel we're messed up people. But really, we're just trying to keep our heads above water and hope that we stay together."

"We really care for each other, Pastor," Emily added, obviously embarrassed and apologetic about my sudden outburst.

The minister looked thoughtful for a second. "You both know that what's going on here is not healthy."

How could I ever explain to Daven the crazy behavior that stems from the loneliness inside? Perhaps he'd have understood if I'd compared it to Christ's encounter with the Samaritan woman at the well and the special request he made of her: "Will you give me a drink?" Indeed, to draw your loneliness up to the surface requires a break in your own conventions and an inspiring amount of faith that the water you'll be offered in return comes from the same soulful depths. You have to anticipate that the person you share your feelings with will be able to accept and relate, without judgment, to the way you describe your relationship to the world around you. And it's not an easy burden to let go of.

The feeling is romanticized enough that it's now a major contributor to your sense of identity, and to put such sentiment into words risks devaluing everything that's precious. So how could I explain to Daven that Emily and I had been developing this trust since the moment we met each other and had created some unusual circumstances along the way?

"What if we requested to be officially married in the church?" I asked.

Emily looked at me quickly, surprised to say the least.

"I'd wish you guys the best. But I wouldn't marry you myself. In fact, until you work through your problems I'd suggest that the ceremony should be performed in a legal venue, not religious."

"You wouldn't trust our judgment and put the matter in God's hands?" I asked.

"In my mind, you two are not what I'd consider to be a devoted couple," Daven said candidly.

"But we'd take the necessary steps," Emily protested, being careful not to sound disrespectful.

"Emily, the problems between you two are well beyond my skills and require a licensed family therapist."

"What if Justin would marry us?" Emily asked. "Would you agree to such an arrangement?"

When she said this, I felt my stomach sink. It made me wince to hear her say his name.

For a second I thought Daven looked a little bit ill. He gave an answer that pacified Emily's request, but obviously stretched his conscience: "I'd have to talk to Justin about it first, but I'd greatly discourage him from doing so."

Emily agreed that this was something to be explored further and then let the subject drop.

Daven, however, didn't seem to be in a huge hurry to leave. He took one last taste of his pipe before setting it down beside him, and then began to drink his coffee, looking much more relaxed.

"Do you mind if I ask you guys something?" he asked.

"Go ahead," Emily encouraged, and I nodded.

"What first attracted you to each other?"

I glanced sidelong at Emily. "Want me to go first?"

She gestured for me to go ahead.

"There are many things, but when I first met Emily I noticed she had a certain way with animals. She lived at home with her family. She had two dogs and a cat, whom she treated like they were her own kids.

"She's also a voracious reader and a much better writer than she gives herself credit for. When I talk about my ideas, she understands where I'm coming from, even though she usually doesn't agree. She's also so simple in her faith. She's the one trying to get me to go back to church. I get the sense she knows there's a better person inside me and that she's willing to wait for him to emerge."

"How about you, Emily?" Daven asked.

"From the moment I met him, I knew he was caring," Emily said, her eyes becoming watery. "In fact, Grant's caring to a fault, and I feel like he'll never give up on me as a person. In my life, that's as much security as I've ever known."

Taking another sip of coffee, Daven asked me whether our parents lived in town as well.

"My father's Marco," I said.

"Yeah, Marco . . . isn't he that tough-looking man who owns the hobby shop downtown?"

I nodded.

"I've been trying to get that man to come to church for quite some time. I bought this remote control car for my son from him and we've been accessorizing it for years: new tires, decals, an upgraded spoiler. The thing's gas powered. Good guy, your dad."

"I suppose so."

"Do you spend much time with your parents?" Daven asked, looking genuinely interested.

"My parents and I don't talk. They were upset when I inherited—what does it matter?"

"It's just that you looked familiar. So you're a Spire? I believe your mother sometimes attends the church."

When I didn't respond, he inquired about my parents' opinion of Emily.

"They really don't know her and I imagine they have no interest in meeting her," I explained.

"What about your family, Emily, are they here in town as well? I'm not familiar with any Arums."

"Yes, they live near the end of Fox Street. Since my father's heart attack, I've been visiting the house more and more often."

"So your family problems have been sorting themselves out?"

"Yes, but slowly," Emily murmured.

Daven picked up the pipe again and began spinning it slowly in his hand. "You know, guys, if you're serious about marriage, Wisdom tells us that to give yourselves the best chance you need the commitment of the individuals, the support of the family, and the hand of God at work . . ."

* * * * *

Aside from Emily, Tamer was my closest confidant and friend. My moral disposition in the world had been irrevocably challenged when I started spending time with him. He was the type of guy who if you told him that you put the goat horns on five married guys in a night he'd congratulate you and give you a slap on the back, but if you threw a pop can in the garbage instead of recycling it you'd never hear the end of it. With Tamer, my sense of right and wrong was perennially being questioned—devil's advocate style. But how could he resist? His Type B personality approach to life and complete lack of concern when it came to women was a stark contrast to my desire for a conventional family.

This well-liked restaurant manager floated about with a smile, surrounding himself with friends he held to minimal standards, and for the most part without a care in the world while I was dangerously near the precipice. From my perspective, it was inconceivable that he was carefree and smiling when we both had so much work to do to get our lives in order. This is why it often felt—despite our openness with each other—like there was an ocean of distance to traverse if we were ever to have a proper understanding.

Later that day we were sitting in the pub together. I had just related to him the events of from that morning, and his response was lackluster, to say the least.

"You look tired today, Tamer," I said.

"Old man, I'm beaten down. I'm going to admit something to you. With all of these women in my life—I don't know if I can take it anymore."

"Yeah, poor you," I said sarcastically.

"No, I'm serious. You know how I'm living with two women right now, and how I have my bed set up in the living room?"

"Yeah."

"It's getting to me."

"What's getting to you?" I asked.

"Every night when I go to bed I wake up to find myself sandwiched between my roommates. I can't even stretch out, with both of them snuggled into me. Not to mention that I have no privacy. I have to—well, you know, take care of myself—on the sly, and I worry about getting caught every time. I'm at the point where it just doesn't matter."

I laughed out loud at the thought of this inconvenience.

"It's not funny, man. Do you realize that I woke up to four women sleeping in my bed last night? Four women. That's way too much cuddling for me. And then I get pulled in for long talks about trivial nonsense like who stole whose juice. Are you kidding me? We had to have a house meeting over beverages in the fridge, with rules laid out."

"Well, you do look stressed."

"It's killing me. It's too much. I need some space."

"Well, I can understand that," I sympathized. "It seems that everywhere we go women are coming up and yelling at you for something or other."

"I know," Tamer admitted. "It's like they all have a claim to me. And if I see an attractive woman when I'm out with these girls, they sabotage. They sabotage, Grant, even though they all have boyfriends. It's ridiculous."

"I can't say I feel sorry for you," I said. "You've brought this upon yourself."

"Well, you could at least keep Emily away from me."

"What do you mean?" I demanded.

"Right after she freaked out at you for showing up like a vagabond in the middle of the morning, forgetting your appointment with the pastor, she came to visit me."

"What did she say?" I asked.

Tamer laughed. "Oh, she was ticked off with you. That Emily really comes out of her shell once you get to know her. She's a fireball alright."

"Tamer, were you the one who recommended that she seek out a pastor to help us with our problems?"

"Old man, crazy as she is, I had no choice but to tell her to talk to Justin. I'm not sure I've ever met a woman like her. Grant, seriously, I think you've been as harmful to her as anything else she's experienced."

"How can you say that?" I said in disbelief. "I took her in when nobody else would and I've tried to care for her the only way I know how. Everything I've done has been at her request."

"Sure, buddy," said Tamer with a wink. "Consider who you're talking to. You can't fool me."

"I've been trying to help her," I insisted.

"I'm not one to cast stones, but you're doing harm to her. Trust me."

"I know . . ." I struggled to admit. "But I love her, Dan."

Tamer got that angry look in his eyes.

"I do. I love her," I repeated.

"Old man, I have seven quid in my pocket and some crowns . . ." he recited, shaking his head in disgust.

"I never should have introduced you to James Joyce," I said.

"Oh, grow up. You should have honored our agreement. You know we're not supposed to use that word in front of each other."

"Are you serious?" I asked.

"I couldn't be more," Tamer replied. "There are three things in life I know to be facts: sex is only a big deal when you're not having it; God reveals himself in dire straits; and love, my friend, is a crock!"

I started to laugh.

"It's not funny," he insisted.

"Look, I won't go all soft on you again," I said reassuringly.

"Be sure that you don't," Tamer warned. "I wouldn't do that to you. Remember, we have a deal. Next time you're buying me dinner."

I just looked at him silently, unsure whether he was genuinely offended or not.

This only seemed to inflame Tamer further: "You're driving me crazy tonight, you serious prick. Just tell me what's wrong and be done with it."

"Something came up in our discussion with the pastor," I admitted.

Tamer had a look in his eye that said he was ready to tear a strip out of me again, but his curiosity got the better of him.

"What have you done?" he demanded, unable to resist caving in.

"Without ever finding the right time to communicate my feelings to Emily, I found myself asking Daven whether he'd consider marrying us."

"Marrying?" Tamer repeated, giving me an appalled look and shaking his head in disbelief, clearly beside himself. "Are you provoking me?"

"No, it happened."

"Old man, when you get the scent you're about as sensible as a bull moose during rutting season . . ."

"You're not helping."

"Fair enough, but I'm certainly not offering," Tamer said. "You realize you're making my skin crawl."

"How about if I do buy dinner?" I offered.

"Not pizza," Tamer clarified.

"Whatever you want."

"Ok, it's a deal. I feel like fish and chips, and I'm awfully hungry."

"So what would you do if you were me?" I asked.

"Wait, I need to get something straight first. So you've never told Emily how you feel about her, and yet you asked about marrying her?"

"Yes."

Tamer lit a cigarette and seemed to muse about the circumstances for a few seconds.

"So why can't you talk about your feelings with Emily?"

"I don't know," I said.

"That's not fair," Tamer warned me. "Don't get me curious and then not fill me in with details. You know it's in my nature to have to know."

"I guess I just don't feel comfortable talking about such feelings with a woman."

"Well, what man is?" Tamer pointed out, exhaling smoke.

"I just wish our relationship could be assumed. Then I wouldn't have to take responsibility when she finds out there's less substance to me than she thought. I'm afraid, after all is said and done, that she'll feel disillusioned."

"Then your feelings for her are conditional," Tamer concluded, reducing everything to its simplest form, another one of his great abilities.

I considered this. "Intellectually, this is true, my feelings for her are conditional on her loving me. From a feeling standpoint, no, I care for her and desire to remain with her with an unconditional intensity."

"You're in a real mess, old man," Tamer concluded. "But I think you just need to ask yourself a simple question: how will my decision, either way, affect Emily?"

"Yeah, but with Emily it's so complicated that I'm not really sure whether I'm harming or helping."

"Oh, you're harming her," said Tamer candidly. "She told me she's trying to become a better person, though—for you."

"She is?" I asked in astonishment, feeling a rush of emotion. "So with our relationship on the line, she's finally making an effort to work through her issues?"

"Whatever she's doing as far as self-improvement goes, it should be for herself. Don't you see the difference?"

CHAPTER 5

ACCEPTANCE IN THE MIDST OF rejection. . . If dogs end up in pounds and shelters because of rejection, what is it that provides them with acceptance? If they are not adopted, it's truly the people who care for them that decide whether the rejection in their lives is exaggerated or whether acceptance is proffered. I recommitted myself to my employment day after day after day. When I woke up in the afternoon, I committed to believing that my contribution made a difference. Every night I went to my shelter and confronted my doubts . . . forced myself to experience the actual hollowness of emptiness, the coldness that seeps past organs and tissue, joints and marrow, right to the soul itself.

This night in question, I arrived at the shelter earlier than usual. I quietly walked into the kennel area and sat down cross-legged outside of Crystal's pen. The young dog was curled up contentedly, obviously fast asleep. Aware of my presence, she flashed a glance at me with one of her blue eyes before scratching herself and resuming her nap. I liked that Crystal was perfectly comfortable with me observing her. Of all my dogs, she was the most psychologically complex, if not the most athletic. She was one of those dogs that made you consider the hierarchy of importance in earthly life and how canine personalities rival humans in uniqueness. When I hugged Crystal, the transference of love was like no relationship I had ever known. She allowed me to experience unbiased, unconditional love, the kind of love that comes from an unshakable faith in the guardian of her well-being.

When Gizzer arrived, he sought me out and helped me to my feet.

"What are you up to?" the kid asked.

"Just spending time with my girl," I explained.

"Don't we have some work to do?" he asked cockily.

Before he could say another word, I gave him a shot to the arm and then swung him around by the collar just to remind him who was the boss.

"Don't make me hurt you," he warned me, holding his fists up defensively.

I raised my fist again and he scampered. "You better run, chicken," I said. "Now go make my coffee."

A little while later, while we were working, I saw the kid was wearing a new set of earphones. Upon closer scrutiny I noticed that somewhere along the lines he had acquired a new iPod.

"Hey Gizz, where did you get that?" I shouted.

Gizzer kept working, oblivious that I was talking to him. In fact, to get his attention, I had to hit him in the head with a clean rag. Only then did he remove the microphones from his ears and look my way.

"Where did the iPod come from, Gizz?"

"Just bought it myself," he said proudly.

"But you've been complaining lately about how broke you are . . ."

"I was . . . until I started working for Tamer. I thought he told you."

"Neither of you guys mentioned it," I said in annoyance.

"I guess we both assumed the other had said something."

"Whatever. So do you like working for him?"

"He's an awesome guy," Gizzer said genuinely. "He's already taught me so much. He even said that I could take a girl over to his new apartment whenever I want. All I have to do is help him with a bit of painting."

"He has a new apartment in the works?" I asked.

"Yeah."

"The fool never told me that either," I said in disgust.

Gizzer shrugged, unable to offer me an explanation.

"It doesn't matter," I said. "It sounds like you guys are getting along. First he renames you and then he hires you. Next thing you know you'll be a regular at his legendary poker nights."

"That would be fine with me," Gizzer said with a confident smile. "When it comes to Texas hold 'em, no doubt I'll be the one schooling him."

This thought amused me. Still, I couldn't help but counsel compassion.

"Be sure you let Tamer win once in a while," I advised. "Because he certainly doesn't get to taste victory when he plays tennis with me . . ."

After we finished up our chores for the night, we let the terrible foursome into the bay for a while. Once we returned them to their pens, I got out the football from my hiding place.

"Hey Gizz, can you throw a football?"

"Absolutely," he said, signaling for the ball.

So we went outside and began tossing the football around. If there's a skill I devoted a lot of energy into throughout my lifetime, it was my ability to throw and catch a football. Gizzer obviously had different pursuits. He had a glaringly weak arm and his mechanics were somewhat of a sorry spectacle. He sure could catch, though. Nice, soft hands, and he caught the ball well away from his body. After we warmed up, I brought the radio outside and I turned up the tunes while we gradually increased the distance between us. I continued his education with some White Zombie and Megadeth and Suicidal Tendencies.

By the time Gizzer left that night, I'm sure he was dog-tired. But I definitely saw some progress. All in all, I gave him a great workout and I was quite proud of my conditioning when I watched him nearly consume a liter of water while I, the old man, hardly worked up a sweat.

* * * * *

Later that night, I felt like a bit of company, and so instead of writing in the office I pulled up a chair alongside the dogs and began to journal about how this current period had to be one of the more episodic in my life: ousted by Megan, condemned by Daven, guilt-tripped by Emily, and confronted by Tamer. If I thought this sudden upheaval in my lifestyle impeded my opportunity to "seize the day," I had no clue how devastating a well-aimed lightning bolt of theodicy could be. Yes, Zeus's bolt pretty much finished me off that evening, with the direct strike of God's justice finding its mark in the form of my charged up father.

It had been years since I had seen Marco, so his silhouette in the window looking into the bay weakened my knees and left me sick. But I motioned for him to come in the moment I recognized him. The materialization of his person in such vivid detail aroused horror and sympathy in me at the same time. He was a big man, at least 220 pounds, with a prickly pasture of two o'clock shadow, the curled lips of one used to barking criticism, and eyes that held an unfortunate mixture of intelligence and malice. Marco had huge, hairy forearms with gorilla hands for extremities and he moved with the confidence of one totally immune to threat, like a gorilla patrolling the forest floor. Despite his simian, menacing demeanor, he was respected in town as an honest, hard-working citizen with a tolerance for hard drink and an appetite for barroom bravado. This was my father, the alpha male with no worthy offspring to continue his lineage.

To really understand my emotions at this time, you have to consider that my father never approved of me. What's funny about the salt of the earth is that they seldom recognize other spices as contributive to a fuller, more balanced flavor. Where my father expected me to come home as an overlord of the playground, I often limped in sporting blood from a fat lip or bleeding nose. For much of my first years of school both my eyes were black, and it's funny to think that I never considered the harsh circumstances surrounding my proletarian upbringing as anything odd. I thought of bullies as a childhood obstacle and nothing more, and I enjoyed the sensation of walking home from school under a sky of shifting clouds in a woodland subdivision where sensual appreciation could be penetrated by violence at any given moment. Much of my psychology was formed in these years, where the perceived autiful surroundings could be destroyed by the ıger lurking at every corner. I knew these things as a child and I appreciated them as necessary obstacles to arriving home from school. It just never occurred to me to take the offensive. To my father's dismay, I was sensitive and thoughtful and accepting. I suppose all these values forced him to evaluate the nature of his own manhood and realize his growing failure as an inculcator of masculine principles. Often if I came home with my eyes still stained with tears, this man would give me another reason to cry. To the woodshed we'd go, in a manner of speaking, and violence compounded left me wondering whether God demanded such perfection of all little boys. It's not that I questioned my father's love, for I always believed that his punishment was for my greater good and a necessary component of life if I was to avoid flaming hell. But now that I'm grown up, I deliberate about why my father couldn't have predicted that the physical blackmail would backfire on him as badly as it did. I am the chemical reaction of a particular set of circumstances and I was activated to be me by the very ape that tried to keep me pounding my chest. Not hard to see why we didn't keep in touch, is it?

Human emotion, though, is as difficult to explore or know as the very depths of the deepest ocean floor. Why, when I saw my father, did I feel such sorrow and guilt in a chemical gush from head to toe? Perhaps I thought he was there to reconcile himself to his estranged progeny and that he had matured and softened. When I chose to leave for university and study philosophy, I thought I was going to be disowned then. When I moved on and studied theology for my Masters, I knew he had given up on me. But when I got my inheritance from my uncle and purchased my house, that was it. And the reason this put him over the edge is that he'd had to work so hard to earn his shelter, paying off his house over thirty years, that he felt insulted that I could accomplish the same feat without scraping a knuckle (or so he thought). My employment, in his mind, involved no discipline and he couldn't classify my occupation as strong, manly work. Therefore, his revile and disgust could no longer be disguised and I eventually became cut off from my family, despite my mother's protests and entreaties.

"What are you doing here?" I asked blankly as he walked toward me.

He didn't respond, just kept walking toward me. In my mind, I was interpreting the scene and I had this literary moment planned. I thought he'd approach me and embrace me and apologize for putting me through such a lonely episode in my life. But according to him I'd been fantasizing since I was born and failing to live up to standards, and it turned out that all my hope in this situation was certainly misguided or born of *naiveté*. When he was near enough that I could make out the expression in his eyes, he mashed me on the chin with a closed, hairy-knuckled fist. The blow sent me flying off my feet and I came down resting against the wiring of Crystal's cage. Dogs were barking in this unified, multi-toned drone and I found it hard to collect my thoughts. The shock was powerful and the hate in my father's eyes burned through the thick cloud surrounding my senses.

"You sick son of a bitch!" he barked, and I thought in that instant that I detected tears in his eyes. "You're capable of anything, aren't you?"

I couldn't understand what Marco meant by this. Even more, I couldn't imagine my father caring one iota about circumstances that in any way involved me. In the heat of the moment, I consciously tried to retreat inward and resist the idea of defending myself. The man who struck me had brought me into this world, and somehow, in some way, my actions must have instigated his emotion. If only I had a chance to consider my father's point-of-view a little more. . . But he began mercilessly kicking me in the ribs, in the face, basically everywhere, so that I was being struck in so many places at once that my mind couldn't process the pain.

All I could hear muttered was something incoherent like, "You sick, artist faggot . . . now go ahead and cry like a girl . . . you sick, get everything handed to you on a plate . . . warped, lazy . . . you know what you've done to your mother!" And he went on and on and on. Everything blended together, the rage, the fluorescent light, the baying of dogs, the gray of cement, the warmth of blood on my face, and I found shelter beneath my arms, which were deflecting blow after blow. One predominant emotion went through my mind during the tirade of punishment: that my father cared enough to come down and personally administer the justice he felt was lacking in my life.

When I came to, Pastor Daven was propping me up and using a handkerchief to sop up blood. As my eyes opened, he tried to comfort me and he assured me an ambulance was on the way. I could barely think, but I had the presence of mind to tell him to call Kelly from a list of numbers in the office. Ironically, Daven seemed very fatherly in those circumstances. Intellectually, I couldn't process human kindness in the face of violence and spite, especially when it came to the concept of "father." God the father, Marco the father . . . Daven the father? The presence of the minister and the compassion he brought left me with a positive impression of the whole circumstance. I was becoming more acutely aware of this as my senses returned while I was carted to the hospital.

* * * * *

Perversion of what's considered normal is the spice of life. The irony is that perversion often feels like the stronghold when it can be the gaping chink in the armor. A person's sense of security in this world is constantly shifting, and it's not always easy to remain rooted in what's normal and healthy. Perversion as a concept is almost always used to describe a dark sexuality, but what I'm talking about is a skewed interpretation of what I have to do in order to feel good about myself. My relationship with Emily was not perverse and I refuse to humor people who have the opinion that the whole messed up situation was the physical manifestation of my messed up mind. Circumstances beyond both my control and Emily's allowed for the events that transpired in our relationship. Just the same, taking what's normal and making it original allows for people to "become" authentically individual. Perversion, then, is mistaking sickness for health and the objectionable as personality defining.

However, Marco had decided that I was indeed a miscreant and a living testament to his woeful skills at sculpting a king. Yes, my father had decided long ago that my interests suggested an enthusiasm for my own gender. So it was my guess that given the opportunity, my father jumped the gun on an assumption he had been entertaining and seething over for years. My father had waited so long for the proof, the demonstration, that he seized the opportunity to vent his fury on me with only my dogs as witnesses.

Marco at least had tried to contact me beforehand. Poor Emily answered the exploratory phone call and spoke to an angry man who demanded my whereabouts. When she explained that I was at work, Marco ended up going into a barking fit on the phone before smashing down the receiver. Emily was scared and couldn't get a hold of me on my cell phone. Then she couldn't get a hold of Tamer, who had the night off. With no other option, she decided to call Daven, who was more than willing to pay me a visit. I think it's a good thing my father reached the shelter before him. There would have been no stopping the machine, and Daven might have gotten hurt as well.

Besides, if these sequences of events had not occurred in the manner that they did, just so perfectly, I never would have met a very dear friend. Brad began as a vague impression on the other side of the curtain in our hospital room. As I gathered my senses, I used his interaction with the nurses to conjure an idea of him as this sixty-plus man that required special attention. At first, the only clue about him rested in this big pair of winter boots arranged neatly against the wall; the man had to be a giant.

As it turned out, he was a forty-year-old ex-clerk of the government, with a big heart and plenty of medical problems.

"I finally decided to get the operation done," said Brad, pulling back the curtain between us after the nurse left, revealing a fairly round face framed by a wispy red beard. He had attempted to feather his hair, but with no real success. His blue eyes were a little droopy and tired, but they were kind eyes that spoke volumes about long nights and rough mornings. "You see, I got this hernia from lifting weights—you know, trying to impress the ladies—and, well, it caused me to have terrible indigestion and so I've been spending way too much money every month on antacids. The doctor said this operation could give me relief for at least a year. I figure the money I'll save in the end is worth taking time off work for."

"I see," I replied.

"Name's Brad."

I extended him a handshake. "I'm Grant."

"Nice to meet you, Grant. You know, I watched them bring you in and it was easy to see that they weren't too concerned. What did they say to you—a concussion, some bruised ribs? Now those are things that we can monitor and observe. But what if you're the type of person who's dying in soul?"

"I'd imagine that there's not much empirical data to provide a cure," I speculated, taken aback by the odd question.

"Exactly. They know I'm hurting and yet they refuse to help me. I mean, can you believe that when I complained about my gout they suggested I stop drinking beer and eating red meat? I said, give me the pills, and then the doctor rolls his eyes as if I'm crazy. I say, live now and if there's a pill to control the discomfort, give it to me. And then my back, they totally ignore that my back is killing me. And my neck, I'm not even going to mention my neck. What's the use? Something good has come from all of this, though."

"Oh yeah?" I asked, inviting him to continue.

"Well, you know, spending as much time in the hospital as I have, I've come to realize something. Surgeries, examinations, needles; being poked, prodded, shaved, and anesthetized. I've come to realize that . . . well . . . that my richest poetry was born in my soul's most desperate hours."

"Really?" I said with a small chuckle, a little surprised this man considered himself a poet. I was very close to laughing out loud, but he looked so sincere.

Brad looked at me intensely. "Oh yeah. I think physical symptoms of illness are manifestations of sickness of soul. In fact, I've been aware of my shabby health since I was very young and it's made me consider the bond between curiosity of the unknown and lament."

"Lament?" I asked, feeling myself turning red. I was a nudge away from breaking out laughing.

Brad nodded. "To lament is to know that you've been given all the tools to achieve greatness and then been denied the constitution to exercise them."

"I see," I said, and then I just started laughing. I laughed until the tears started flowing. He just stared at me with a confused smile on his face.

"What's so funny?" he asked.

"You just reminded me of someone I used to know. It's uncanny."

"But I'm serious, Grant."

"I believe you."

"I worked in the government. I was all set. And then another party gets elected and three-quarters of my colleagues and I are out on our cans. I had to leave the city and move back to White Sands. I don't have the tolerance for pain to do manual labor. But I can't seem to get another office job in the city, either. I have all the skills, but my constitution is weak."

"What have you been doing for work, then?" I asked.

"I was delivering pizzas, but they cut my hours," Brad explained bitterly. "It was a good time to get this done."

"Do you like this line of work?" I asked.

"It's good money for around here."

"Let me make a call. We could do an interview right here."

"Doing what?" Brad asked.

"Delivering pizzas full-time for my buddy," I said. "He's been complaining about a lack of reliable drivers."

"Get him in here," Brad said with enthusiasm. "I just want full-time hours with two full days off a week. That's all I want."

I called and woke Tamer up. He complained about me calling him at the early hour of one o'clock in the afternoon. I pretty much told him that I was in the hospital, close to last rites, and that he needed to haul his butt out of bed. It didn't take long for him to arrive.

"This is Brad," I said to Tamer the moment he walked in the door.

The two characters shook hands.

"So what happened?" Tamer asked me.

"My father finally expressed himself to me last night," I explained.

Tamer just started laughing. Clearly he thought this was a hilarious turn of events.

"What, you got your ass kicked by an old man?" Tamer asked in disbelief with a huge grin.

"Ha, ha," I replied, truly amused.

"It's funny," said Tamer. "I ran into your father recently and I told him how we spend a lot of time together."

"Thanks for reminding him of me, Tamer," I said acidly. "It's all worked out so well."

"Your father did this to you?" Brad asked in disbelief.

"It appears you're never too old for a lesson," I said.

"A harsh lesson at that," and Brad shook his head.

"Hey, Tamer," I said, changing the subject, "by the way, here's your next delivery boy," pointing at the bearded giant. "He's experienced and looking for lots of hours."

Tamer sized him up. "Well, you look like a Brad, but you need a little more spice to your name if you're going to work for me."

"People always have to give me a nickname," Brad said.

"You're . . ." Tamer began thoughtfully, scratching his chin.

"Red beard?" I suggested.

"You know I hand out the nicknames for my staff," said Tamer. "Brad, you're . . . I got it . . ." Tamer turned to me. "You're going to like this, Grant." Then he turned back to the expectant giant. "Welcome aboard, Brad-to-the-Bone."

Brad reached out and grabbed Tamer by the hand, pulling him into a crushing handshake. "You won't regret it, Tamer, I promise."

"What do you think, Grant?" Tamer asked, once he freed himself.

"Brad-to-the-Bone it is."

"Just to make sure, your car's reliable, right?" Tamer asked.

"It's a 2005 compact."

Tamer thought about this for a second. "Can you even fit in the car?"

"It's surprisingly spacious," Brad explained.

"And what are you in here for? Is it chronic? I don't want to have to always worry about finding people to cover your shifts."

"Terrible indigestion. One-time surgery, I swear."

"Fine, you're in, Brad-to-the-Bone," Tamer concluded. "But I have to run. Heidi's coming over and I'm going to be taking some pictures of her feet."

Brad began to chuckle. "What, you collect feet?"

"Doesn't any sensible man? My album is growing and very much a beautiful thing. You should start one of your own."

"That's about enough, Dan," I finally intervened, shaking my head. "Off with you."

"Have it your way," said Tamer. "Brad-to-the-Bone, it was good to meet you. Come see me next week and I'll get you on the schedule. Old man, hope you get over your ass kicking. You are delicate, you know."

Tamer started laughing again and he could be heard singing on the way out of the door: "Brad-to-the-Bone. Br, Br, Br, Br, Br, Brad. Brad-to-the-Bone . . ."

As soon as Tamer's voice trailed off, Brad turned to me. "I appreciate you doing this for me. He seems like he'll be a great boss."

"He'll be a great boss to you all right."

Brad then looked at me as if he wanted something.

"Is there anything else I can do for you?" I asked him.

"Well . . . I'm here for at least two more days. Do you think you can sneak me in some beer? Maybe some magazines, too?"

"I don't know," I said, considering the appropriate response. "Definitely no magazines—if I catch your drift. I don't want to be seen with those things."

"Don't tell me Tamer wouldn't have some," Brad suggested.

"I'm not bringing you any," I repeated.

"Well, what about beer?"

"I don't know."

"Oh, come on," he urged. "Nobody will find out."

"All right, I'll bring you one beer. I'll visit you tomorrow, but you can't drink it when I'm here."

"I can live with that."

Just after we had agreed to these terms a police officer walked in and said he had some questions for me. Brad rolled back the curtain between us and finally shut his trap. The officer was a young guy with a mustache.

"You're Grant?"

I nodded.

"I'm officer McNally," said the policeman. "I'm here to take your statement."

CHAPTER 6

It was early the next morning. Having returned to work the same day I was released from the hospital, I was finally in my own bed, trying to fall asleep with an affectionate Emily next to me. She was observing me in very close proximity while I worked on emptying a mind that refused to stop churning out thoughts. A beam of sun had penetrated the blinds, revealing a streak of auburn in her otherwise glossy dark hair, adding a sense of newness and discovery with this woman I had known from so many perspectives. In the moment, I felt such closeness to her that it verged on being unreal, and with the exception of a nascent plot to remove her clothing forming in my mind, I felt pretty satisfied with my situation.

"I didn't realize I could be so concerned about another person until last night," she said, propping her head up against mine and kissing me on the cheek. "And I've never felt so relieved, either."

Her appreciation for me was familiar, yet different. Things had immediately changed when I admitted to Daven that I was willing to dedicate my life to Emily. I mean, physical love, when compared to the possibilities that this type of closeness presented, paled in comparison. When I thought of all my sexual experiences and how there was a little bit of boringness behind all my encounters, I knew that I had made the right decision to focus on the one bright spot in my life that Emily had become. It's baffling to think that I was impatient with her for consistently resisting my advances while trying to figure things out.

"You never have to worry about me," I replied. "I'm resilient, you know."

Emily smiled. "Even Tamer says you're sensitive."

"And Tamer's the final authority?"

Emily laughed. "No . . . I'm the final authority, you know that," and then she began tickling me under the sheets.

I endured for a few seconds before wrestling her hands away and pinning her beneath me.

"Now what are you going to do?" I asked her.

Emily positioned her knee between my legs and gave me an impish grin.

"I wouldn't do that," I said.

"Why not?" she asked, beginning to squirm.

"Because now you've put me in a position where I have to kiss up to avoid the consequences," I said.

"You have it all wrong, Grant," Emily explained with a gleam of challenge in her eyes. "My knee is there just in case you trying anything of the sort."

This was all I needed. Before she could even smile she was being kissed. I began to tug at her shirt, but she stopped me.

"What are you doing, Mr. Spire?" she asked in a voice of mock disapproval.

"Don't you trust me?"

She looked up at me. "It depends."

"Well, do you?"

She nodded, but unconvincingly.

"I've waiting for this moment for so long," I confessed, "and finally there is nothing that can stop us . . ."

Then we kissed again and my hands started to search her body.

"Grant," she protested.

"What?" I asked, kissing along her neck, starting to gain some momentum.

"Grant, I hate to burst your bubble, but your timing is off the mark."

I stopped. "That time of the month, you mean?"

She smiled. "No, silly. It's not special enough," she explained. "I dreamed of this moment and it felt a lot different."

"Well, if you ask me, this seemed like the logical progression of all we've been through together," I argued.

"Let's not cheapen it. Have patience. Come on, let's just go to sleep. You've had a long day."

"If that's what you truly want," I conceded, but unable to hide the disappointment in my voice. I still hoped she would have compassion on me and change her mind.

"You're an understanding man," she said with an indifferent smile. Then she gave me a soft kiss before cuddling up to me and falling asleep.

I just lay there for a while, waiting for my body to relax. I tried to think innocent thoughts so that I could finally drift off to sleep retaining that feeling of satisfaction I had experienced only a while earlier.

* * * * *

"Grant," I heard suddenly, feeling myself shaken from sleep, Emily still lying by my side. "Were you serious when you asked the pastor if he would marry us?"

I rolled over to face her. Looking into her eyes, I felt a surge of conviction.

"Absolutely, Emily."

"What came over you?" she asked.

"I love you. I didn't want him to separate us like he wanted."

Emily smiled. "I love you, too. I think we should get married."

"In a way, we've been married for a long time. Our meeting with Daven opened our eyes. It seems like it's not only the logical next step, but the right thing to do."

There was silence between us for a second.

"You won't make me wait too long, will you?" Emily asked.

"Of course not."

"I'd do it tomorrow if we could," she said, kissing my cheek before turning her back to me, settling under my arm, and drifting off again with a peaceful look on her face.

My dream world, though, wasn't as ready to welcome me back. In a gush of emotion, I had finally expressed my love for her with no resistance of pride, nor fear of rejection—and I was taken aback by the ease with which my true desire overcame my historical reluctance to give my feelings for her a voice. Now all I had to do was acclimate myself to my decision . . .

* * * * *

"I just wish I had a cigarette to go with this," said Brad-to-the-Bone, admiring the can of beer I had brought him. "You have to understand, it's hard to have one without the other."

There I sat in the hospital room that afternoon, feeling the assault of sterilization and white walls, fluorescent lights. I was contemplative about the progress in my relationship with Emily and none too pleased that Brad had dishonored our agreement. Fortunately, he was thought provoking enough to make me stick around.

"Well, Brad, it's strange to come here and find out that you've already had like six coffees today, each one of them loaded with sweeteners and cream. It's nice I can provide you with yet another pleasurable outlet."

Brad's tired eyes looked thoughtful, my sarcasm missed. "Yeah, thanks, I appreciate it. You don't know how much of a relief it is to crack a beer."

"It's psychological," I said.

"What is?"

"The crack of the beer," I explained. "I imagine that you're probably already feeling the relief before the liquid even touches your tongue."

"You nailed it," Brad admitted.

"So are you getting out of here soon?"

"At the end of the week," he replied. "This is supposed to be a surgery that you're in and out for, but with my medical history they wanted to make sure that everything was ok. When my appendix exploded last year, it really gave us all a scare."

"You've had your appendix removed as well?"

"Oh yeah," said the red bearded giant, pouring his beer in a cup and handing me back the empty can, which I crushed and stuck back in my pocket. "It's fortunate that I lived. It was like three days of not taking a shit and I had this little cramp. So I decided to the go to Emergency to see what was going on. They told me if I'd arrived a few hours later I would have died."

"Wow," I replied. "That's called providence."

"Sure is," Brad agreed. "You want to see the scar?'

"Who wouldn't?"

Brad-to-the-Bone lifted his shirt so that I could see, beneath the hair on his belly, this red incision line.

"My appendix was like up here," Brad said, pointing up near his rib cage. "Now I don't take any chances."

"I don't blame you."

"My mother says that it's better safe than sorry. Secretly, I think she enjoys me being away from the house for a while."

"You live with your mom?" I asked.

"I live downstairs. It's mutually beneficial because she's getting so old. It makes me feel good to know that I'm there for her."

"Yeah, that's quite a sacrifice," I said. "Is she uncomfortable when you bring women home?"

"Oh, I haven't had that problem. It's hard to find women around here that I like."

"Maybe Tamer could help you with that," I smiled.

"Hey, I'm always open for suggestions," the giant said, looking hopeful. "My friend and his wife from the Harbor are always on the lookout for a girl for me as well."

"If I can think of anyone, I'll let you know."

"What about you?" Brad asked. "Are you seeing someone?"

"I think I'm newly engaged," I told him.

"You think?"

"Ok, I am engaged, but it feels kind of weird," I admitted. "It's going to take a while for me to become comfortable with the idea of being so committed."

Brad seemed to inspect me for a second. "No offense, but you don't seem the sort to be engaged. I imagined you were smarter than that, I guess."

"It's a strange engagement. We haven't really . . . well, you know . . ."

"You haven't what?"

"I've agreed to marry her and yet we haven't had sex. There, I've said it. Curse your ship to the bottom of the ocean, Brad-to-the-Bone, for being so easy to talk to."

Brad took a long swig of his beer, like he needed a strong drink after my confession. Afterwards, he seemed to mull the situation over.

"Hmmm . . . it seems to me that no matter how you spin it, the whole thing is risky."

"I know," I agreed.

"So why have you committed to her without knowing the crucial details?"

"It's complicated."

Brad thought about this for a second before saying, "Speaking for myself, I wouldn't marry into complication. Then again, I believe all women are nuts."

I looked at the gentle giant in shock. "What did you say?"

"They're all so unpredictable, so—"

"Whoa, Brad-to-the-Bone," I interjected. "Maybe you shouldn't go work for Tamer. You two could feed each other's fire."

Brad laughed. "Why, does Tamer feel the same way?"

"Pretty much," I nodded. "But you're kidding with me, right?"

"No, deep down they are all insane creatures, I tell you."

"Oh Brad, you've allowed your experiences to taint your beliefs," I said, shaking my head.

"Hey, that's how I feel. They're all crazy. And your situation doesn't discredit my view."

"Why is that?"

"I imagine Emily has slept with some men, right?" Brad asked.

"Yeah, at least one that I know personally."

"She probably thinks that it's something special, or she's convinced herself it's a moral decision, or perhaps she isn't ready. But no matter how you spin it, you can't help feeling that she's withheld something from you that's she's offered to other men, and this makes you feel like you haven't been fully accepted by her. Am I right?"

I looked at him. "You're pretty close," I admitted. "I haven't had the same access as other guys."

"There you have it: craziness."

"You must have met a few girls who you thought were sane," I said.

Brad scratched his beard. "Yes, once I did. She was the fiancée of my friend. I met her and then realized she was ideal for me. It was a cruel trick of nature that she was my friend's girl when we could have been perfect together."

"Well then, I'm sure you can see where I'm coming from. If you thought she was perfect for you without having relations with her, doesn't that prove something?"

"You got me, I suppose," the giant admitted with a shrug.

"So maybe it's not so strange that I'm engaged to this woman?"

"Yeah, but if I was with her I certainly would be satisfying my needs. To me, your situation suggests a problem. And the moment there was even a hint of a problem I would have been gone. I don't have time for sickness."

I laughed.

"What?" Brad asked, oblivious to the irony.

"Forget it," I said. "I'll tell you this. As of right now, I don't regret my decision."

Brad gave me a warm smile and then said, "There are ways to hold yourself over. I have a phone number for this agency in the city."

"Not another word," I warned.

"Then hear, hear," said Brad, lifting his cup. "To uncharted territory." He then gave me a nod before downing the last of his beer while I couldn't help but laugh.

* * * * *

On my drive home from the hospital, I felt this overwhelming desire to bite the bullet and pay my old friend Justin Fancy a visit. Besides, I couldn't justify waiting any longer. After parking the car, I found myself walking up the steps to the church with a growing feeling of dread. Once on the landing, I opened the door as quietly as I could, peered in cautiously, and then moved stealthily down the hallway, hoping to avoid an encounter with Daven.

With the door to Justin's office partly open, I could clearly see him typing away at his desk with three or four open books scattered around him. Fancy wasn't the tallest of fellows, but he was thick. Most often he had a shadow of beard on a face marked by slightly hawkish features, and piercing blue eyes that always seemed to detect the truth. He looked up from his work and broke into a welcoming smile.

"Come in, come in," Fancy said in a delighted tone. "I knew you couldn't stay away forever."

When he reached out to shake my hand, I took a step back.

"You still don't have any boundaries," I said accusingly, trying to hold back my anger. "Right now, it's all I can do to not punch you in the head."

"What line have I crossed this time?" Fancy asked, half smiling. With the exception of Marco, there wasn't any guy in town who could take him.

"You just had to get involved with Emily again."

Fancy shook his head in disappointment. "If you don't learn how to let things go, you're only going to drive yourself to an early grave."

"Why did she come visit you?"

"She just wanted to talk," Fancy explained indifferently. "I referred her to the senior pastor."

"I don't believe you," I snapped. "You can't help yourself."

"If you must know, Miss Arum wanted some advice on your relationship. I told her it's none of my business."

I started to pace around the office. "Your library has grown," I observed.

"I'm a different person," Fancy insisted. "I'd like it if we could work things out and be friends again."

"Of all people, why did she have to come see you? She knew if I found out it would upset me."

"I just think she's comfortable talking to me," Fancy offered.

"I can't forgive you. I can't make myself."

"You're the one that Emily loves, my friend—not me."

"It's just so unfair," I said bitterly, turning to look Fancy in the eyes. "I met her, I cared for her and devoted so much of myself to her, and then when she decides we're better off as friends she gives you what she has always withheld from me."

"I can't explain it. I'm just as confused by women as you are."

"How can I possibly make sense of this? Still to this day we haven't slept together."

"How many times do I have to apologize? I'm sorry. If letting you punch me in the head would clean the slate, I'd let you do your worst. But I assure you, nobody is harder on me than me."

I collapsed into the chair facing Justin's desk. The midafternoon sun had the office half lit. There was a mustiness to it from the books, and yet there was a floweriness as well from a mixture of cleaning solutions and Fancy's cologne.

"My father appeared at my work and jumped me," I confessed, permitting my eyes to rest on a shelf devoted to his collection of football trophies.

"I heard about it," Fancy admitted, appearing sympathetic. "That's crazy."

"Have you heard anything that might explain this?" I asked.

"Perhaps, although I didn't make the connection until now. I have bumped into Marco because he's been meeting with Daven. I know that his yard was recently vandalized and that there was some disturbing writing spray painted on the front of his house."

"Really?" I said in disbelief. "Who would dare mess with Marco?"

"I asked myself the same question."

"You said he's been seeing Daven as well? Do you ever talk to him?"

"We exchanged some pleasantries, but that's about it."

"It's strange to think of Marco pouring out his heart," I said thoughtfully.

"Grant," Fancy began seriously, "I have to ask—did you vandalize your parents' property?"

"Of course not," I said defensively. "That's ridiculous."

"I believe you," Fancy assured me. "It didn't seem like your style."

"What do you mean by that?"

"When you're angry at someone, you cut them off rather than dealing with the situation."

This comment angered me. "You put a knife in my back, Justin. You think I can just forget?"

"I know this may be a shock to you, but there was no conspiracy on either of our part to hurt you. It just happened."

"Tell me exactly what Emily said," I demanded.

Fancy shook his head. "You know it's confidential if she talks to me here. What's the matter with you?"

I looked Justin straight in the eyes, unable to beat around the bush any longer. "Did you sleep with her again?"

Justin laughed. "Take it easy. She loves you. Did you hear me? She loves you. I never knew you were that insecure."

"Yeah, she loves me . . ." I repeated cynically. "I admit, her coming to see you has made me uneasy. I can't stop thinking about the fact that she still considers you to be a confidant."

Fancy shrugged. "I never encouraged it."

"Did Daven talk to you about the possibility of marrying us?"

"No, I haven't heard anything. So you two are engaged then?'

"Yes, we plan to get married."

"Well congratulations. I do think it's a risky move, though. I'm of the opinion women don't tend to change. Regardless, will you endeavor to join me for a beer?"

"I came here to tell you to stay away from her."

"And you've done that. But I'd like to talk to you about a book I began writing."

"About what?" I asked.

"To be honest, the shattering of our friendship was the result of the single most destructive decision I ever made in my life, and so I started to think about my mindset at the time."

"What does that have to do with your book?"

"Well, I wondered whether we all gravitate toward and nurture this part of ourselves that craves suffering. So I polled a sample demographic of people about (a) whether they acknowledged a conscious desire on their part to knowingly bring harm upon themselves, no matter how small, and (b) if they did, the manner in which they fulfill this desire."

"And what did you discover?"

"The majority of those surveyed hardly considered a need to nurture this sense of self-destruction, but openly acknowledged that it must be there because they couldn't avoid satisfying it. The manners varied, from drug use to cigarettes to alcohol abuse, amongst many others. Some took advantage of the confidentiality, admitted to cutting and purging and all sorts of twisted behavior."

"Why would anybody want to read this book?"

Fancy looked at me very seriously. "Because the temptation to walk with one foot in the water of your own destruction can be balanced by a powerful sense of self-forgiveness."

I found myself slightly nodding as I contemplated his point.

"Now let's go get a beer . . ." Justin said.

*****

By the time I returned to the house that afternoon, Emily had disappeared. I found a note on the counter saying she had gone for a walk. Since it was probably one of the last beautiful days of the year, it was likely she had made her way to a spot that had become very special to us. To find your way to this hidden location, you began in the shadow of trees in our backyard—an eclectic arrangement, including a white birch, an oak, an assortment of fruit trees, and even a beechnut tree—before crossing a large meadow to the edge of the woods. Here, if you knew where to look, there was a path concealed in the tall grass that you could follow into the woods. Under the canopy, you would follow the trail until you encountered the Old Maple. This marked the point where you had to exit the path to the right and go cross-country until you reached a secluded pond that had a large stump by the waterside. From such a position in the forest, you could see bluish hills peeking up over the trees. Sometimes I would wake up and do some writing in this oasis because I found the sights, fragrances, and sounds of the woods inspiring, especially in autumn.

So after I greeted my dogs, I put my hiking boots on and took a walk into the woods. Sure enough, Emily was sitting on our stump. By this time, it was around four but it was a particularly warm October day. I stood there and observed Emily for a few seconds. To me, she was breathtaking. There was a self-reflective quality about her that I found so attractive. There she was, sitting in the sun, wearing blue jeans and a red plaid flannel shirt, gazing out over the pond. I could tell she was lost in her own head. It would almost have been better to capture the image with a camera rather than approach her because it seemed she was in her natural habitat whereas I was the tourist. She accepted nature, while for me the grandeur was meant to be interpreted.

When Emily heard me coming, she looked over and smiled, then shifted over a bit and patted the stump by way of invitation. I sat down and put my arm around her. My movement made the ducks in the pond take flight, their wings creating a panicked flapping as they disappeared over the trees.

"It's so beautiful," she said.

"I was watching you," I replied. "God made this day for you, you know: the beautiful autumn colors . . . the incredible sky . . . the blue hills rising in the distance."

"Stop it, Grant," Emily said, enjoying the flattery.

"So what are you doing?" I asked.

"Just thinking."

I stood up and began to scour the ground for stones to throw. "About what?"

"About us," Emily admitted.

I found a smooth round stone that felt comfortable in my hand.

"Watch this," I said. "I bet you I can throw it to the other side of the pond."

Emily didn't seem receptive to being impressed. Not discouraged, I took a step forward and launched the stone as far as I could. It seemed that the stone was going to make it to the other side easily. The trajectory was right, the power seemed sufficient, and then we heard the faintest plop, with a splash about a foot from the other bank.

"Nice try," said Emily.

"Why don't you give it a go?" I suggested, tossing her a similar sized stone with a bit more weight so that it could carry better.

"I don't feel like it," she said, placing it back in my hand.

"Then try to hit that rock in the middle of the pond," I suggested.

"Maybe another day."

In one motion, I turned, stepped into the throw and delivered. The stone was a laser and hit the rock in the middle of the pond with an emphatic "tick" and then shot up about fifty feet in the air before finding its final resting place at the bottom of the pond with a resounding plop.

"Impressive, eh?" I said with a big grin.

Emily shrugged, clearly indifferent. I sat down and put my arm around her again and she leaned into me. I kissed her temple. Then she turned to me so that I could kiss her mouth. When I kissed her, she suddenly assumed a passion I had never experienced. She leaned into me further and then used her weight to break my balance, taking us to the ground. While on top of me, she pressed her body on mine with all her strength while kissing me with an intensity approaching desperation. Her hand found its way beneath my shirt and with great enthusiasm she tugged at my belt. I didn't quite know what had hit me and it was all I could do to keep up. I ran my hands over her body, and finally began to understand that a connection between emotions and physical contact could exist. Her eyes looked deep into my own with a knowing, penetrating quality I had never witnessed in her before. It was as though I had been introduced to the concept of intimacy for the first time.

And just . . . just when I thought my waiting was over . . . and that our first time together would be at such an appropriate spot . . . Emily composed herself all of a sudden and disentangled her body from mine, leaving me on the ground.

"What?" I said, getting up. "What did I do?"

Emily pulled her jeans up, sat back on the stump, and began buttoning her shirt. She wouldn't look at me. I made similar adjustments and then sat down next to her. I physically turned her face so that she could look me in the eyes.

"You didn't do anything, I promise," she said quietly.

"You're driving me crazy," I said. "How am I supposed to take this?"

"We're so close to being married. Why wouldn't we just tough it out for a few more months?"

"Because those are a few months we can never get back," I offered.

"That was a taste of what's to come," Emily explained, clearly unmoved.

"It was a fine taste, but you have to understand how rejecting this feels," I said, hoping for the slightest sign of empathy.

"It's for your own good," she said flatly, her face expressionless. "It's for the good of our relationship."

"I don't see how," I replied in disbelief, my heart sinking.

Emily had no further explanation, so we sat there for a few quiet minutes with the sound of squirrels scurrying and chattering amongst themselves in pursuit of nuts. Winged insects hummed, and birds—perhaps blue jays or crows—were calling intermittently into the still air. I have no idea what Emily was thinking, but I sat there trying to make sense of the messages I was receiving. She had nearly taken my head off with her passion, and yet she'd cooled off like a bucket of ice water had been poured over us just as quickly as the fire had started. It was confusing to try to make sense of this contradiction while we sat there in the October sunshine.

"You didn't tell Pastor Daven the whole truth," Emily suddenly said, accusingly.

"What do you mean?"

"You didn't sleep with that girl to make me jealous. That may have been part of it, but it's not the whole truth."

"I don't know where you're going with this."

"I've thought about it for a while and I figured it out," Emily went on. "It's the most beautiful thing anybody has done for me."

I stood up. "You can talk to me when you're willing to make sense," and I began to walk away.

Emily followed after me.

"Admit it, you slept with her because you knew it was the only way I would agree to marry you."

I stopped and turned back to her. Emily was looking straight into my eyes, as serious as she could be. "You knew this, Grant. It was the only way for us to be on the same level."

I put my hands on her shoulders. "You don't know what you're talking about."

Emily didn't budge a bit. "I know it's true because of your values beforehand. You're changed. You changed yourself to make me forgive myself with you."

I stood there for a second, staring into her eyes, reluctant to admit anything. Then it dawned on me that my deep down motivation might have been hidden, for in my heart I knew that I could never have convinced her to marry me without creating some common ground.

"Maybe you're right," I said.

"I am right. I know it now."

"I can see why it was the only way for you to be comfortable with me . . ."

"I love you for it," Emily said. "I can't believe you'd do that for me."

"We've hurt each other equally," I acknowledged. "There doesn't have to be guilt between us now."

Emily wrapped her arms around my waist and I held her tightly in my arms. I held her knowing that her intuition was remarkable. It was her observation that allowed me to recognize the truth, attaining insight into myself that was like a religious awakening. My true love for Emily Arum was beginning to make sense to me.

CHAPTER 7

IN THE WOODS BEHIND OUR house we had awakened suddenly, as though from a foggy dream. I would have been on top of the world now that Emily and I had this new understanding, but behind the blue October skies and the changing leaves was the beginning of an anxiety that threatened to bury this startling joy like the first snowfall covering a ball diamond. I couldn't quite put my finger on the source of this uneasiness within me, but that aside, I was as happy as I had been in years. How could I not be? My feelings for Emily had migrated into something I could finally explain. First she had persevered her way into my imagination, then into my heart. And finally, after months of struggle, she persevered her way into my confidence. It's no wonder, then, that a few weeks later this confidence was symbolized in the engagement ring I presented to her on one knee when we returned to our special spot with the large stump beside a quiet pond concealed by the woods around us.

Later that month, Emily approached me with a request. While working at the restaurant one night, she had connected with an old friend who'd grown up in White Sands as well. Ever since, they had been texting and calling each other nonstop. For Emily, it was only natural to readopt her best friend from years ago. For me, it was about getting accustomed to hearing "Avery this" or "Avery that" as the predominant topic between us. Not that I discouraged her at all. It had been a long time since Emily spent time with someone of her own gender that she felt such a kinship with and I wanted her to deepen this friendship as well as expand her social circle.

The request itself was quite simple. Emily thought it would be a good idea for me to take Avery out for a night on the town in order for us to get acquainted. This seemed reasonable enough to me, so we set it up for a Saturday night, since this was when Emily made her biggest tips and Avery was only able to come up on weekends. My guess is that Emily had designated Avery her *fiancé* inspector but was uncomfortable describing our time together in terms of an interview. In truth, I didn't mind the pretext because I was curious why this woman was so special to Emily in the first place.

Avery was a striking contrast to Emily, being fair-skinned and blond, with very pretty blue eyes. She showed up at the house late in the afternoon and insisted on driving. Our first order of business was to visit Emily in the restaurant's lounge before it got busy. After the two girls greeted each other with a warm embrace, they finalized their plan to go out for drinks once Emily was off. It was obvious that Avery was supposed to share her opinion of me. After observing them, I was sure Emily was fishing for some high praise from her friend. Anyway, with the particulars now decided upon, Emily released us for the night. I suppose we could have eaten in the lounge, but Emily insisted that I endure my interrogation in a venue where she didn't have the temptation to eavesdrop or pry.

In the end, we decided on having Italian food. When we arrived at our destination, my companion and I were fortunate enough to get a good booth and we found ourselves in this romantic lighting with happy couples surrounding us. I felt a little stupid—perhaps even a little dishonest to those around us who assumed we were together—while she was obviously enjoying the importance of her task.

"You're good looking," said Avery. "Emily's done well for herself."

"I feel so lucky to be with her," I replied, opening my menu. For some reason, I felt the burden of making Emily's friend approve of me.

The waitress then came by and we ordered our beverages.

Avery had a rough and tough exterior, like she had survived many hardships in the course of her life—and yet there was a warm light in her eyes that suggested she wanted to volunteer some information. I hoped she wasn't one of those girls who's willing to get too personal too quickly on a date.

"Is there something on your mind?" I asked.

"How did you know?"

"I'd have to be soulless not to," I replied lightly.

"Ok, I'll let you in on something," she said with a sly smile. "But you have to promise not to tell Emily."

"Agreed," I said, somewhat intrigued.

"I have an ulterior motive for being in town this week," Avery whispered.

"Oh?"

Avery nodded. "There's this guy in town that I've been seeing. He comes to visit me in the city and I come here as well—I mean, we meet in a hotel close to here. We've been on and off for like five years and I think he's starting to view me as someone he might date exclusively. And guess what? I stayed at his apartment last night. He says he doesn't care who sees us together anymore."

"That's great, I'm happy for you," I said honestly.

"I'm so excited," Avery continued. "He's like the best guy. He's so good looking and he does well with kids. It just goes to show that if you have faith, everything will work out in the end—just like with you and Emily."

"You believe that?" I asked.

Avery nodded enthusiastically. "Absolutely."

"That's good," I said. "I'm glad it's worked out for you."

"You know, it's taken some time for me to mature like this. Emily and I went to this wedding several years back and it was shocking to realize that we had slept with pretty well every man in the wedding party. It was the wake-up call that I needed."

I sat there staring at Avery, feeling a little sick. "What do you mean?"

"Well, it was the point where I decided that I couldn't live like this anymore and that better opportunities had to be out there for me."

"Were you and Emily alike?" I asked.

Avery assumed an almost flirtatious tone with me. "Now Grant, I don't want us spending our time talking about Emily. She's our common ground. I'm not going to make this easy on you."

"If that's how it has to be, then so be it," I conceded, wondering how I could get the truth from her.

The waitress brought us our drinks and set a warm loaf of bread in front of us. After we ordered our food, I automatically began buttering a slice, trying to interpret the truth of Emily's history from the cryptic expression on Avery's face. I found my appetite had disappeared, totally replaced by that nervous trembling in my stomach.

Avery continued. "But with Justin in my life now, things are looking up. I know I can commit to him and that we'll be happy together."

"Justin?" I repeated. "Justin who?"

Avery seemed enthused by my interest. "You might know him. Justin Fancy. Does the name ring a bell?"

"Are you kidding me?" I laughed. "Justin Fancy. Of all people you're dating, it's Justin Fancy?"

I watched Avery's disposition change to concern. "What, you know him? You don't like him?"

"Listen, Avery," I began sharply, "I don't get involved in other people's lives. If you love Justin, that's your business. I could explain myself, but Emily might be a better person to talk to."

Avery looked at me in surprise. "I didn't realize Justin could be such a sore subject for anyone."

"Well, there's more to Fancy than you know," I explained. "But that's between you and him. Just promise me that you won't bring him around Emily when I'm not there."

"That's a strange request."

"I mean it," I said seriously. "Look, I think you're a wonderful person and I'm happy that you've turned your life around and that Emily has friends that care about her. But please respect my wishes."

A confused Avery nodded, not quite sure what had gone wrong between us. But our food came and the tension between us dissolved. Avery changed tactics and began asking me questions about myself, and I, in turn, did the same. She really was a nice girl and I kind of felt bad for her, misplacing all her hope in such a selfish man who could never care for her.

Afterwards, we went out for a drink. I felt it was the most passive form of entertainment since the noise in the bar would reduce the need for much exchange between us. During moments when our conversation did succumb to the loud music, I thought about Emily's relationship with Avery and tried to process the potentially disturbing information about Emily's past that her friend had so carelessly related. Later on, after Avery and I ended our encounter with a token embrace outside of the restaurant where Emily worked, I hooked up with Tamer at the pub for a little bit of insight.

We were perched on stools, drinking beer around one of those tall tables you'll often find in bar lounges—a little too close to the pool table if you ask me. Cooper, one of my childhood friends, had joined us, and he was definitely on the hunt for the only woman in the bar. He had just moved back to White Sands after a drawn-out breakup up with his girlfriend across the province. Also with us was Darren, who had recently broken up with his wife of two years. Darren seemed intent on drinking himself to oblivion. Both of them were blond-haired and blue-eyed and covered in tattoos, but the noticeable difference between them was that Cooper carried himself like a superstar. He had returned to town as a bit of a celebrity, trying to make it as a musician.

The problem with being famous and visiting your hometown is that people's perceptions of you tend to be pretty much set in stone, even if deep down they are grateful to you for putting their town on the map. Cooper had arrived to find that he was welcomed with open arms, but the reverence he had been expecting due to his numerous accolades was lacking. Most people, including myself, had a difficult time viewing him as anything more than the abundantly talented, likable garage band guitarist who entertained people in high school gymnasiums.

Darren, on the other hand, made no claim to greatness, preferring to use his wit when it was needed and always managing to inject his biting cynicism at the least appropriate times. For the most part, Darren liked to smoke and drink and complain. For onlookers, his contrast to Tamer's jovial spirit and good nature always made for an interesting evening. From Tamer's point of view, Darren seemed to amuse him about as much as he annoyed him, while Cooper's narcissism got the hair standing on the back of his neck. Cooper's tactic with women was simple: present all of his promise in one sales pitch, impress the socks off the smitten admirer, and then whisk her to his bedroom before she thought better of it. Tamer—who considered himself an artist when it came to such things—was not at all impressed by this strategy, describing it as an embarrassment as well as amateurish. In fact, he likened the performance to the "spray technique" of an untalented salesman. We watched Cooper introduce himself to this young woman playing pool by herself and soon after we could hear him talking to her about all his ambitions, all his promise, while she gazed at him with a look that certainly wasn't admiration—perhaps confusion, definitely dismay. Cooper seemed to assault women with this desperate desire to impress, while Tamer used his knowledge of women to secure their interest and eventually gain their affection.

"This is making me sick," Darren said with disgust, watching Cooper's painful struggle.

"He's making an ass of himself," Tamer added. "I bet my bottom dollar that even Gizzer could do better."

"At least Cooper's not afraid to try," I defended lamely.

"So you approve of this embarrassing display?" Darren asked me.

I shrugged my shoulders. "Well, I'm ready to turn my back to it, if that's what you mean . . ."

"He's digging his own grave," Tamer observed, taking a drag from his cigarette.

"Why don't you just put the poor guy out of his misery then?" I asked.

"Yeah, I should."

"No, do it," Darren urged. "Teach him a lesson. Take the girl."

"My friends," Tamer began seriously, "it's too easy, there's no challenge. Cooper's actually made my chance of success a foregone conclusion."

"I have an idea," I said. "To make it more interesting, I'll bet that you can't coax the girl away from him without leaving your chair."

Tamer smiled. "I know I can. You have yourself a bet."

We shook hands while Darren laughed and lit another cigarette.

I swear, within two minutes, Tamer had the girl coming back and forth to our table, laughing and touching his arm while she spoke. He hardly even said a word to get her interest. From my point of view, he merely smiled at the girl and she was utterly enchanted. Cooper, stunned, witnessed this success and desperately tried to regain control of what he thought was a promising encounter. He even followed the girl back to the table when she made her third or fourth visit.

"Sorry, I should have introduced you. This is my friend, Dan Tamer," said Cooper by way of recovery, as though Tamer was one of his lackeys. But he knew the power had shifted and his attempt to provide evidence of his leadership in the group came across as futile and desperate.

"I know who is," the girl said, never taking her eyes off Tamer.

Realizing all hope was lost, Cooper opted for greener pastures. "This is boring, guys, maybe it's time we moved to another bar."

Tamer and I were pretty comfortable, so poor Darren got dragged away for the encore performance. As for the girl, Tamer got rid of her shortly after, preferring to leave himself with no prospects for the evening. When I questioned him about it, he insisted that he just didn't want to be seen with a woman of her reputation. He also explained that there were too many women in his life already. This worked out well for me, I suppose, as it gave me the chance to take advantage of Tamer's undivided attention.

"It's the dates Avery provided that don't add up," I explained. "If Emily hooked up with Justin two years ago, that would mean their affair intersected Justin's relationship with Avery. And I know for a fact that Emily and Avery were close before she moved to the city, which would have been around two years ago."

"It's in the past," said Tamer. "So who cares?"

"You don't get it," I replied. "Avery obviously worships Fancy. If this encounter between Emily and Justin took place during this period, I'm concerned. It's such a gross breach of friendship that I can hardly comprehend it."

Tamer shook his head in disappointment. "Old man, you have so much to learn about women. You know the motto,

'All is fair in love and war.' You realize this applies to every woman, don't you?"

"You think so?"

"Do you know how tentative the friendship between women is when it involves a man?" Tamer explained in an almost condescending tone. "You're a good fellow, but naive, my friend, naive."

"No, I'm concerned," I clarified. "If she's capable of this type of deceit, how can I marry into this?"

"If this bothers you so much, then talk to her about it," Tamer suggested. "You'll never know the truth until you get her side of the story."

"You're right. It's the only solution."

I noticed that Tamer looked a little tired, like the natural enthusiasm that defined him had been tempered with a more negative mindset—something approaching disappointment. The fact that he'd dismissed the girl without hesitation indicated to me that something deeper was going on.

"I'm feeling the burden, old man . . ." Tamer confessed and then took a big gulp of beer. "I'm tired of living up to this reputation that has become bigger than life. I need a vacation, I suppose. Such weariness. Why can't women see that I'm human?"

"So you're saying that you might find yourself a real girl-friend then?"

"Whoa, Grant, let's not read too far into this," Tamer cautioned, holding his hands up. "I'm just tired of having to perform like some porn star stud night after night for these loose-lipped girls. The legend has finally become too big for the man, I suppose."

"Then maybe it's time to settle down."

"There's no such thing as love," Tamer stated, "so I want to be clear about this. I believe in the possibilities afforded me just by waking up each day. In fact, I believe that men that settle for one woman are either sheep or they're lazy or uncreative or conservative—just to be clear . . ."

I smiled. "I'm not insulted to be lumped in with such men, but what about under a different category? How about idealistic?"

"More like stupid," Tamer replied. "Because you know in this world that stupid and idealistic are one and the same."

"What about Justin Fancy? You know the history we have. Has he been playing it right?"

"All I know about him is what you told me, that he charmed many a woman before he became a pastor. I respect that . . ."

"He's such a jerk, Tamer. How can you admire that?"

"I didn't finish," Tamer replied. "I don't think there's anything wrong with being a seducer of women—it's part of being a man—but I have a big issue with any guy who screws over a friend."

CHAPTER 8

THE CONVERSATION THAT I NEEDED to have with Emily was forgotten as a more pressing concern finally found its way to the surface. I suppose the good news is that I was finally able to account for the anxiety that had been keeping me on edge the entire month. The situation was so horrifying that for weeks I procrastinated and refused to acknowledge my feelings. And now, the sun had risen to reveal that the dreaded day had come, yet I found myself unprepared, stuffed with butterflies, and as close to the edge of sanity as I had ever been in my thirty years.

It was a Wednesday afternoon and I was at home by myself, sprawled out on the couch; all was silent with the exception of the breathing of three dogs as they slept in various places, in various positions, on the floor. To be exact, it was probably about two hours before going to work, and I was now face-to-face with the denouement of a spiritual dilemma my subconscious had been wrestling with for weeks. I remember lying there, trying to find the energy and motivation to overcome this temptation to take the easy path out of the predicament I found myself in.

I began attempting to motivate myself by recalling my intention when I first started working at the shelter and how I'd had this magnanimous vision: I was to be an advocate for innocent dogs and bring healing to everything I touched, including the feeling of emptiness inside myself. So I'd volunteered at the shelter for a few months and taken some courses. Once I'd earned my way to night operations, I lobbied to be responsible for the welfare of the dogs, using some creative strategies derived from my business experience. Initially, I took on projects aimed at attracting potential adopters within the community. I considered this a form of proactive marketing. But it seemed that the more aggressive I was about finding potential homes for these dogs, the harsher the fiscal responsibilities became. My efforts seemed to have a counter-effect that I had never considered: more people were abandoning animals as the larger community became more aware of our presence. This left me wondering whether I should have dedicated my efforts to educating the public about the necessity of spaying and neutering as a preventative measure. Regardless, at this point we couldn't provide the space and no initiatives could keep up with the operational expenses.

Given that my efforts alone could not save these animals, the consequences for opting to pursue this line of work in such an environment were brutal. I now had to shoulder the painful burden of knowing that every dog we destroyed was paying the price for failing to find love in his or her lifetime. But I found that if I administered this "punishment" myself I could be secure knowing that my presence ensured these dogs were experiencing love and kindness and sensitivity in their final moments. This brought me a measure of comfort as well. And admittedly, the very fact that I cared about each animal and took this pain upon myself allowed me to make leaps and bounds in my own view of God. Much of what we believe about God is a great injustice to his character. While there are many sins in this world, I now understand that an absence of belief isn't one of them. Not everyone can choose, and not everyone can be chosen.

Still, as I considered these things while lying on my couch, I couldn't help but question my own limitations as I realized that my choices had caught up to me. Had I finally reached the point where I could no longer see hope's silvery glimmer? Did I finally understand that the human capacity for love isn't big enough, that it implodes when strained to its utmost definition? It was dawning on me that my capacity to love had been stretched across the horizon and, despite what they tell you in science classes, the edge of the world marks a drop off into eternal black space. And as I was stretched, I had continued to hope and pray that something would come up, like the telephone ringing in the last hour with the message of pardon. I had called the Humane Society and OSPCA, put out classified ads, put posts up in local animal hospitals and veterinarian offices. I'd even spent countless hours posting ads and searching for potential families on the Internet. My last resort was trying to network using my circle of friends. Manifestly, it just wasn't in the books for Crystal to be adopted. Because she was unable to find a religion in life, in protest against my very soul it was time to say goodbye to her . . .

So as I lay there trying to motivate myself to get up from the couch and follow through with this despicable policy, I was still clinging to my overall conviction that every dog was to be given equal opportunity and held to the exact same standard. In this particular case, the problem was that the consequences had become excruciatingly personal. I had come to love Crystal like a daughter, and the very thought of killing her was invoking every instinct to protect and defend her as though she actually was my own flesh and blood. In an attempt to mitigate this anxiety, I couldn't help but draw my dogs around me at home so I could kiss them and hug them and use their physical warmth as a reminder that no harm could come to them now that they lived within the safety and security of my walls.

In the end, I needed to talk to somebody about my internal conflict, and so I decided to seek out Emily at the restaurant. As I walked across town, my anxiousness grew and I found myself trembling, feverish, and not thinking straight. In all honesty, I would have preferred to die myself than go through with such a horrifyingly demanding expectation of me.

By the time I arrived at the restaurant, I was a sweaty, inconsolable wreck. Emily was tending to the bar, with a few scattered patrons enjoying her service.

"Hey, honey," she said, very surprised to see me. "You look hot. Can I get you a drink?"

"I need to talk to you about something," I said.

"You look sick, Grant. You should take the night off," Emily suggested.

She leaned over the bar and felt my forehead. "You don't seem to have a fever. What's wrong?"

I shook my head. "It's this dog at work," I said. "I—"

"I told you never talk to me about this," Emily warned, her eyes suddenly flashing angry.

"I have to," I insisted.

"Give me a second," Emily snapped and then disappeared. Another woman came over to tend the bar. Emily then took me by the hand to a booth.

"What's going on, Grant?"

"My faith has been shaken," I said to her, my eyes filling with tears. "I can't go through with it tonight. Not tonight."

"Did you think you were superhuman?" Emily asked in disbelief. "Did you think you could infinitely give of yourself this way?"

"I didn't plan on doing this forever," I said. "But where do I draw the line? I mean, where's the cutoff? I invest myself in each dog that comes in."

Emily shook her head in dismay. "I told you your job was killing you, but you didn't want to hear it, did you?"

"I'm begging you," I said, my hands clasped together.

Emily began to shake her head.

"Please, can't we just adopt one more?" I pleaded.

Emily looked at me sadly. "Oh honey, you know we can't. We have three dogs that we can barely take care of as it is."

"But we can take her home and then just give me time. I'll find another home for her, I promise. Just give me a month."

"There's no way," Emily said sternly. "Are you out of your mind? I mean, where does it end? We have three dogs already."

I felt like I'd been punched in the stomach. I remember letting out a deep sigh and putting my head down on the table.

"What are you feeling?" Emily asked.

"This is beyond me," I admitted, looking up at her. "I'm not strong enough."

I felt a tear trickle down my cheek and I wiped it away, but my eyes just kept watering.

Emily took my hand in hers. "I want to point something out to you."

"What?" I said, sniffling like a child.

Being in the comfort of Emily's presence, I just wanted her to hold me and allow myself to lose my composure for once, even with all these strangers around us. The internal conflict was unbearable and the desire to shelter Crystal from the consequences of her failure plagued me.

"If you aren't faithful to your task with this dog, Grant, then you've diminished the meaning of the other dogs' lives who might not have been as special to you. I think that she might be the most important experience you've had at the shelter to this point."

That was the last thing I wanted to hear. I sat there for a few seconds with a downcast gaze—contemplative, miserable, and feeling highly exposed.

"You're right," I said finally, looking into Emily's eyes.

Emily got up from her side of the booth and sat next to me, putting her arm around me and pulling me close.

"It's going to be ok."

I was too choked up to say anything, so I nodded, and yet this was a silent lie because I did not agree in my heart.

Emily continued in a consoling voice, "I know how much you love your dogs and I recognize that you've taken a lot upon yourself. Maybe after this it's time to move on."

"Perhaps it is time," I whispered in a cracked voice.

Then we both stood up and Emily gave me a hug before I departed the restaurant, stomach in my throat. I was a mess. Nothing mattered to me at this point. I could have been accosted at gunpoint and I would have felt no fear. Walking to the restaurant, I had been counting on Emily's compassion to overthrow my idealism, but now I was walking away alone to face an impossible task.

When I got to the shelter that evening it was unfamiliar. It was mean, rotten, and cruel. What had happened to the proffered acceptance that had made this place bearable? It was cold, and the cement feeling penetrated to the marrow of my bones, almost like my eyes had been adjusted to see the truth for once, and the grayness and cement and industrial dark had worked its way past all philosophy to the core of my beliefs.

When Gizzer arrived, I immediately told him to go home.

"No," he said with great resolve. "I know how much Crystal means to you. It will be better if I'm here," he insisted.

"You're off tonight," I repeated.

"Please reconsider, Grant? It's not about you."

For a second, I did consider his advice.

"Get lost, kid," I finally said. "I appreciate your support, but I have to do this alone."

He was not to be deterred. "What, it's ok for you to see me get emotional, but when it's you all bets are off? No, I'm staying and we're going to do this together."

"Get lost, before you get hurt," I warned, shoving him up against the wall. I was beginning to lose it, trembling, I was so spiritually shaken.

"Fine, have it your way," Gizzer agreed, pulling away from my grasp. "You're a hypocrite, you know."

He slammed the door and I was left alone: a hypocrite.

Despite the distraction, I still tried to follow the schedule. I put on the pot of coffee, fed the damn innocent lizards, and then found I couldn't type out my notes. Feeling like my body wasn't my own, like I was a puppet, I entered the hollowness of the bay: wire caging, dogs whining and barking, the prevalent smell of dogginess that I loved. Everything I saw resounded with the language of devotion and the very sincere joy of those ecstatic to see me.

Crystal, as always, was unmoved by my entrance, curled up in the corner of her cage. One blue eye slit open and then she stretched limb by limb and came over to give me a lick. She had no clue about her fate. If any animal in the world was hand-created by God, it was certainly Crystal—down to her bleached white muzzle, to the calico pattern of her coat, down to her bushy tail, dainty white paws, and crystal blue eyes. She was a canine meant to streak through the fields of the heavens. More than any other dog, Crystal had become symbolic of everything I had wanted to experience in a relationship with a wounded animal. At first she had been withdrawn in my presence. Then I began achieving a working trust with her. There had been times when she was so excited to see me, and yet there were other times when I'd show up at night to find that she had reverted to her own withdrawn ways. She was a confused, unloved animal psychologically working through her own relationship anxiety. And there was no reason that she should ever trust again, considering that she had been abused to the point of being at death's door. Her marred ear was a small, living testimony to her previous life, and her attitude was representative of the growth experienced in the friendship she had developed with me. And now, was I to be the one to ultimately betray her? Or were we both casualties of an unfair system?

From my jacket I took out a package that I had picked up at the grocery store earlier, and produced a large steak wrapped in paper. I took the paper off and handed the young dog the most luxurious meal of her life. I watched in silent despair as Crystal ate it down with the zeal of one expecting many such meals to come in her long life ahead. Once she was done, I had her follow me into my office. I sat beside her and stroked the soft fur behind her floppy ears. I even found myself hugging her repeatedly. The grieving process had already begun and during this hazy interval of pre-mourning my only focus was to continue milking out every last second from the clock.

Instead of going through with the procedure immediately, I ended up leashing her and taking her into the night air. I wanted her to see and smell the world for one last time. For me, it was a melancholy walk, but for Crystal, who didn't know any better, it was the greatest of pleasures: everything was new and fresh and worthy of being sniffed. We circled around the block once, twice, and by the third time I noticed it was quite chilly. I was happy the stars were out for our last night together, for nothing connected the ancient past with the indeterminable future like the lights of the night sky. I walked slowly the whole time, allowing Crystal to sniff absolutely anything she wanted. Neither did I object to her marking any territory that she decided to overwrite as her own. And during this walk I mourned internally because the tragedy was entirely avoidable if I simply abandoned my values and took her home with me that night.

When we returned to the shelter, I realized I could no longer prolong the inevitable. I picked Crystal up carefully and carried her like a shepherd carrying a lamb. We walked across the bay together and it felt so surreal. It would be easy to bend the truth and claim that I was strong in my limbs as we moved together, but in actual fact I was sick from the stomach to the knees and my head was plagued with temptation. Starting with Crystal, I could build a resurrection community in the "here and now" and ensure that not one more of my animals would die prematurely. I would solicit donations day and night; I would buy a farm for the animals I couldn't find a home for and give them the lives they were meant to experience. I would petition for stronger animal rights laws and more severe penalties for those in our area that hurt the weak and abandoned their responsibilities at the slightest discomfort. All these things I considered as Crystal trustingly allowed herself to be transported from the bay and into the room of departure.

When I put her on the table, I considered her life, the strides she had made—and all for what? She had never known what it meant to be an integral part of the pack and she had never known normal, healthy life among a human family. I was sick for her and at the same time I was sick over the precarious life I had erected for myself. What was wrong with me? Did God really demand of me this type of torment? I, myself, had chosen my vocation and in some ways I was certainly responsible for breaking off my relationship with my parents.

As always, I noticed Crystal's collar and I considered her concept of possession. A collar, when you think about it, becomes an extension of a dog's personality, and the kicker is that a dog has its collar chosen for him or her. I don't know why, but considering possession in the face of departure always invited my greatest sadness.

Finally, mercifully, the moment came, and I grabbed the instrument of her passing. I walked over to Crystal, who trustingly discounted the sharp point of the needle, and I brought the tip close to her paw. When I went to insert it . . . I stopped. I couldn't do it. I just couldn't. My love for Crystal transcended my own will. The conditions would be bent and rewritten to accommodate this flaw in myself. I could see it now: Crystal running through fields and streams, gnawing bones, and sleeping peacefully by the fireside while Emily and I watched television. All these things would come true and I'd see to it that she'd be exonerated of a canine's worst sin: failing to find love. Love would find her. At this decision, I felt such a wave of relief that it brought tears to my eyes and my soul let out a relieved sigh. From this point on, things would change. My own religion would evolve. It would have to. I would find a new job and I would aspire to health and long life. Maybe I'd even start exercising and stop eating meat.

 I even got so far as to take Crystal off the table, place her on the ground, and walk her back into the bay. She snooped like nothing out of the ordinary had occurred. But as I walked her back to her cage, I thought twice about my decision, swept her into my arms, and put her back on the table. I looked into her trusting, somewhat confused blue eyes, and I felt tormented by my conflict again. I needed a second to recompose myself. In the end, I had to run to the wash station to puke my guts out. Even when I returned to my task, I still had to take some deep, steady breaths. Finally, I overcame my desire to protect—my personal reluctance—by focusing on doing the right thing given the circumstances. In opposition to my very nature, I grabbed her paw, brought the needle to it, and began to press.

 This was a pivotal moment in my experience. Despite my resolve, there was a physical force rendering me incapable of proceeding further. Of all unforeseen obstacles, it was Gizzer's presence that proved the toughest to overcome. He had slipped in undetected when I was absorbed in the task and now he was holding my arm back with all his might.

"Stop, Grant!" he cried. "You'll never forgive yourself."

I pushed him away. "Defiant little bastard. If I don't do this, it will devalue the life of every other dog that's gone through the same thing."

"What about you?" he pleaded with great emotion. "Is it worth your happiness?"

Enraged, I grabbed the boy and pulled him towards the door. Crystal began howling, clearly in disapproval of the confrontation. Gizzer was not so easily dissuaded. He fought back for the first time since I had met him, slipping through my grasp then reversing his grip and spinning me to the ground by my arm with a great display of emotional strength. This was simply too much for Crystal. She had jumped down from the table and was now barking defensively at the boy, standing protectively between my attacker and me.

"When I get my hands on you, you're going to pay," I threatened, rising to my feet with a renewed anger and purpose.

"Just listen to me," Gizzer pleaded, backing away.

But I was not reasonable. I was overcome by my emotions. Now that I had the boy cornered, I hauled him to the ground by the collar and began dragging him kicking and protesting to the door. Crystal by this time was going absolutely nuts. Once again, Gizzer managed to rip away from my grasp and he scuttled against some cabinets like a panicked crab.

As I stood hovering over him, just about to get a hold of him again, my senses began coming back to me. I looked down at the kid sprawled out at my feet.

Gizzer had tears in his eyes. "Don't you get it, I've come to adopt her?" he pleaded, holding his hands up to protect himself. He looked absolutely pathetic, with his face contorted in emotion.

"You're what?" I demanded, taking a step back. I was absolutely numb.

"I'm adopting her, you maniac!" Gizzer cried.

Silence. I didn't know what to say at first, although I could feel my blood settling. The stillness in the room was torturous.

"You came back for her?" I asked in a choked up voice, almost unable to comprehend it all.

The kid looked at me in disgust. "Don't you get it, I'm adopting her for you, Grant."

Slowly, instinctively, I reached my hand down to help him up, but he batted it away and got to his feet on his own strength.

"I'm sorry, Brent," I said, putting my hand on his shoulder. I just wanted to break down and surrender to my exhaustion.

"Don't touch me," he warned, brushing my hand away.

He then put Crystal's collar back on her, wiped his eyes, and leashed her. At this point, I had dropped to the floor and was leaning against the cabinets with my face in my hands. As they were walking away, Gizzer thought better of it and turned back to me.

"As soon as you sent me home tonight, I called my dad and forced him to understand the exceptional circumstances," he explained. "Do you know what I had to go through to get him to agree to this?"

"I feel terrible," I said, all choked up and looking up at him, still dizzy from the roller coaster ride of emotions. "How can I make this up to you?"

"By pulling yourself together, old man," Gizzer said. "You're a wreck."

"I don't know how to thank you . . ." I whispered, unable to find my voice behind the constriction of my emotion. I'm not sure he even heard me.

"I'll see you tomorrow tonight," he stated, before adding, "By the way, if you put your hands on me again I'll knock your teeth out. I mean it."

Then they departed together, man and dog, leaving me alone to process this incredible sense of spiritual relief—like the world had been taken off my shoulders. It was the type of relief that prompts worship, like getting down on your hands and knees and genuflecting before God from the very depths of your soul. It was the type of relief that reminded me that I was truly powerless before fate. It's true that when I had the needle in my hand, at the drop of a hat I would have easily exchanged my life for Crystal's, but at that moment there'd been no higher authority in the universe whom I could even approach with such a bargain. And then Gizzer arrived like an answer to a prayer that I would never have had the courage to voice. Never had I felt more grateful in my life, or more existentially cared for by the universe.

CHAPTER 9

Brad-to-the-Bone had been released from the hospital with no complications. Now that he had under his belt a few weeks of delivering pizza, his days were beginning to glide along smoothly, like a great blue heron descending into the lily-padded surface of Wye Marsh. I was so encouraged by his progress that I talked Tamer into adjusting their schedule at work so that the gentle giant could join us at the pub for a few rounds. Since we all got such a kick out of Gizzer, I encouraged him to join us as well. The kid seemed amenable to the idea, but warned me that he'd have to catch up with us later due to a prior commitment that certainly took precedence over the alcohol induced banter and mindless conversation that were sure to define the occasion.

Once we arrived at the pub, we secured our preferred table in the corner and began to reacquaint ourselves with the menu. Poor Brad didn't get much of a chance to look before Tamer pressured him to get off his butt and haul us over some drafts. I noted that the line between employer and employee most likely had little distinction outside of the workplace. It wouldn't have taken much persuasion anyway, for in the pub atmosphere the big man really seemed in his element.

Although Brad was slow to recognize his responsibilities as a newcomer, once he caught on he didn't see the need to argue the point. With his departure, Tamer and I caught up a bit.

"I just want to thank you," Tamer began, his eyes accusative. "Brad-to-the-Bone is not only the slowest delivery boy I've ever had, but he takes forty-five minutes to eat his dinner and then follows it up with half an hour in the bathroom."

I started laughing.

"That means I pay him a full seven hours, when he works five and three quarters," Tamer complained.

"And that's probably maximizing his time," I added, fanning the flames.

Tamer continued, "He insists on wearing these hiked up blue jeans despite our dress code. For some inexplicable reason, he wears these big winter boots that he stomps around like an elephant in, tracking mud everywhere. And that beard, I'm not going to even start telling you about customers' reactions when that jolly face goes up to the cash register to take an order."

This made me laugh even harder.

"It's not like I can fire him either. I have Smoker, who comes in so stoned that he sometimes forgets he's delivering pizzas while on the road—even with a stack of pies piled beside him. Then I have Trenton, who shows up when he feels like it. I really have no choice but to keep your friendly giant as my number one man. But you've really screwed me this time, old man."

"I love him," I said. "He's the nicest guy I've met in a long time."

"Did you know that he hates kids?" Tamer asked in disbelief.

"Nothing surprises me about Brad," I said.

"This guy's a real piece of work, but he's lovable . . . I'll give him that . . . Customers talk to him twenty minutes at a time. I can't let him answer the phone 'cause I can never get him off once he's started . . ."

"You'll thank me some day, Dan."

"Believe me, I'll be thanking you with my fist," Tamer growled.

Brad strolled back to the table carrying beers in his hands, a big grin on his bearded face, blue jeans hiked up to his chest, boots up to his knees.

"Here you go, fellas," he said in a cheerful voice, painstakingly setting the drinks on the table, his good nature absolutely infectious.

His jolliness only seemed to irritate Tamer.

"Quit screwing around and decide what you want to order!" Tamer barked before Brad could even take his seat at the table.

Brad nodded and smiled politely before beginning to snail his way through the menu with no added urgency to speak of.

"You probably won't believe this, guys," I said. "The police visited me a week or so ago to question me about some vandalism. My parents' place got trashed with spray paint and it seems I'm one of the suspects."

"Did you do it?" Tamer asked.

"Of course not," I replied, looking incredulous. "Does that sound like something I would do?"

"Certainly the work of a highly immature person with lots of motive, so I wouldn't rule you out," Tamer said with a smile.

I continued, "Well, if you add this suspected vandalism to the incident at work with my old man, I've come to the conclusion that the police have their sights on me. There's a cruiser that drives by my house a lot now, I assume because they suspect my injuries were drug-related. It's not like I provided them with Marco's identity . . ."

"Tough break," said Brad. "I guess we can forget smoking some fat ones out on your porch, at least for a few months."

"Well, if you guys could keep your vices within the law, we wouldn't have a problem, would we?" I pointed out.

"Yeah, old man, speaking of venues, that reminds me," said Tamer, changing the subject, "you still haven't taken the time to visit my new apartment."

"I keep forgetting," I admitted, surprised with myself for not going over.

"You're going to love it, old man," Tamer promised. "I have this room where I get women to come over and paint their feet on it. I'd say the room is truly a robust, colorful work of art. Who would have known that I had such a creative spirit in me?"

"I've seen it, old man," said Brad. "It almost inspired me to pull up a chair and write poetry in that room the last time I saw it."

Tamer was beaming in pride, apparently pleased with himself.

"It's a beautiful collage," Tamer agreed. "The only glitch is that—believe it or not—I think I met someone, Grant."

"You met someone?" I repeated, unsure whether I'd heard him correctly.

"Yep," Tamer replied, a smile tugging at the corners of his mouth.

I looked at him for a second, as if I could divine the truth.

"Yeah, sure Dan . . ." I said with doubt in my voice, starting to laugh. "You almost had me . . ."

"No, I'm serious. She's an amazing girl," Tamer said with enthusiasm. "I can't invite her over, though, because she'll see that room. I'm sure you can appreciate my struggle: on the one hand I have my artistic integrity and on the other I have the desire to explore this relationship without a significant strike against me."

"Who's the girl?" I asked.

"That's her over there," said Tamer, pointing to a girl working the bar. She was blond and round with a pleasant face.

"Really?" I asked, shocked. "She's so plain I never noticed her here before."

"You know I like plumpers, old man. Besides, there's just something about her."

"True, you've always made it clear really skinny girls aren't your preference."

"She's pretty hot," said Brad, quick to add his two cents. "Quite a rack on her, eh?"

"And you've asked her out already?" I asked.

"No, no, no," said Tamer, shaking his head. "Next summer I intend to make her a happy woman. I've got plenty of time. The thing is, in the meantime my masterpiece is only going to get more elaborate as I recruit more females of culture."

At this point in the conversation, Gizzer decided to join us. He was accompanied by four dazzling-eyed women who hung on his every word. These young vixens piled around our table while Tamer's zealous *protégé* proved beyond a shadow of a doubt that he was taking his apprenticeship to heart. Tamer and Brad seemed incredibly impressed, while I sat there silently, suddenly feeling miserable for some reason. Gizzer casually sat down and joked with us—all the while charming the girls with his quick wit and growing confidence.

"I thought you had a girlfriend, Gizz," I whispered.

"Told you, man, women flock to me now," he replied.

"So you broke up with your girlfriend?"

The boy nodded. "She let herself become boring."

At that point, Tamer decided to take over the party before I got a chance to question him further.

"Listen up, ladies and gentleman!" Tamer shouted, standing up at the head of the table with his glass raised, banging a spoon against it. "Take a seat everyone. I'm about to propose a toast, so quiet down."

"Hey Tamer!" shouted a voice from the back of the room. "Can't a week go by in this boring town without of one of your stupid toasts?"

"Give me a break, it's been at least a month," Tamer shouted back, grinning from ear to ear. "Now take a seat and shut up Jimmy B. so I can say my piece, got it?"

Everyone quieted down and gave the popular restaurant manager the respect he quite naturally elicited from new acquaintances. This silence was only interrupted when the girls spontaneously began giggling amongst themselves. Tamer winked at them, gestured for silence again, and then assumed a very serious demeanor.

"I'm glad so many of you are here tonight because I want everyone to know that Grant Arthur Spire—an absolute fool in my opinion, but a good man—has announced that he will be marrying a woman who is a very dear friend of mine. She's not just any woman, mind you. Grant is marrying his soul mate, which means that they were meant to be together since the beginning of time. I congratulate him for finding her. Everyone, please congratulate him."

Then he made a big show of pointing at me to ensure that my identity could not be mistaken. He even had me stand up so that he could lead a round of applause.

"You tricked me," I said to him. "This was supposed to be Brad's night."

Tamer merely grinned at me.

He then continued, "You know, folks, I'm not sure there has ever been a man more patient with a woman than Grant. There's a term that comes to mind, to be frank. It's called attrition. This man ground the will of the universe to a malleable pulp because he determined from the moment he met her that they were destined to become a couple."

I had to think about what he meant by this, and by the look of the faces around me, so did everyone else.

"So my toast is to the old man, Grant Arthur Spire," Tamer shouted triumphantly, raising his glass high and surveying the scope of the room, "a true sucker for punishment!"

"May he have a long life . . . plenty of offspring . . . lots of flow to his member well into old age . . . and . . . most importantly . . . still have time for tennis with the people in his life he can always count on: his friends!"

Tamer then raised his beer, winked at the same girls again, and smashed his mug into Brad's before swallowing the entire pint down like a Viking. Everyone else clanked glasses and drank deeply. From my point of view, I couldn't but question his sincerity and motivation—I mean, taking into consideration Tamer's low opinion of relationships. The only part I could take seriously was the plea to continue playing tennis with him.

It wasn't over, though. Tamer walked around and encouraged everyone at the bar to line up and congratulate me in the form of a hug. He was like a sheepdog nipping the flanks of the flock. Funny thing is, almost everyone surrendered with very little protest. In one sense, it was almost unbearable, but there wasn't much I could when baaing sheep were lining up to congratulate me on the heroic achievement of transcending time and space to pluck my love from such a small patch of white sand in the universe.

For ten or so more minutes, people I had known for most of my life continued coming over to our table to shake my hand or give me a pat on the back. It seemed that once Tamer had opened the floodgates the support would never end. Several congratulatory beers later, after things died down a bit, Megan, of all people, appeared beside me, a little wobbly from one too many beers of her own, and asked whether anyone had a smoke. Without a blink, Gizzer produced a cigarette that he'd snatched lightning quick from Brad's pack, lit it in his own mouth, and passed it to her.

Megan gave Gizzer a look of unmistakable interest that I had certainly not seen in our own encounters. She even put a hand on my shoulder and whispered into my ear: "It's good to see you, Grant. Congratulations. Who you marrying? You'll have to excuse me for dismissing myself to the bathroom instead of giving you a proper hug."

"It's good to see you, too," I replied. "Actually, I'm marrying—"

"Who's your friend?" she interrupted, shamelessly eying little Gizzer.

Naturally, before this could go any further, I sent her away. I didn't want my young friend having anything to do with the older woman. Besides, the beauty of the four women that had arrived with him that night made Megan's appearance seem rather ordinary. But if I'm honest with myself, there's a good chance I got rid of her because I felt a twinge of jealousy.

After Megan disappeared, Tamer thought it would be a good idea to have Brad reveal his appendix scar to everyone. Without a second thought, Brad, no inhibitions at all, stood up on a chair and lifted his shirt for everyone in the pub to see. He was met with looks of initial fascination that turned into a chorus of groans that seemed very satisfying to him.

While everybody was reacting to this, their collective elevated mood more evident by the minute, Gizzer got my attention and drew me to the side.

"Who was that girl you were talking to?" he asked.

"We used to see each other," I answered. "Believe me, Gizz, you want nothing to do with Megan. You could never compete with her penchant for getting high . . ."

The kid, unfazed, didn't feel the need to question me further, obviously interested in forming his own conclusions about Megan. He tracked the fresh trail without a second thought, leaving us older guys to entertain the wild young women he had abandoned so impulsively.

Before I left that evening, I looked across the pub to see Gizzer and Megan side-by-side on barstools. He had his arm across her shoulder while he spoke closely in her ear. To me, it looked like he was offering her comfort and counsel. No doubt the nature of their conversation had become quite personal. Even Brad remarked about their beautiful harmony together before heading home to work on one of the neverending projects he used as an excuse to escape. Tamer didn't seem to notice, though, or if he did, he certainly didn't show it. He was more concerned with being the gentleman, which he demonstrated by volunteering to escort the girls to his apartment for a nightcap and the prospect of adding to his collage of feet.

I walked home along the street lamp lit streets, considering Gizzer's recent behavior. He had saved me when I most needed saving and now he was giving Megan the type of attention every woman deserves. No doubt, like any other teenager, he was vulnerable to peer pressure and certainly not above trying to come off as cool. Still, armed with a powerful sense of empathy and no shortage of courage, he certainly had the right combination to continue making an impact in the lives of those who had the fortune of crossing his path.

* * * * *

Sunday night, my one night off, and Emily called while I was putting the finishing touches on my dinner, already reaching for a plate as I picked up the phone. She insisted that I visit her at work right away, since she was bartending and couldn't leave. Concerned by the urgency in her tone, I turned off the stove and decided that I'd have to postpone feeding the dogs until later as well.

When I arrived at the restaurant, I was impressed, as always, by the atmosphere in the lounge. It seemed so American, with jerseys and plaques on the wall as well as big plasma televisions visible from any seat in the house. On this night, many of the patrons were playing an interactive trivia game that could be seen on select screens, while others sat there shouting, eating wings, and draining mugs of beer with the four o'clock football game still raging on.

Once I was comfortably seated at the bar, Emily approached me, an ominous dark cloud engulfing her features. I knew whatever she had to say wasn't going to be pleasant.

My smile was met with ice, so I tried to test the water with delicacy.

"What's wrong tonight, sweetie?" I asked.

"Do you want a beer or what?" she replied coldly.

I nodded. "Sounds good."

I watched her expertly pour my favorite brew from the keg—very little head—before slamming it down on the counter in front of me so that a tiny splash wet my beard.

"Smartly done," I said, trying to be funny.

Emily looked at me with scalding eyes. Things were heating up.

I dared to ask her again, "So what's wrong?"

"It's that Avery . . ." she said through gritted teeth.

"What did she do?" I probed, watching Emily pick up a mug and wipe the counter where a customer had been sitting.

"I'm not on speaking terms with her anymore," Emily muttered with little emotion in her voice, and yet she looked irritated by the question.

This caught me by surprise, but I recovered.

"So what happened?" I asked gently.

Emily sighed loudly, like it took great nerve for me to ask.

"It's nothing, Grant. She called me and freaked over something insignificant."

"Then why worry about it, sweetie?"

"Because it's not fair, I didn't deserve it," she hissed.

"What's not fair?"

"Oh, she got all upset when she caught wind of me and Justin," Emily confessed, her frustration mounting. "It was two years ago, won't anyone let it rest?"

I began to feel a little bit dizzy and nauseous.

"Emily, when I was with Avery, it became clear that she's been highly involved with Justin for five years or so," I began slowly. "He keeps a lot of his stuff to himself, so I never could keep track of all the women he ran with."

"Yeah, so?"

"Well, if you and Avery were best friends, can you blame her for being disappointed?"

"Are you accusing me of something?" Emily asked, visibly becoming livid. "Are you taking her side?"

"No, I just want to know the truth," I replied calmly.

"Look it, Justin approached me. I wasn't going to turn away the man I thought I could possibly marry because of her. Besides, at the time, I really thought it was possible. You know, it just seemed like two screw-ups like Justin and myself were meant to somehow be together . . ."

"But you told me that you only went out once. Something doesn't jive. I'm not getting the whole story here."

"I'm not the same person I used to be. I know you're idealistic, but a date with anyone but you pretty much implies sex afterwards. That's just the way it is. There's no responsibility to take. He asked me out and I accepted, fully aware of what was going to transpire later. But I thought he could be the one."

"And that excuses it?"

"What do you mean?"

"Forget it," I replied, perhaps a little too sharply, becoming frustrated myself. "We're not accomplishing anything by having this conversation."

"Well, you don't have to worry about hearing about her anymore. I've blocked Avery's calls and her emails as well. If she wants to be a bitch, she's messing with the wrong girl."

"How you want to deal with it is up to you," I conceded, prepared to wash my hands of it all. "But I have to go. The dogs are waiting."

"Leave then," Emily encouraged. "It's quite nice of you to get me all fired up and then take off when it's convenient for you, while I'm stuck here."

"I'll see you at home," I stated, standing up to leave.

Emily then looked at me with really sad eyes. "Wait, Grant. That's not why I asked you to come here tonight."

I stopped. "What is it then?"

I felt a hand on my shoulder. Justin Fancy had arrived and now took the stool next to me. The timing of his arrival couldn't have been better or worse, depending on your point-of-view.

"Have a seat," he said invitingly. "Let's have some beers together."

Left with little other choice, and feeling like the victim of some well coordinated subterfuge, I surrendered my pride and resumed the seat offered to me by my former close friend, now sworn enemy.

"It's good to see you guys in each other's company again," Emily said with a smile, setting a beer down for Fancy. "It's about time."

"I don't feel like I've been given much of a choice here," I grumbled.

Emily looked at me impatiently. "Listen, Grant, we need to figure out some of the details of the wedding and I doubt you would have come here otherwise. Let's just try to be mature about this."

I nodded and took a sip of beer. I couldn't help sharing my opinion with a hint of bitterness, though. "Fine, but it's just weird for me to think that the pastor who's going to marry us has a more intimate knowledge of my bride than I do."

Justin laughed. "It's strange, I admit. But I've heard of more awkward situations."

When he saw that I wasn't nearly as amused, Justin tried to be reassuring. "Whatever happened between us has faded from memory."

"Me as well," Emily added, glaring at Fancy with a hint of insult to her expression.

"I don't want to talk about it anymore," I said, getting fed up. "Let's just forget about it and move on."

"It's interesting to see you jealous," Emily observed. "I like it."

"I'm not jealous," I insisted. "I just know that it's important to you that we get married in a church. At this point, I wouldn't even care if Justin was part of the wedding party if it meant that we could get this conversation over with."

"It's ok," Fancy said, trying to keep me calm. "I understand. I'm here to do whatever you guys like."

"Emily and I talked about January," I said.

Emily had to drift away to serve a customer some beer.

"Before we get into it, would you like an update?" Fancy asked me, momentarily changing the subject.

"On what?" I replied, a little curious.

"I think they found out who vandalized your parents' property."

"Really? Who?"

"What are you guys talking about?" Emily interrupted, afraid she had missed something in the nanosecond she'd been gone.

Fancy responded to us both. "The truth is that Marco had an affair with a married woman. The husband found out and vandalized your parents' property in retaliation."

"Naturally, I was the one who had to pay for it," I said sarcastically.

"Grant, I heard through the grapevine that your parents have split up," Justin said seriously.

"Really?"

"It's about time," Emily piped up. "I don't know how anyone could stay with that beast."

"My mother was raised to believe that divorce meant a ticket straight to hell," I explained. "Don't be too hard on her."

"Perhaps she's changed her views," Fancy said. "Either way, I think you should give your mother a call and find out what's going on. No offense, but it's common knowledge that your old man's the type to dip into other men's cookie jars. If your mother has finally pulled the plug, I thought you'd want to know for sure."

Fancy was wrong. Although I was estranged from my family, one of the constants in my life was their commitment to each other. I had mixed feelings and preferred to remain unenlightened until things worked themselves out.

"It's not my business," I finally said. "Let's just sort things through so that Emily can get back to work and I can get home to let the dogs out."

"She's not busy," Fancy said playfully, giving Emily a wink. "There's no hurry. What's your pressing need? The dogs? They can wait, I'm sure."

Emily joined in. "Yeah, Grant, would you have me believe that you treasure your nights away from me?"

"You know better," I replied.

"Don't contradict yourself, my friend," Fancy teased. "Just last week didn't you say that you needed a night to yourself to recover from a week-long headache?"

"Is that so?" Emily asked. "Well, maybe I'll confide more in your friend, Dan Tamer, the only man who knows how to ease a woman's headache."

"She's not joking anymore," I explained to Fancy, feeling a twinge of envy. "Tamer knows just what to say."

Emily seemed to take offense to this. "Grant, all I needed from you tonight was a bit of empathy. Sometimes you're just supposed to listen."

For a second, we just glared at each other. She was doing everything she could to scald me with her eyes.

"So do you guys want me to do this wedding or not?" Fancy asked, breaking the silence. Obviously, he was disturbed that our discussion had accumulated such tension.

Emily turned her angry eyes from me and then softened her look when she turned to Fancy. "We were thinking January would be good, what do you think?"

"Works for me," said Fancy. "If I can talk Daven into it, I should be able to get the church booked for the end of the month with zero difficulty."

"That would be great," Emily said in relief. "In the meantime, it's important to me that you two settle your differences. I want you both in my life, and you were friends long before you met me. Grant, you realize you wouldn't have gone to seminary if it weren't for Justin. And Justin, you might not have your position at the church if Grant hadn't talked you out of abandoning your studies at one point, remember?"

"I'm all for reconciliation," Fancy said. "It's about time, I say."

"I need more time . . ." I protested, not even close to being ready.

"Whatever, let's get the hell out of here!" Fancy cried, tossing down some money for our drinks. "Let's get our next drink at the bar, bury the hatchet."

"But . . ."

Once we were outside, Fancy was joyous. He spun around in his trench coat and then came to a stop with his arms raised to the sky, no doubt enjoying the cool night air and the slight breeze and the freedom he was experiencing.

"This is great," he said, looking at me with a big smile. "I can't believe you and I are hanging out together like this, just like old times."

"Listen Fancy—"

But he laughed and interrupted me. "Let's just start a new chapter, you stubborn zygote. We're more alike than you think."

"No way," I objected, shaking my head.

"I feel so good that we're outside, I just farted in the wind," he exclaimed, ignoring me. "Remember that beautiful girl we tortured in the bar? I asked her if she farted very often and she gave me that strange look. So I said, 'Hey, hey, we have a woman who's about to explode here,' and then she turned three shades of red in front of all of her buddies."

Justin then grabbed me by the shoulders and shook me affectionately. "Woohoo! We're free, buddy, the night stands before us!"

"Let go, you freak," I protested, but I couldn't help but laugh.

"It was oppressive in that restaurant with Emily, wasn't it?" Fancy asked.

"Sure was."

"Good God, what a depressed atmosphere in there. It's like my soul was being constricted."

"When Emily's in a mood she can turn a carnival into a morgue."

We began to trudge along the path that ran by the waterfront.

"So be honest, you really love that girl?" Fancy asked, giving me a bewildered look, as if loving Emily were inconceivable.

"Absolutely," I replied without even having to think about it.

"Why?" he asked. "How?"

"There are so many reasons."

"Like?"

"Like the way she demands the best from me—she won't let me underachieve," I began, "or the way she sometimes looks at me with those mysterious brown eyes. I guess it's how she makes feel in general. She's like my own little wildflower."

"With lots of thistles, buddy . . ."

"What do you mean by that?"

"Do you even know her? I mean, really know her?"

"Sure, I've known for her years," I said. "I live with her. I interact with her every day. I share her problems."

"She's so guarded, though," said Fancy. "So secretive . . . so unapproachable. The girl puts up walls at every turn—at least for me. She doesn't do the same for you?"

"Getting to know Emily requires commitment. She has a big heart and I've seen glimpses of that soft underbelly below the toughness she portrays."

"I think you're confusing love with something else. I know you love her in a general, caring sense, but how can you love someone in the way you profess without understanding her?"

"I understand that she wants to be with me and that's enough," I replied casually.

"Well, you realize that by marrying you guys I'm paying my dues. You know deep down I can't support this wedding. But for a clean slate, I'm willing to exchange one guilt for another."

"I'm not making any promises."

Fancy gave me a weak smile, like he wanted to argue further. Instead he lit up a cigarette.

"Take one," he said.

"No thanks."

"Damn it, just take one," he insisted. "You never turned one down before."

"Ok," I shrugged, lighting up and passing him back his lighter.

"This is great," Fancy said again, stopping and resting his arms on the driftwood fence that ran parallel to the path, so that he could look out over the bay. It was a clear night, with moon and stars. "We should get together at least once a week, don't you think?"

I stood beside him and said nothing. We were both contemplative for a moment, slowly puffing away.

"Remember when we went to seminary?" Fancy asked, disturbing the silence. "We were so idealistic, so confident."

"Yeah."

"But by the time we left, we could no longer believe in a system. In a sense, we left with too much knowledge for a regular faith, and yet we couldn't exactly share that from the pulpit. But what we've learned is far more beautiful than any religious system. It was worth it, right?"

"Your point?"

"Is that why you abandoned the idea of ministry and opted to work with animals? Because you're too honest?"

"No," I replied slowly, considering his question. "I think it's because I wasn't sure what I believed anymore."

Fancy chuckled. "When it comes to spirituality, at some point everybody has to acknowledge the mystery. It's honest. Why should you be more secure than anybody else?"

"I never thought of it that way," I admitted.

"You're strong enough to admit to yourself that you're actively feeling for the truth that's behind the everydayness of our lives. Besides, it's each person's responsibility to make their own beliefs meaningful."

"That still doesn't make me a confident leader, though. It makes me uncertain and indecisive."

Justin shook his head in complete disagreement.

"People want to worship this idea of God in their heads because it's comfortable," he explained. "It's our job to make it easy for them . . . and yet stretch them gradually to the point where they can question their beliefs . . . weigh their beliefs versus their experience and incorporate all the knowledge they've learned throughout their lifetime. I feel like a professor and a philosopher and a healer and a counselor and a writer all in one. I love my profession and I'm good at it because I know how we must walk the line between expressing what we truly believe and what we teach."

"But are you able to live up to the moral standards required of the position?"

"I've changed, my friend. Why can't you see that?"

"Well, what about Avery?" I pointed out, putting him on the spot. "She thinks you're ready for a commitment. Do you intend to follow through with your word?"

Fancy looked at me like I was insane and then broke into a grin. "You know that women have always been my weak spot. Avery and I have had some good times together, but I know I wouldn't be doing myself any favors by being with someone like her. I'd have to be nuts. But you know this already. How is this helpful?"

"If I've learned one thing in the past two years," I explained, "it's that you never take someone who cares for you for granted."

"Good advice, my friend," Fancy replied with warm enthusiasm, "but there's a young lady that started to come to our church that's much more in line with the type of girl I would marry."

I sighed in frustration. His logic reminded me of Emily's.

Justin looked at me with curiosity, like he couldn't understand why I was vexed.

"I need you to co-write that book for me, Grant. I lack your skill, but the ideas are all there. I don't want to settle for a regular ministry. I want to help others. I want them to see the symptom in all of us that resembles . . . no, imitates . . . Christ's passion for the cross. I want you to write my theology of destruction."

I started to walk away. He threw his cigarette down and caught up to me.

"It was no accident," he said, grabbing my arm to stop me.

We stood there looking at each other.

"What wasn't an accident?"

"I had to hook up with Emily so that you could be free, or at least that's what I thought. I can see how she plays you, how she tortures you. I thought if I slept with her that we'd go through a rough patch, but you'd be better for it. But now, in hindsight, I suspect that I did it as much to hurt myself because you are one of the few people that I consider my friend. And I still do."

His explanation infuriated me. "You took advantage of the opportunity. You tasted the one thing that you knew she denied me. This is what makes your act such a betrayal."

"I agree!" Justin shouted. "I agree!"

"Then why give me such an excuse?"

"Because that taste cost so much. It was a violation against my own soul, to make you hurt like that."

Before I could protest, Justin's cell phone went off. He answered it and said, "Yes, yes, ok, ok, no problem . . . I'll be there in ten minutes."

"You have one of those new BlackBerrys?" I asked.

"Yeah, what you got?"

I showed him my phone, one of those sliders. He took it from me and seemed to inspect it with interest. But that was only a ruse. Before he gave it back, he dialed a number and then tossed me the phone while it was still ringing.

"I just dialed your parents' number," he said with a very serious look. "It's time you learned the truth."

He broke into his usual smile, reached out and messed up the back of my hair, and then tore off into the night, leaving me panic stricken, not knowing what to say.

My mother answered.

"It's Grant," I managed. "Tell me you left the monster . . ."

CHAPTER 10

THE SHELTER WAS NOT THE same the next time I punched in. Without Crystal's personality to draw inspiration from, I'm not even sure I could call it a shelter. In fact, it now resembled a pound. There seemed to be a more penetrating hollowness to the place—a deadness that saturated the atmosphere and made the routine seem alien, like a relationship you wake up to one day that suddenly feels cold, distant, and unfamiliar.

When Gizzer arrived at the facility, he sensed my mood was dark. To help ease the tension, he released Pete, Tory, and Lady from their pens. He figured the only thing that could combat the oppressive atmosphere was the instant infusion of energy that comes from canine jubilation, and he was right. After watching the dogs snoop around and explore the bay for a few minutes, I left them in his care and made my way to the office. It felt like an appropriate time to close Crystal's case file on the computer.

When I sat at the desk, a sober feeling washed over me again. I wasn't quite as ready to write as I had thought. Instead, I sat there examining the reptiles, trying to get my bearings. The iguana, Otis, was motionless, only his dilating and contracting pupils betraying the life within. Pinecone and

Mussolini, my anoles, were pretty active, cocking their heads and looking up at me with a deceptive appearance of wisdom. I surmised that they were expecting a cricket or two. Hector remained curled up and didn't seem to notice me; the snake's only indication of life was the flick of his forked tongue. Over the years, these reptiles were the only witnesses to the records I typed on this computer. They were also probably the only residents of this building, including myself, held to no conditions of survival.

When I began to type out the details of Crystal's adoption, it felt like I was writing lines of soulful poetry. It was her story, a beautiful story, with an ending that signified an open-ended beginning. I liked that. I had expected more such endings and beginnings when I started working at the shelter, and the opportunity to close Crystal's case with a positive outcome still had its price. Honestly, I felt drained and in need of a vacation. But the first step was making it through the night, so to bolster my spirits, I poured myself a cup of coffee and pulled up a chair to watch Gizzer play with the dogs.

Each dog had a unique approach to the game that was immediately discernible. Pete's eagerness for the rough and tumble activity, as well as his contagious excitement, immediately caught my attention. From the moment we were introduced, this trusting, unattractive mutt eagerly pursued my friendship. I felt like I had failed him by being unable to find him a worthy home. Ugliness is a matter of perspective, and Pete certainly was worthy of affection and adoration from the inside out. He was never able to contain his joy, nor did his joy ever seem to diminish.

Tory, on the other hand, had always been uninterested in having me as a friend, but I do think he grew to tolerate my presence. His defining attribute was his need for the company of other dogs. His obstructed breathing was almost symbolic of his obstructed understanding of my love for him. Just the same, I had provided for Tory as best I could and explored many avenues to find a home where he might fit in. If he had been a few years younger, I'm positive he would have been adopted early on.

Then there was Lady, who was fanatical when it came to my attention. I think it was her fear of me abandoning her that kept her so dependent on my affection and made her incapable of experiencing joy outside of me. From the reports I heard, this long-snouted collie was a different dog when I wasn't around. Although I knew this type of hyper-devotion could be transferred to someone else, anybody we got to come in and meet her found her to be intolerable and unfit for adoption. I just wished a loving family could see her potential. Given some security, there was no doubt in mind she'd become the type of dog to reward her new family with an endless supply of gratitude.

After observing them playing with such intensity for a few minutes, I felt my dark mood dissipating. It was hilarious to see the determination in each set of eyes. Such serious business. Once they had worked themselves into a frenzy, they put their ancient wolf lineage on display, leaping around, barking and growling and trying to outmaneuver each other with ferocious bared teeth. And Gizzer stoked their passion by waving a rawhide strip at them from his sprawled out position on the floor, always managing to pull it away from one of their death grips.

It's incredible how watching highly charged dogs always makes me laugh. I can't help myself. There is just something about their single-minded focus that re-energizes my spirit no matter how heavy the atmosphere.

The moment I took a step to join them, I heard a familiar snarl. "Playing computer games again, dogs out of their pens again . . ."

I had been so contemplative that I didn't even hear him enter the facility.

I turned to face him, resigned to my punishment, and was met by the glare of disgust on the pallid Inspector's face.

"It doesn't matter, Grant, your fate is sealed," the old man continued.

Kelly walked in behind him and stood at a distance, with a mixture of shame and malice replacing the normal cheerful expression on her face.

"What's this about?" I asked, feeling somewhat defeated. The dogs had sensed the new visitors and were beginning to bark. I closed the door to the bay and signaled to Gizzer that it was time they go back in their pens.

The Inspector looked at me with contempt. "Kelly rightfully informed me about the incident several weeks ago and we considered the matter thoroughly. We've decided that it's time to let you go."

I was shocked. This was a possibility I thought could never happen.

"On what grounds?" I stammered. "You can't blame me for the incident that left me in the hospital."

"Grant," Kelly began, "you are responsible for everything that takes place here at night."

"This is ridiculous," I said in disbelief. "Kelly, you know that nobody can do a better job here than me. You know this."

"I've had Kelly keep track of all your missteps over the last six months so that we could bring a strong case against you," the old man intervened. "We have so many grounds to fire you."

"But—" I tried to object.

"This was merely the straw that broke the camel's back," he sneered.

I looked at Kelly, feeling utterly betrayed, and couldn't devise a plan to convince the man that I was deserving of another chance.

The Inspector continued, "I told you weeks ago to get rid of the damn lizards. I told you to stop using the computer on my time. I told you to stop allowing dogs to roam the bay freely. Don't act like we're in the wrong. You're the one responsible for your actions and you never chose to be compliant."

I felt like collapsing in despair. My hands and legs were trembling. Why were they doing this to me?

The Inspector looked me up and down without emotion and added, "Your transgressions have gone beyond repair. Now get your damn lizards out of my office and pack up your belongings."

"The reptiles are cold-blooded," I replied, keeping my voice calm and steady.

"So?" the Inspector replied.

"It means I need someone to pick me up."

After a pause to consider, the Inspector nodded curtly.

"Very well, young man. Find a means of transportation quickly."

I called up Tamer at the restaurant and asked him whether he could spare Brad for a few minutes since Emily had taken the car to work. While I was on the phone, the Inspector summoned Gizzer and then told him go home for the night and report the next day if he was still interested in finishing his term. The boy gave me a sad, concerned look as he strolled by. Kelly immediately assumed my duties and began to take care of the dogs. As if to pour salt in my wounds, she started letting the dogs out fifteen minutes ahead of the schedule I had implemented over the years.

I began the process of cleaning out my office by carrying Otis's aquarium over to the door for when Brad arrived. I did the same with Pinecone and Mussolini's, then brought Hector's cage over as well. Each movement seemed like slow motion. Looking back, the experience was like a bad nightmare where I couldn't wake up with that overwhelming sense of relief.

It had always been my intention to resign from my position. But when I did move on, the plan was to leave the shelter with great provision for the dogs I left behind. Since I wasn't leaving on my own terms, everything was a blur and I found myself in panic mode. When Brad showed up fifteen minutes later in his Echo, his presence was definitely comforting, although he didn't say two words in front of the Inspector. While we loaded up the car we could hear the old man giving Kelly instructions now and then as they went through the files. They totally ignored us while we began to carry out the computer and the rest of my stuff.

By the time we started to take out my personal effects, I was still concentrating on finding a solution to the quandary I found myself in. It wasn't the job that I cared about. The problem was plain and simple: if I allowed myself to walk quietly out of this building tonight, I could no longer facilitate my dogs' futures. Their lives depended on how I handled the next ten minutes. For all my sacrifice, nothing had changed. I had never made a difference.

A dog's life in a human world is so uncertain, and yet there is a beauty behind it: they're completely unaware. A dog can have a child bite his ears, pull his tail, hit him with sticks and kick him around for months and the whole time we know that one moment of aggression on his part could label him as dangerous—ultimately spelling the end of his life. Or a dog can be a huge part of a family for years and then be dumped off at an animal shelter on a whim, or given to a farm, or handed over to strangers.

It's such intolerable insecurity for a human mind to comprehend. And here I was, packing my belongings, on the verge of making them feel abandoned once again—as if they hadn't been through enough.

After the last of my stuff was placed in the trunk of the car or on the backseat, I was feeling desperate. When I reached to close the door to the facility, it happened. I was struck by a life-altering innovation. It was like forks of white energy had been shot from the heavens and passed through my body. For the first time in my life I had become the conductor for an ideal beyond me that I was suddenly able to see myself fulfilling.

Now knowing what I had to do, I walked back into the shelter and reclaimed it as my own.

"I'm adopting all of them," I told them.

When I said this, Kelly looked visibly pleased. She couldn't hide it.

"Very noble," the Inspector said coldly. "But do you want to know why I opened this shelter?"

"Yes, I've always wondered," I stammered, quite shocked by his sudden willingness to open up.

"When I was a boy, my dog ran away from home. We looked for him everywhere, but no luck. It was months later that I learned he had been picked up three towns over and euthanized when nobody claimed him."

"I'm sorry that happened to you."

"You were brought in because I thought you exhibited the same concern, only I didn't realize you were deeply flawed. You'd rather play with the dogs than save them."

"Then it should please you that I want to help all of them," I pointed out.

"No, it doesn't," he growled. "It shows me you're incapable of looking at the bigger issue."

"If you force me, I'll have every friend and acquaintance I know come here tomorrow morning to adopt them on my behalf," I promised.

The Inspector actually smiled. "Well, that's what you'll have to do then."

Face-to-face, I looked right into the Inspector's feelingless gray eyes behind his gray-rimmed spectacles and witnessed the soul of a man who would always value structure over compassion.

"They're my responsibility," I said.

"You can't save every dog in this world, Grant," the Inspector pointed out.

"I'm not sure you get it," I said scornfully.

He smiled coldly. "Get what?"

"Not one more dog in my care will fail to find a loving home."

CHAPTER 11

I WOULD NO LONGER PERMIT it. My dogs would never again be allowed to fail. I became what I should have been all along, my dogs' one guarantee in a horribly irresponsible world. On a personal level, this decision was the logical extension of my experience at the shelter and the realization of a very demanding journey through the desert of my mind. However, the damage I had done to myself in the process was irreparable. The fact that I'd had a part to play in the death of many innocent dogs was a wound to the soul that would continue to bleed for a lifetime. Given the choice, though, I would never want to forget anyway.

The new community was built in my backyard using funds borrowed against the equity in my house. At first the dogs all lived in my basement. Then the portable kennel was erected once I had all the proper permits. The inside had a very different atmosphere from the cement and wire caging that constituted their old home in the shelter. It was warm and welcoming—and it didn't take long for the place to have that doggy smell—and I enjoyed being personally responsible for these animals in the freedom of my own values and principles.

During the next two months I finally felt some conviction in my vocational sense of direction, and I found that my newly acquired freedom allowed my relationship with Emily to be catapulted into the stars. At first it began as a trickle, but then I started to tell her things, even deep feelings that I had never shared with anyone before. The closeness that I now felt to her eased a sense of security into my life in a way I had never known. To top it all off, Gizzer, good kid that he is, ended up uniting me with Crystal once and for all. And believe me, after what Crystal and I had been through together, she would never have to worry about leaving her place by my side. This left me on top of the world, sharing my life with my two precious girls: one brown-eyed and beautiful, the other blue-eyed and beautiful—both vying for the position next to me when we went to sleep at night.

In early November, the first flakes of snow began to sprinkle and cold, steel skies replaced the deep blues of October. The dogs all had their chance to play in the snow as the season progressed into Christmas time. It was actually during the holidays that we felt the reality of our decision to marry each other. I suppose the concept of adding permanence to our living circumstances was coming into being much faster than we had expected. But with all the details ironed out by this point, we decided to celebrate the New Year with champagne at the pub, where on New Year's Eve it underwent a makeover that left it resembling more of a nightclub.

Poor Tamer couldn't join us because of his seasonal curse. He was destined to wrap up the year and begin the next one hard at work while the majority of his fellow White

Sanders got together for a drunken bash. We would have to visit him later for a pizza slice and a Coke. Going to the pub turned out to be a rather fortunate decision, as we reconnected with Gizzer after he had retreated into his own world for the previous couple of months. In fact, the last time I had seen or talked to him was when he dropped Crystal off. Naturally, he was joined by Megan. It was pretty comical when I first noticed the preposterous couple sitting close to the bar. Gizzer was sitting on a chair with a cigarette dangling from his mouth, a mug of beer sloshing in his left hand, while Megan was straddling him and kissing along his neck. The boy had this ear-to-ear grin on his face. They were clearly oblivious to everyone else around them. People even bumped up against them and danced on by, and yet nobody paid them any attention. Some probably found their comfort in each other to be more fascinating than offensive. They were like fixtures in the place, a table in the way or a barstool. It was strange to see the impact Tamer had made on Gizzer in their short time together. This quiet boy had been transformed into a man with a voice and now he was going to behave in the manner of his choosing . . . and no one was going to tell him differently. Public opinion no longer existed for him.

"You're in the way!" I shouted in Gizzer's ear, hardly able to hear myself speak over the loud music and all the jubilation around me.

His reverie interrupted, he met my gaze before breaking into a welcoming smile.

"As long as she's comfortable," Gizzer replied, pointing at Megan.

"Good to see you, too," Megan screamed at me, getting to her feet.

"Hi Megan," I shouted.

Megan drew closer and said in my ear, "Where's your roommate, or should I say fiancé?"

"She's in the ladies' room," I explained.

Megan looked at me as though she was going to offer an opinion, but decided to let it go.

"I'm going to fetch me a drink, you guys want anything?" Megan asked.

Both of us declined, so Megan left us to ourselves.

"Well, old man . . ." Gizzer said in my ear, "it's been some time, hasn't it?"

"I've tried to call you, Gizz."

"It's too loud," he observed. "Let's catch up outside."

So with a motion to Megan indicating that he'd be back momentarily, Gizzer carved a path through the crowd for the both of us. On the way, we bumped into Emily, which was fortunate because I imagine she would have been equally interested in my whereabouts. Then we walked out the front doors and into the frosty evening. An arctic blast met us the moment we got outside.

"Ah, I can hear myself think again," he said with relief.

"So why haven't you returned my calls?" I asked, my breath coming out in clouds.

The stars were out and shone very white against a cold, black sky. It was so cold that the air was flecked with microscopic crystals that captured the light of the street lamps as they floated to the ground at a languid pace.

"Sorry, Grant, I've been busy," he apologized, lighting a cigarette. He now looked kind of miffed for some reason.

"What's with the smoking?"

"Megan's made me see the value of exorcising your anxiety at the end of the day," he explained with an embarrassed smile.

I chuckled, amused that this easygoing kid was starting to feel the pressure.

"So Tamer told me you quit the shelter and then the restaurant shortly after?" I asked.

"Yep, I didn't have to work at the shelter anymore to know that I'm going to be a veterinarian some day," he explained in a somewhat condescending tone. "It all just seemed to come together in my mind."

"You're going away to school, then?"

"That's the plan," he said, making his boredom evident.

"What's wrong with you?" I demanded, growing frustrated with his attitude. "Why are you giving me the cold shoulder here?"

Gizzer smiled. "Do you really want to know?"

"Out with it," I snapped. "If you have a problem with me, I want to know about it."

"I believe I've discovered something, Grant . . . something that might be too difficult for someone like you to grasp."

"Try me," I challenged.

"I've discovered something very special about Megan . . ."

He almost looked serious and somewhat sober when he said this. The boy had me fascinated. I couldn't tell the smoke he exhaled from his own breath in the cold.

"Go on," I encouraged.

"It was something I found rather obvious."

"What is it then?"

"You would know yourself if you ever took the time to talk her—I mean really talk to her."

"Get lost, we talked all the time," I scoffed.

"If you'd been really listening to her, you'd know how lonely she's been."

"Lonely?" I repeated, having a difficult time imagining it.

"Yeah, and for a long time."

"Is there a reason you're telling me this?"

"I was a friend to her. I spent time with her and asked her questions—made her feel comfortable enough to share her feelings. The point is: if I'd have written her off for being so messed up like you did, I never would have experienced the authentic Megan, the one I'm now in love with."

"So you guys are in love?" I asked in amazement, trying to process the significance of this admission.

"You shouldn't patronize me," Gizzer said, sounding insulted. "I'm heading back in—too cold."

I grabbed him. "No, I didn't mean to insult you . . . you just surprised me there, that's all . . ."

"I'm trying to share something with you because you obviously overlooked something in her."

"I'm sorry, I was out of line, Gizz," I admitted.

He nodded. "I guess what I'm trying to say is that I found Megan's true beauty by peeling away her layers of insecurity. I know who she is now and I'm blown away by what I see."

"If only it were that easy," I said, suddenly becoming thoughtful.

"What do you mean?"

"Given Emily's situation and all she's had to overcome in her life, she's revealed very little about her inner world to me. Even when she used to disappear for days at a time, she'd never give me a straight answer afterward."

He looked at me accusingly.

"Look, I know it's my fault," I admitted. "I've never been convincing enough to get her to confide in me."

"Perhaps you've been afraid to go deeper because you're afraid of what you're going to find," Gizzer offered.

"I didn't ask for your help," I said, suddenly ashamed at the realization that I was getting explanations for my problems from a kid. "Remember, I have a lot more experience with women than you do."

He smiled at me. "Really? Then you should know that exploiting a vulnerable woman is wrong—especially when you're fully conscious of the mess you leave behind. Someone like you should certainly know better."

Right away, I understood his point; it was now clear why he had become so distant. But since only a few months earlier he had been gravitating toward Tamer's kind of lifestyle with such eagerness, this was the last accusation I had expected from him. Gizzer believed I had intentionally pursued Megan because I knew she was an easy target.

"I completely agree with you," I replied. "I've done many things lately that have been out of character for me."

He nodded and looked at the ground, not ready to forgive me.

"Is this why you never returned my calls for the past couple months?" I asked.

"Perhaps," Gizzer replied, his voice betraying the truth.

"There was more to it than that, Brent," I tried to explain.

"What do you mean?" he asked, giving me a confused stare.

"I found Megan to be interesting and spiritual. I thought the circumstances of our relationship were unique and that I might learn something from her as a result."

"Then you got it all wrong. From what she told me, you always treated her like an afterthought. She said she was never lonelier than when she was with you."

"Those are her words?" I asked in disbelief.

The kid looked at me with the accusative eyes of someone defending his lover.

"I just wonder—if you had taken the time to talk to her, and if you had been willing to let her open up to you, I wonder if you would have made the same discovery as I did. Megan has to be one of the deepest, most caring, most sensitive, most spiritual women in the world, if given an actual opportunity."

"I'm happy you two have such a connection," I said supportively, but at the same time I couldn't help but wonder why Megan had held so much back with me.

"Whatever. Just realize there's so much more to a woman than the sum of her problems."

"You're right," I said, extending him my hand. "So are we ok?"

"Yeah, I suppose we are," Gizzer conceded, shaking my hand. "But going forward, I expect you're going to treat Megan differently. If not, you'll have to piss off for good."

* * * * *

The following Sunday, Emily woke me up fairly early in the morning and convinced me to take her to church. For whatever reason, Emily's enthusiasm had an effect on me, and I had a sudden desire to hear Daven speak. I also was curious to see whether he would now be more supportive of our plans to marry at the end of the month. I was proud of the way our life together had evolved since the morning he'd counseled us, and I felt that attending the service together would provide us with an opportunity to showcase the strides we had made as a couple. So we ate a quick breakfast, bundled ourselves up, and after a drive across town through gusting winds and snow squalls we entered a church for the first time in several years.

As usual, we were late, so we slipped in and seated ourselves in the back row. At first I was disappointed; it was Fancy, not Daven, commanding the pulpit. I could tell he noticed us come in, and his eyes betrayed a certain sense of relief that I couldn't account for. After pausing momentarily so we could make ourselves comfortable, he went on to deliver a beautifully crafted sermon expounding on the New Year's theme of beginnings. As I listened, I was impressed by the evolution of his skills as a speaker and how he was able to coerce me into reflecting on my life.

Then, as he approached his conclusion, Fancy's tone became noticeably more personal.

"We've spent this morning contemplating how our spiritual journey involves countless crossroads, and how each can afford us a new beginning," he began. "But before I wrap things up here, I want to talk about the significance of this morning's message to me personally and how I've managed to apply it to my own beliefs."

Fancy started to pace back and forth, betraying a look of nervousness; he also appeared to be fighting back tears.

"Like anybody, I've been far from perfect," he resumed, composing himself, "and along the way I have hurt many people. As part of my desire to create a new beginning out of my entire life, I want to apologize to someone here today that I wronged in the past—someone whose friendship means the world to me. I have suffered tremendously as a result of my actions, and I'm willing to take ownership for what I have done."

Fancy didn't look at me when he made his apology, but I knew he was talking to me. As he spoke these words, I felt Emily squeeze my hand.

"Over the past few years," Fancy continued, "it's become essential for me to believe in God as a natural expression of who I am, not only for my future, but to help me deal with the repercussions of my past. I needed my faith to become less intellectual and more real to me. I realized, to have any chance at all, I had to change my approach to the way I believed and take responsibility for my role in the process.

"To help illustrate what I've come to call the 'mindset of transition,' I think it's appropriate that I conclude this message by sharing a story with you based on the experiences of a friend of mine working deep in the trenches of a local animal shelter."

"This should be interesting," I whispered in Emily's ear.

"Shhh," she replied. "Listen to what he has to say."

"Several years back, two identical pups—best friends from birth—were adopted together," Fancy began. "These floppy-eared brothers were brought into a home where they began their new life as the center of attention, but once their novelty wore off—as is the case with so many dogs—neglect became the replacement. They were fed irregularly, often with unhealthy foods, and were isolated the majority of the day. There was also evidence they were physically abused. The one brother, Lagoon, was stronger-willed, and from his scars it was obvious the consequences for his attitude were more severe. Cower, on the other hand, was much more submissive, and adored his master unconditionally. For the slightest bit of attention, he'd do anything to please him.

"It's hard to know the exact details, but I suppose one morning the family forgot to close the door when they left for the day and Lagoon seized the opportunity to make his escape. Since all these brothers had ever had in life were each other, I imagine he did everything in his power to try and coax Cower into joining him. But in the end, Lagoon failed to persuade his cautious, more intimidated twin to embrace such an uncertain future by his side, and so he was forced to set off without him.

"When Lagoon first appeared at the animal shelter, my friend marveled at the poor condition he was in. So he was bathed, groomed, fed, and nursed back to health. He also proved to be a quick study. In a few weeks, he was socialized and even house-trained. I imagine for the first time since he was a pup, Lagoon was enjoying some stability. But this was only the beginning of his fortunes. Not long after he settled into his new routine, his circumstances were about to improve even more.

It so happened that a friendly gentleman vacationing from out of town felt compelled to visit the shelter. From my friend's account, the man and dog had an instant connection—so much so, that Lagoon ended up going home with the kind stranger that very afternoon. Somehow, and in a roundabout way, Lagoon's decisions led to a whole new world of possibilities to explore with a loving family to support him.

"The reason my friend was able to piece this story together was because Cower ended up in the shelter as well. After additional years of trauma and abuse, this shell of a dog was dumped off when the family couldn't stand the sight of him anymore. The man described the twin brother's disappearance a couple years earlier and how Cower had never been the same dog since. When his master left him that day, Cower trembled and cried for a week. It was only after my friend cleaned him up that he recognized him to be the spitting image of Lagoon. But, unlike his brother, Cower had deteriorated beyond the salvage point. He resisted socialization, and with his will broken beyond repair he was unresponsive to training.

"Cower ended up being put to sleep, a sad, broken-hearted dog incapable of letting anybody care for him. Two brothers, the same circumstances, two very different paths."

Fancy paused for a second to let the story sink in.

"As we start the New Year, I want you to consider your own spiritual predicament. For me, the door opened when the need became unbearable. I seized my opportunity and resisted looking back. You could say I embraced the life of a 'stray' and spent my own forty days in the desert, willing to endure all the necessary hardships in an effort to make sense of my beliefs, values, and the world around me.

"Sometimes, in order to come to a new understanding, we have to reach the point where we're willing to lose the very things that keep us secure in our faith. By permitting ourselves the right to explore our own hearts, we just may end up with a more tolerant master . . . we just may end up in a more loving home." Fancy gazed out over the congregation, then bowed his head. "Let us pray before we go out this week . . ."

Fancy's apology touched me, and I appreciated both the direction of his sermon and how he had used my challenges in the shelter to articulate some of the things that were on my heart. He was making a great effort to communicate with me. This made me wonder how long I could continue hating him as much as I did when we had such common ground. As for the rest of the congregation—for the most part older and set in their ways—I wasn't sure that his message would be as well received.

With the sermon over, I started to relax. The nostalgia of being in church again began to warm me from the inside. I even found myself enjoying the singing and my surroundings. I entertained myself by glancing over the internal structure of the sanctuary with its arches and angles, the natural wood support beams, the murals, and the unique position of the windows on the ceiling that refracted the light to create the impression of rays from heaven. While the service was winding down, I felt moved by my experience that morning in the context of the wonderful ambiance created by the sanctuary and the snowfall outside.

After the service, Emily and I walked out with the rest of the congregation and waited our turn at the end of the line to shake Justin's hand and be dispersed into the community. Daven, however, was greeting people on their way out instead. There were at least twenty people ahead of us, with clusters of conversations all around and children running reckless and wild between them. When we finally got to

Daven, he shook both our hands and said he was happy to see us in attendance.

"Interesting sermon, eh?" I said.

"That's one way to put it," Daven replied, visibly turning red.

"It meant a great deal to us," Emily said, sensing Daven wasn't as impressed. "I'm sure it wasn't easy for Justin."

When Daven was about to respond, one of his young boys, freshly released from Sunday school, ran over and clung to his leg. The pastor picked him up and held him for the duration of the conversation.

"He's a shy one," Emily observed. "What's your name?"

The boy buried his face in his father's shoulder.

"This is Simon," said Daven. "Can you tell them how old you are?"

"No," said a quiet voice.

"You can't tell them that you're three now?" Daven urged.

"No."

Daven looked back at us and said, "I suppose he's more interested in me getting him home to watch the football game this afternoon."

"We wanted to invite you to attend the wedding reception at the end of the month," I said. "It's going to be small, and we're still going to send invitations out, but we wanted to ask you personally."

"Of course," Daven replied with a smile. "Congratulations."

"I also wanted to thank you for being there for me through that whole ordeal with my father," I added.

"No need, Grant," he replied.

"I'm glad my parents are staying together. My mother told me that my father's been having sessions with you for a couple months now."

Daven nodded. "Marco sought counseling on his own."

"Good for him," I said honestly. "Did Justin tell you that I was looking into getting involved in ministry again, too?"

"Really?" Daven asked, looking surprised. "Justin said nothing of it."

"I feel like I have a calling—only I think I needed to have some experiences in order for me to throw myself into it again. And with Emily to support me now, I feel especially confident."

"Whatever," said Emily sarcastically, but she showed some pride in her smile. "Pastor, I can say this honestly. Grant has been a lot more pleasant since he moved the shelter into our backyard."

"That reminds me," said Daven, "I've been wanting to drop by and adopt a dog for the family anyway. I'd want one, say, less than fifty pounds and friendly, preferably male. You'd like a little howler, wouldn't you, Simon?"

"Yeah," squeaked the little boy.

"I got the perfect one for you, Pastor," I started, "he's house-trained, great with kids—"

"A perfect addition to any family," Fancy cut in, approaching from behind and putting his arms around both of us. "It's awesome that Emily was able to drag your skinny butt here today. I was counting on her being persuasive."

"You didn't disappoint, Justin," Emily said with a smile. "It was worth the battle getting him up this morning."

"You know, guys, I can definitely see myself getting back into it," I said with conviction, making a show of inspecting my surroundings. "I even find the music less offensive than I did when I was younger."

Pastor Daven laughed. "Offensive? Many think the music's the best part."

"I like the music the most, too," Emily agreed.

"I was always concerned that the bad theology in many old hymns was being internalized," I explained. "It seemed like dangerous osmosis to me."

This observation seemed to get Justin excited. "Just recently I was saying something along similar lines . . . wasn't I, Pastor?"

Daven shook his head and mumbled, "So this is what the young people now heading into ministry are like . . ."

"Your message this morning, Justin . . ." I began, stumbling for words, "I . . . I was touched you'd go to such lengths, to be honest."

"But did you like it?" Fancy asked, looking at me expectantly.

"Absolutely," I replied. "Somehow we ended up on the same page. You could say my own days in the desert were spent in the shelter."

"Speaking of your sermon," Daven interrupted, pulling his briar pipe out of his pocket and pointing it at Fancy, "I'd like to discuss it with you before you leave today."

"Definitely. I especially look forward to your feedback," Fancy replied confidently.

"Daddy, when are we going to watch the game?" Simon whined, unburying his face from his father's shirt.

After he asked this, he turned his accusing gaze directly on Emily. The child was cute, with little blond curls and big, blue, inquisitive eyes.

"Well, we shouldn't hold your dad up any longer, Simon," Emily said, running her hand through his curls. "But if we're to leave now, it'll cost you a kiss."

So before we departed, Simon stretched out from Daven's arms and kissed Emily on the cheek. I appreciated the little exchange between them because it was one of the only times I had seen the maternal side of the woman I was soon to call my wife.

CHAPTER 12

A FEW DAYS LATER I was out back attending to the dogs when I heard a knock. Since I had talked to Daven earlier that day, I expected a visit, but instead I found Justin waiting for me patiently in the gusting winds. He was standing there with a brown paper bag in his right hand, while snow accumulated on his woolen toque and his jacket.

"Hey buddy, can I come in?" he asked.

"Sure, get in here."

"Daven wanted me to come get his dog for him," Justin explained, stomping to get the snow off on the mat at the door and beating his hat against the wall. "I love doing such errands for the church. I guess it's part of my probation."

"Probation?"

"The next time I deliver a sermon Daven has to read my notes beforehand," Justin explained. "Keep it biblical. He's been giving me these shitty jobs, too. He even had me clean the bathrooms."

"Would you give the same sermon again?" I asked.

"Absolutely," Fancy replied with a big smile.

I walked over to one of the pens.

"It took a great deal of convincing, but I was finally able to talk Daven into allowing Pete to become the newest member of his family," I explained.

"Pete?" Fancy echoed.

"What do you think?" I asked, opening up the door to Pete's pen so that the troublemaker could scamper out.

"Pretty ugly dog, Grant," said Fancy after observing him for a few seconds.

"Oh, come one, he's a good ugly," I insisted. "He's the most adoptable animal I've ever known."

"I've always wanted one of those little bulldogs. I figured I could feed him a steady supply of chili and parade him around. A stumpy, smelly, frypan-faced little beast would bring some attention to himself, and he'd certainly be able to clear a room."

I laughed. "Please don't adopt a dog any time soon."

Justin opened the bag and took out the blue collar and matching leash that Daven had purchased, and handed them to me.

"You look great, pup," I said, admiring Pete with his new collar. Pete's tail was wagging back and forth and he was looking up at me expectantly. "No, I'm not taking you for a walk. Justin is."

Pete started to snoop around the room, smelling everything from the sealed barrels of dog food to Justin himself.

Fancy couldn't contain himself anymore. "Listen, I've been considering something . . . and I have some advice to give, although, in all honesty, I feel like it's not quite my place . . ."

"All right, I'm listening."

"You and Emily need to talk."

Immediately, I felt my stomach sink.

"Why do you have to do this now?" I asked coldly, my good mood quickly dissolving. "Didn't you notice I was starting to warm up to you?"

"Fine Grant, have it your way, be a fool," and then Fancy made a move toward the door.

"Ok, ok, let's just talk," I said.

"There's something about Emily you need to know," Fancy warned.

"It's still hard for me to trust you when it comes to her," I confessed. "What should I say to her?"

"If you were smart, you would sit her down and ask her whether she really is prepared to go through with this," Fancy suggested. "Tell her you want to be aware of any reservations, of anything that might suggest she's not ready for this marriage."

"Has she been confiding things to you again?" I asked.

"Not exactly," Fancy replied, but unconvincingly. "Just trust me. I'm trying to do the right thing this time."

"Let me ask you this: if I ask her this question, will I still marry her?"

"I don't know," Fancy replied honestly. "It depends on her explanation, I suppose."

"This is a real fine time for this," I said sarcastically. "Thanks for all your help. You've been such a dedicated friend."

Fancy let out a defeated laugh.

"Fine, keep being your stubborn, oblivious self. Don't you think there hasn't been a day that's gone by that I haven't lived with regret?"

"I don't know whether you're capable of remorse."

"Then there's nothing more to say," Fancy concluded.

"You're right, there's nothing," I said flatly.

Fancy bent over to grab Pete's leash and proceeded toward the exit. He then stopped and turned back to me one last time.

"There is one thing I'd like to add, come to think of it."

"What's that?"

"I'm very well aware that the decision I made years ago cost me my best friend . . . but what about her role in it?"

"What about it?"

"Do you know how you referred to Emily as your wildflower?"

"Yeah."

"Enjoy the beauty of the wildflower. Smell the wildflower. But for God's sake, haven't you learned by now that a wildflower really belongs in the field?"

"She needs someone strong, like me," I protested.

"What about intimacy? How can you ever have a sense of closeness with a woman like that?"

"With patience," I replied. "You have to earn your way through the layers of her heart in order to enjoy the reward."

"You're crazy," Fancy stated. "You've become more and more suited to write my theology of destruction."

"What do you mean by that?"

"Without destruction there's no redemption, my friend . . ."

"But—"

"Talk to her!" Justin ordered.

Before I could get anything more out of him, Justin tugged on Pete's leash and led him out the door without so much as a goodbye. Thanks to Fancy, all of my joy in one conversation had been replaced with an anxiety that I had no choice but to address.

* * * *

The next day, I invited Brad to join me for coffee. Of all the people I could turn to, I opted to discuss this matter with the giant because I was too ashamed and secretive to bring it up with anyone else. Besides, he had to be the most easy-going person in all of White Sands. And I just needed someone instead of Tamer to bounce some ideas off.

Most of the tables around us were filled to capacity with the elderly, clanking their spoons and talking in a hybrid of English and French for a deaf audience—but we were oblivious to our fellow coffee drinkers anyway.

Once we had our drinks and were seated, I explained to him Fancy's ominous warning and my current distress as a result.

"It's hard to figure out what Fancy's motive might be," Brad responded, rubbing his beard. "Here's the risk, though. Do you want to look like you're distrustful of Emily so close to the wedding?"

I thought about this for a second. "It all depends on the wording and how I could spin it without offending her."

Brad considered this before saying with confidence, "You know, I wouldn't worry about it. She's crazy about you. And if she's been talking to Justin about cold feet, what's the big deal? It is a big step, you know."

"That's true," I agreed.

"Besides, some things you just don't want to know until it's critical."

I took a sip of coffee and considered this. "Fancy talked like it was critical, though. That's what scares me. It might be more than just cold feet."

"Here's the progression of questions you have to ask yourself before you approach her, then."

"What are they?"

"Do you trust Emily enough that she will confide this information to you when she deems it necessary?"

I thought for a second, before answering, "Yes."

"And if this is so, does it really matter when it comes out, even if it is years down the road?"

"I suppose not," I concluded after some thought.

"And if Emily thought this information would make you call off the wedding, don't you think, given her integrity, she'd have raised the issue by now?"

I considered this for a moment. "You're right. Emily has the best character of anyone I know. Perhaps this is just another test of faith."

"I agree," Brad said encouragingly. "And to be truthful, this Justin guy, he has no investment in you anymore."

"I don't know whether he does or not," I replied.

Brad shrugged. "No offense, but to me his involvement at all in your wedding seems preposterous. I just can't believe that this philistine is involved in ministry," the giant added, shaking his head sadly.

"I don't know what to think of him these days," I explained. "He's always been intense, and what's most perplexing is that I believe him when he insists that he cares for me still."

"You really believe this?"

"I have to," I admitted. "He's marrying us, remember?"

"Well, I think you should leave it alone. But you're the one who ultimately has to decide your next move. The flip side is that it's almost always better to have the sickness diagnosed than to go about your days unaware of it. How else can you get your hands on the so-called cure?"

"That's true as well," I agreed. "I guess my decision is still up in the air, but it feels good to talk about it. I appreciate it."

"No problem," Brad said with a smile. "Did I tell you that I've written a poem for your wedding?"

"That should be interesting."

"Well, I thought about the 'unknowing' factor with Emily and how you're still willing to marry her. I really think that what you're doing is worthy of poetry. It's like renaissance beautiful."

"That's enough. You know it's not by choice."

"Just the same, you're prepared to leap into the unknown. It's quite inspiring."

"Well, what about you? What are you working on in your own life that's inspiring?"

"Well . . . I bought this DVD recorder and I've been transferring all my sci-fi on video to disk. It takes up a lot of my time, but it sure is worth it."

"You know who likes sci-fi?"

Brad shrugged. "Who?"

"Dan Tamer," I lied, knowing the hell this would cause the restaurant manager.

"Really?"

"Sure, big, big fan. I'm sure you two could watch hours of it together and never get bored."

Brad looked at me in confusion. "You know, funny thing, Dan never mentioned it all this time."

"Tamer's aware of the stigma associated with watching that stuff, so he stays in the closet about it. You know, with the ladies around him all the time, he has to portray a certain image. You just need to bring him into the open with some of your old school flicks, like old Star Trek and Buck Rogers."

"Definitely," said Brad before taking a long, deep sip of coffee. "That's insane . . . You think you know somebody . . ."

"Every person is capable of surprising you," I said, envisioning Brad and Tamer spending long nights together in the furthest reaches of the galaxy.

Brad then became very sincere. "Remember when I talked about my poetry being born in the soul's darkest hour?"

"It's something I'll never forget," I replied, trying not to grin.

"Well . . . since I started working for Tamer, I've been happier than I've ever been—and if anything, I've been more prolific. Maybe I had it all wrong."

"That's interesting."

"Anyway, I feel like I need to thank you for introducing me to that gregarious bastard."

"Nonsense, Brad. It should be Tamer thanking me."

* * * * *

Later that day, I was agonizing over what to do. I considered asking Tamer whether he would gently probe Emily for answers in my place. This way I wouldn't feel I was personally betraying any mistrust or loss of confidence. One problem was that Tamer would need to be filled in about this mysterious piece of advice I'd received from Justin, which meant I'd have to endure another painful diatribe about my foolish need for a female companion in the first place. Of course, letting Tamer do my dirty work would make me a detestable weakling, especially before myself. But with the wedding only weeks away a decision had to be reached. I didn't want to be put in a situation where I had no choice but to call the wedding off, and yet even more, for my soul's sake, I didn't want to find out what Fancy thought it was crucial I know.

After I debated the matter thoroughly, I decided that I'd confront Emily myself. So I waited until later that evening and then, following dinner, joined her on the couch.

"Can I talk to you about something?" I asked.

"Sure, Grant," said Emily, moving over to my side of the couch and cuddling into me. I put my arm around her.

"I—I'd like to think that I can talk to you about anything," I began, not even knowing what I was going to say.

"Of course you can. What's this about?" she asked, searching my eyes.

"I have to ask you . . ." I began.

"Ask me what?" Emily coaxed.

I just couldn't form the words in my mouth. There was too much on the line, and in my heart I wanted to forget that the conversation with Justin had ever taken place. In the end, I decided the information, whatever it was, could not be helpful to me in any way. Fancy was a fool.

"I have to ask you, Emily . . ." I started again.

"Go on, spit it out," she urged, looking confused but expectant, perhaps even a little impatient.

"How long will we wait before we have kids?" I finally asked, thinking on the fly.

"Why, do you want kids right away?" she asked, looking surprised. I think the question took her a bit off guard since I had never brought up the topic before. My own question certainly took me off guard.

"No," I said truthfully, "I was just wondering what your expectations were."

Emily seemed to think about this for a second, somewhat puzzled.

"Well, if you want, I could start going to Planned Parenting now to check my cycles. I mean, is this really important to talk about right now?"

"Not at all," I said.

"Well, let's save this conversation for six months from now," Emily said.

"Sounds good to me," I agreed.

Emily then got up and turned on the television. When she returned to the couch, she had me stretch out so that we could spoon together. Moments later, she rolled over to face me and then hugged me with all her strength.

"I'm so blessed," Emily said.

"I feel the same way."

"It's already like we have our own little family, isn't it?"

"Yeah, I suppose in a way we're already surrounded with children," I said, looking at the dogs sleeping lazily around us.

"And I've been thinking . . . Once we're married, I'd like us to join a gym. We can work out together and I'm going to cook for you more often. We're going to eat super-healthy."

"I'd like that," I smiled.

"And if we get any money as gifts from the wedding, I think it would be great if we got you a beautiful, wide-screen television, with theater speakers and everything."

"Are you serious?" I asked in excitement.

"Definitely. You know I intend to make you the happiest husband in the world."

As she talked about our future together, it was like a drug coursed through my veins. I felt amazingly fortunate. Even more, I felt very special and provided for—like Emily had waited for me her whole life and then taken the necessary steps to ensure I was the only man allowed to approach her castle and slay the dragon. And here she was, so content to be next to me. It was intoxicating to know I could make Emily happy, and I convinced myself this was all I needed to know.

So I ended up watching television for the rest of the night while Emily napped beside me. I enjoyed her closeness and that fact that in a few short weeks she would be eternally mine.

* * * * *

Although I wasn't comfortable with it, I agreed to join Fancy for a pint at the pub later in the week. He'd been insistent. We sat there for a while, just talking about the NFL playoffs and the Leafs, drinking beer, and scarfing back some hot wings.

When we finished eating, Fancy ordered us a round of beers along with some shots of Jägermeister.

"Cheers, brother," he said.

"Cheers."

We clanked shot glasses, and he then downed the Jäger and chased it by gulping down his entire beer. Afterwards, he wiped his mouth and decided it was time to get down to business.

"So you did talk to her?" Fancy asked.

"Sure did," I said. "In all honesty, I don't care. I don't see the big deal."

"So you're going to marry her?" Fancy asked, looking concerned.

"Definitely," I said.

"I'm not sure I understand you."

"You know the feeling is mutual."

Fancy shook his head. "I accept that you'll never forgive me. But this time I'm just trying to look out for you. Please believe me."

"I don't choose my feelings," I explained. "Every time I see you I relive the betrayal. The logical solution is to avoid you and the negative feelings that surface by seeing you."

Justin nodded, as if he understood this perspective, but then provided his counter-argument. "I hate to point it out again, but the woman you're marrying had something to do with it. It's amazing to me. You clutch one of us even tighter while you cut the other completely out of the picture. How can such thinking make sense?"

"I can't help the way I feel," I said.

"You're so afraid of being alone that you ignore the parade of red flags in front of you. It's become a quest to you, hasn't it? You're willing to do anything or believe anything because it's more comfortable than going out on your own and believing what you see and feel."

"It's love, Justin, something you could never understand."

Justin rubbed his forehead and chuckled. "It's laughable. You use love as your excuse to indulge your own self-destructive tendencies."

"Then put it in your book."

"I plan to. But I just can't believe it."

"Believe what?"

"There's you, who idealizes a woman so much he's incapable of seeing her faults, and then there are ignorant men that write all women off as being crazy because of a few bad experiences. Whatever side of the coin you're on, it's proof that testosterone makes us the crazy ones."

"I think each gender finds it hard to understand the other."

"True, but us men, we have this unstoppable force that makes us seek out the easiest women to get in their pants, and then we get all jaded when we develop feelings for them and they cheat on us. Who's crazier?"

"I never thought of it that way."

"But you . . . you . . . have taken insanity to a whole new level. You work in an animal shelter, for God's sake, and then you deliberately take steps to marry someone who can't love you back."

"Don't talk about Emily that way. You don't know her like I do."

"When are you going to be honest with yourself?"

"Can't you let it go?" I replied, starting to tremble with anger.

"My friend, remember—we've met pastors that are scoundrels. They teach what they don't believe themselves because it's what they're trained to do. Others are afraid to look deeper because it threatens their livelihood, so they become friends with ignorance."

"Your point?"

"I'm not one of those pastors. I'm more honest than that."

"There's a reason you're telling me this, Justin."

"I wanted to talk to you today because I talked it over with Emily. My conscience won't allow me to marry you guys."

"What?" I said, surprised by this turn of events.

"Nothing's ruined," Justin assured me. "I talked to Daven about it and he agreed to do the service now. I just can't. You may be able to accept Emily's explanation, but I can't."

This news actually made me happy.

"So what does changing pastors at this point entail?" I asked.

"Pretty much that your marriage classes are going to have to be fast-tracked and with Daven now. He won't marry you without spending time with you guys."

"I don't mind," I shrugged.

"You really love this girl, don't you?" Fancy asked once again, still in utter disbelief.

"I do. I've always felt we were meant to be together," I explained. "Behind closed doors she handles me so delicately compared to the rest of the world. She looks out for me and I know she has my best interest in mind. From the moment I met her she's tried to protect me—to shelter me, in a way."

"From herself or from the world?" Fancy asked.

"Look it, Justin, I know Emily better than anyone," I stated in no uncertain terms. "We both have overcome so much to be ready for each other."

"You'll never convince me. I'm still against it. But that's my opinion."

"Then you're not welcome there," I said.

"You know I have to be there. It would disappoint Emily if I wasn't."

"And she knows you disapprove?" I asked.

"Definitely."

"Why are you so against us being together?" I demanded, but not really wanting to know.

"My friend, do I even have to say?" Fancy replied, getting up to leave.

"I suppose not," I said. "Don't worry about the bill. I'll get it."

"No, I'll take care of it," he insisted, throwing down some cash.

He stood up to leave, took a step toward the door and then hesitated.

"Look, Grant," he said, slipping back into his chair, "I'm not saying Emily's not a fun girl and doesn't have her admirable qualities. She can drink most men under the table, and she's as amused by a loud fart as much as the next woman. That's pretty cool in my books."

"She's not a party girl anymore," I insisted.

"Regardless, as your pastor I'm asking you to please, please do the right thing and break it off with her . . . And then you have my permission to go out on the town with your pal, Dan Tamer, and do what my position at the church doesn't allow me to do: start ripping it up. Life is too short, my friend."

"I've made up my mind. I'm not going to change it."

Fancy stood up to leave again, but couldn't help offering one last tidbit of advice: "Just remember, until you say 'I do' you can always change your mind."

He then walked out of the pub without another word—in every appearance of disgust.

With Fancy gone, I was left alone to experience this rustling of guilt inside, and yet I felt relieved that the conversation was over. Regardless of what anyone said, I had to believe that a certain breed of leopard can choose to change its spots. Emily was living proof of it. And it wasn't a desperate desire to be right that made me determined to prove some people have this capacity to change; it was because I cared for Emily so much that I wanted everyone else to see her for her true beauty.

Now that Fancy was out of the picture, there was no way he could come between us again. Brad was right: I never should have allowed myself to trust this shifty fellow for a second—no matter what my instincts were telling me. Even after all these years, it was obvious that Justin Fancy still felt a claim to Emily. Well, he wasn't going be the one to keep us apart this time. We were going to build a life together, with children, dogs, and travel, and everyone was going to see that our togetherness was imminent, like it had been written in the stars. And all this was to become true because I allowed Emily to come to me on terms that could be described as her own.

CHAPTER 13

THE MONTH OF JANUARY HAD frozen completely. It was as if a primer had been brushed over all the landscape and water. Even the evergreens had been buried in white, with only patches of branches managing to add some color. Because it was so bitterly cold and the snowfall had been so relentless, it was a relief to envision the airplane ride that would transport us from the clutches of winter to the sunny destination for our honeymoon. We'd agreed on taking two weeks to enjoy the Florida sun before continuing to build our life together in White Sands.

It had been an eventful month. Along with meeting Daven twice each week for marriage classes, I had been in touch with my parents. Since the night Fancy had put us in communication again, I had spoken to my mother about seeing her, but she would not budge on that reconciliation with the family began with my father.

With no time to spare, I agreed to meet Marco right around peak coffee drinking time at a heavily frequented café; knowing the location and timing would keep our conversation somewhat civil. This meeting took place two days before the wedding and it was paramount that the issue be resolved so that I could turn my attention from making amends to the formality of commitment—all the while trying to keep my emotional stress and excitement in check. I guess before I could actually see myself participating in the ceremony at all, I had to feel comfortable with my parents' presence during the most important event in my life. I know it seems far-fetched to include them after experiencing such a long period of isolation, but I wanted things to be different now. I needed a family presence again to support me, and my new vision of life included having a relationship with my father like any other son.

When my father entered the café, I notice that his mannerism seemed a bit different and the look in his eyes was unfamiliar to me. In many ways, Marco looked humbled. He still carried himself with confidence, but there was humility present as well. On top of that, he appeared aged, like his best years were behind him. On the other hand, he seemed somewhat softened around the edges. Knowing my dad all my life as the toughest old bird that walked the streets, it was almost unnerving to see him as a man capable of being wise and gentle.

After easing himself into his seat with noticeable strain, he nodded to me and grabbed a menu. He even took out a pair of reading glasses.

"Figure out what you want, eh?" he said in a gruff voice.

"I'm just having coffee."

"No, eat something. It's on me," he insisted.

"I'm having coffee," I repeated.

"Suit yourself," he said, then flagged the waitress over and ordered himself a big breakfast of bacon and eggs.

"What's done is done," he said, seeming to look past me, quick to dispense with the pleasantries. He made split-second eye contact here and there, but it was obvious he was uncomfortable in my company. He had always been.

"Is that your way of apology?" I asked.

"I'm getting help for my anger. Isn't that good enough for you, eh?"

"Should it be?"

"It's the best I can do," Marco said, making no bones about it.

"And that's all I get after being excluded from my own family for all these years?" I asked in disbelief. "I don't get it."

The old man looked worn. "You never listened to me. The son is supposed to listen to his dad. It's a lesson you needed to learn."

I laughed at how set he was in his ways and how ridiculous he sounded. Still, I found myself taking the bait.

"I made my own decisions, Dad. You, of all people, should respect a man being a man."

"Your coffee's getting cold," my father replied, making a drinking gesture at me, furthering fanning the flames of my anger.

"And coming to my place of work and not even giving me a chance to answer for something I had nothing to do with." I said in disgust. "You know, I was convinced you came in like a belligerent gorilla because you decided I was attracted to men."

Marco shrugged, refusing to concede any ground. "Never hurt a man to learn a lesson by force, if that's what it takes, eh? Wakes him up. Motivates him. Toughens him up."

"I never asked to be toughened up."

This reality finally evoked some emotion from my father. "Listen, son, you fooled around and went to your prep school and wrote your poetry, eh? It still burns me up . . . because that's not the way I raised you to be."

"I suppose, then, that you raised me to be unfaithful to my wife," I said, holding nothing back at this point.

My father chuckled.

"I love your mother, but you can't cut out a man's nature, eh? There's a word for that, eh?"

"Like what . . . castrated?" I asked.

"Don't call me that," he warned, pointing his finger at my face.

"I can't believe you, Dad," I said. "Is that what you consider yourself now?"

"I'm not proud of myself," Marco admitted, taking a deep drink from his coffee. "But you can't question my love for your mother. She understands me like no one else in the world."

"You're right about that," I said bitterly.

My father looked at me for a few moments, like he was about to say something. His jaw was tight and I noticed his fists were clenched.

"You want to hit me right now, don't you?" I asked.

The old man shook his head. "I had plans for you when you were born, eh? You were going to grow up and take over my contracting business. We were going to develop this town together. Then you were going to inherit it and then do the same thing with your son, eh?"

"That's preposterous," I said. "When I worked for you as a kid, you knew that I wasn't mechanical. Why would I purposely choose to be all thumbs?"

"I know," the old man admitted. "But it was disappointing, eh? It was unacceptable. You're not like my father, or his father, or your great-grandfather."

"No," I said. "I'm like your brother."

"Then you think you should have been his son, eh?" my father speculated, looking suddenly like a tired old man.

"Let's not kid ourselves, my life would have been a lot better if I had been," I said candidly.

My father nodded in agreement, but this thought obviously upset him.

"Your uncle enabled you to continue this lifestyle of yours," he said with resentment. "I'll never forgive him for it, eh?"

"But Dad, you loved your brother. You accepted him for who he was. You protected him all his life. Where were you for me? Why didn't you protect me?"

Marco was unapologetic. "Mike was weak, very frail. He needed helping. You were strong and you had the blood of a lion coursing through your veins. You had all the advantages and it all comes down to one thing. You ran away from work hard, eh?"

"No I didn't," I protested. "You have no idea how demanding my work has been."

Marco dismissed my objection, opting to finish his thought. "Well that character flaw of yours—that aversion to work—I view it as my failure as a father, eh?"

The waitress brought out Marco's plate. He began dipping his toast into the eggs, his appetite just as hearty as ever.

"In my mind, I work as hard as anyone," I argued, trying to be convincing. "What do I need to do to prove that I share this same value?"

My dad looked at me, appeared thoughtful for a second, and then said very deliberately and with great sincerity, "Take over my business."

I just about fell out of my chair before bursting into laughter.

Marco didn't laugh. "I'm serious. My shop does very well and I retire soon. Take over the business, eh, and continue to build our name in White Sands."

"You're serious?"

"You and your wife can run it together. Keep it in the family."

"This is all it will take to make you happy?"

Marco nodded. "You might think I'm a stupid brute, but you hurt me too, eh? You do not share even one of my values. Well, I'm giving you a chance now. Take over my business."

I thought about this for a few moments.

"I'll talk about it with Emily," I said. "Given the circumstances, that's probably the best I can do for now."

"That woman of yours," said my father, "she's a keeper, eh?"

"She's the best thing to ever happen to me."

"Does she know her place?" Marco asked.

I scoffed at how little regard he had for political correctness.

"No, she keeps me in place."

I think I actually saw a gleam of amusement in my father's eyes as he purposefully contradicted himself. "Then she's a good girl in my books. She'll keep you working, eh?"

"Right until the day I die," I agreed, finishing my coffee.

* * * * *

"Brad's losing it," Tamer said, sitting with me at the pub later in the day. "Somehow he got in his head that I like science fiction, so he's bringing movies into work for me and trying to get me to go to these lame conventions. He's preposterous."

"You'd think he'd figure out that you're all about documentaries, war movies and westerns," I offered, trying to keep a straight face.

"Yeah, you'd think . . . anyway, I hope you don't mind, but I went out on a limb and told Brad that he had to take his friend from the Harbor as his guest to the wedding."

"Why did you do that?" I asked.

"Because I'm convinced that this Harbor friend is fictional and that Brad uses getting together with him as his excuse to blow us off all the time."

"Brad wouldn't do that," I said in disbelief.

"Oh, Brad lies when it suits his purpose," Tamer explained matter-of-factly. "He's sneaky all right—the king of excuses, hemming and hawing . . . Oh, I can't come over tonight because I have to mess with the furnace . . . Or, I have to do laundry tonight . . . Or, my friend from the Harbor is coming over for beers."

"So why do you think he blows us off?"

"I made a connection. Every time he tells me that he bought a new porno he ends up canceling our plans."

"So let me get this straight. Brad has an imaginary friend as a built-in excuse to watch porn? Do you hear what you're saying?"

"The man's a great guy, but he's deceitful."

"But to watch porn?"

Tamer nodded. "Did he tell you that when he was in the hospital for one of his million operations his mother had to go downstairs to take care of his cat. But he left in such a state of emergency that he forgot to put his porn away. The funny part of the story is that his mother never said anything about it, but there was some awkwardness between them for a few weeks afterwards. Brad didn't know how to talk about it, so he just let things remain uncomfortable until it went away."

"For the nicest guy I've ever met, Brad is actually kind of a badass in his own way," I observed. "And he's perhaps one of the more self-indulgent people I know."

"Happiest man in the world!" Tamer said with conviction.

"No way," I objected.

"And you want to know why?" Tamer said, beaming.

"Enlighten me, Dan."

"Because he doesn't bother with women. Maybe you should consider that big, happy, bearded smile before you go through with this wedding of yours. It's not too late, you know."

"I appreciate your wisdom. I really do. But I know what I'm doing."

"I'm just saying, old man, as long as there's no 'I do' you are committed to nothing."

"Dan," I said, lowering my voice and looking around to make sure nobody was listening, "my biggest concern is the wedding night, to tell you truth. It's been so built up . . . and it's been so long since the last time I've done it . . . that I'm kind of nervous. I want the first time to be defining for us."

"I've been thinking about that, too," said Tamer. "I mean, I considered what I would do if I was in the exact same circumstance. The solution's really quite simple. Near the end of the reception, we'll sneak out and smoke a joint together. That'll settle you down, I promise."

"You think?" I asked.

"Absolutely," Tamer assured me, nodding confidently. "Nice long encounter, with the edge taken off. She'll think that she married a god."

"You're an odd duck, Dan Tamer," I said, extending my hand to him. "But definitely a good friend."

"You wait for the bachelor party, old man," replied Tamer, shaking my hand with a warrior's grip. "Even Brad has no excuse to miss this."

* * * * *

The day before our wedding arrived and there was still much to be done. We began that morning by frequenting discount stores in search of additional decorations and wedding accessories. Then, with the help of family and friends, we spent hours decorating the church. Next, we had to have the final fittings done. Emily's bridesmaids were a hodgepodge of waitresses from the restaurant, including her maid of honor, Brandy. The girls all went to the boutique to have last-minute adjustments made to their dresses. As for my crew, I'd had no problem convincing childhood friends to return from all over to White Sands. The group included Tamer, Darren, Cooper, Sweet Johnny (who flew in from BC), the big Italian, Milano, and Clue. I also asked Brad and Gizzer to help out as ushers. We were scheduled to be at the tux shop a couple of hours before the rehearsal.

By the time we started the rehearsal, Emily was stressed, bossy, and mean. I exchanged looks with Tamer several times in response to Emily's theatrics and pressing agenda to get things perfect. I found it amusing, though, when Tamer finally pushed her off the deep end and into despair. When we were standing in position at the front of the church's sanctuary, Tamer signaled for a time-out and then went and stretched out on one of the pews, informing everyone it was time for a breather. Emily was livid and told my good friend that he should have checked his attitude at the church door. I didn't blame Tamer because there was so much discussion about arrangements and music and timing that it was hard on the feet and really quite boring. It's not like he pushed for a cigarette break.

When I made the mistake of laughing during the altercation, Emily's acid tongue fell on me. "We have to get this worked out tonight," she scolded. "This childishness is unacceptable—not funny at all!"

"But we're making such a big deal of such small details when we should be having fun with this," I instinctively complained.

No sooner did the words leave my lips than I regretted them. Emily gave me a look that would have exorcised the possessed. I shut my mouth and got with the program.

Not only did Tamer and the rest of us quickly come to understand Emily's unnatural demand for perfection, but we all used "principles of reason" to conclude that every detail had to be accounted for in order for her to feel comfortable. It was to be the woman's wedding day—the day she had dreamed about all of her life—and who were we to get in her way? We were only the insensitive groom and his pain-in-the-ass best man.

Pastor Daven, however, did a good job of keeping everything under control, and proved to be a stabilizing presence. Otherwise, Emily would have prolonged the rehearsal all night. Besides the wedding party, there were the onlookers. Once Emily had announced our engagement, her family had become even more involved in her life, just as mine had. In fact, her mother walked around the sanctuary, making little adjustments here and there, and certainly wasn't afraid of adding her two cents. Emily's father, on the other hand, pretty much recovered from his heart-attack scare, reclined in his pew and didn't let the bickering impact his blood pressure. Marco did likewise, the model of patient behavior. My mother used her calmness to diffuse any tension the best she could. Many of the wedding party's significant others also looked on while we debated where a plant might sit and how each individual involved had to be infused seamlessly into this grand production. It was quite tiresome and all of us were starving. I didn't blame Brad for dismissing himself to go to the bathroom about five times, and he had no problem announcing to everyone that something he'd eaten earlier just wasn't sitting right.

Finally, the major work was accomplished and only slightly behind schedule, so by the time we finished the rehearsal dinner a noticeable relief could be seen in the language of Emily's entire body. I think she was just anxious about everything and wanted every detail accounted for and out of the way. Regardless, Emily had calmed down and seemed to be feeling better, so I left her that night feeling quite good about her state of mind and looking forward to spending my last moments of bachelor freedom with my friends.

When I dropped her off at the house to gather with her bridesmaids, I walked her to the door like a true gentleman. It was arranged that she would have our house to herself for the night and I—after some convincing on my part—was to stay at Tamer's place after he'd thrown together a little bachelor party for me.

"Our last premarital kiss," I said, opening the door for her.

"You could have been more helpful today, you know," Emily replied, turning back to me in the doorway.

I shrugged. "I probably could have."

"I'm not going to be able to sleep tonight."

"I expect I'll be passed out one way or another," I said, trying to be funny.

"If you're hung over, I'll kill you," Emily warned. "I mean it."

"Relax, honey, I'll be fine."

"I mean it. I'm holding our wedding night over you."

"I'm only going to have a few drinks, Emily. Now give me a kiss."

So I kissed her goodbye and then drove over to Tamer's apartment to drop my car off and meet with my friends for a night on the town.

After we assembled, we made our way to the pub as a group. Everyone seemed remarkably festive and enthusiastic. I felt so grateful for each one of them and it was surreal to have such attention cast my way. Once we arrived, Tamer, the perpetual employer, gave Brad the responsibility of keeping the pitchers flowing with beer. Wings, sandwiches, baskets of French fries and other pub foods were set out before us. Cooper was given special permission to bring his guitar and had set up some equipment in advance so that we could have live entertainment. He had Jean-Marc, another one of our good friends, show up with some drums, and Sweet Johnny—

the smooth, quiet charmer—had brought his guitar along with him as well.

And then we started pouring the pitchers. Soon laughter and loud music filled the pub. Brad drank like it was going out of style. There was more cigarette smoke in the place than even on New Year's Eve. Gizzer sat at my side and made it his personal mission to ensure my glass always remained full. And Tamer was truly the life of the party. Even my friends from out of town, like Milano and Shawn, were encouraging him to keep rhyming off names of local women he'd hooked up with that we all knew growing up. Although I was unsure exactly what Tamer had planned for me, through the grapevine I'd heard that one of the highlights of my night was supposed to be the poem Brad had talked about writing in my honor. I had no idea what kind of poetry the bearded giant could write, and this made it even more compelling.

As things played out, nobody could keep up with the amount of beer Brad was guzzling. And he almost did it effortlessly; he poured himself a glass and then the liquid disappeared without anyone ever catching him taking a sip. Cooper, meanwhile, was playing his guitar and singing covers that brought us back to high school: Metallica and Pantera, Soundgarden and Pearljam. Jean-Marc was a hummingbird of activity on the drums, the gleam of his glasses barely visible behind his whirling arms. Clue sometimes would join them to pipe in with his harmonica, while Johnny and Darren took turns playing rhythm guitar. Overall, the music was loud but better than anything I could have imagined. What made it utterly perfect was that these guys hit the right nerves with the songs they chose—and I couldn't help but reflect on the events of the past year. It was music that transported me back in time, making me feel overwhelmingly sentimental about all my friendships and what it had taken for all of us to come together that night.

For the toast, Brian—our light-on-his-feet, metrosexual server—passed out a special round of beers that Tamer had ordered for everyone. Tamer called them dark and tans, where beer was mixed with Guinness. Gizzer, a little too enthusiastic—perhaps not thinking—took a sip from his glass before we could toast. This was met with a chorus of disapproval. Of course, Gizzer had to pay the price and down his whole glass by way of punishment. The guys' jeers turned to cheers when the boy tipped the glass back and poured it straight down the hatch, making a man of himself before our very eyes.

After Brian brought out another drink for Gizzer, Tamer, master of ceremonies, stood at the table to address the crew. After he managed to get everyone's attention, he began to speak in his assumed speech voice loud enough for everyone in the bar to hear him.

"Good evening, gentlemen. I hope everyone is enjoying himself. I'm not going to waste your time toasting to a long and fruitful marriage, huge helpings of happiness—you know, all that inane dribble that belongs at the wedding reception. We all know that tonight's about something different.

"I'm the last person who'd like to admit it, but this is one of those occasions we can't take lightly. One of us has chosen to take the proverbial 'plunge.' Now that's a powerful decision, isn't it? So I just wanted to lay it all out on the table so that everyone's aware of what's exactly at stake: tomorrow one of our own, as we know him, will be gone forever."

Tamer let this sink in a bit, inviting a collective pathos into the room.

"It's a bitter-sweet thing, isn't it? We're all happy for the old man here, and yet it's a sad reality—knowing that things can never be as they once were. Change is the price we pay for entering into marriage. Not that I'm knocking it, for this is what all romance aspires to and it's expected of every one of us here."

"Except you, Dan," Cooper said with a laugh.

There was a stir of agreement.

Tamer grinned. "He's right—except me. But, gentlemen," Tamer continued, picking up where he'd left off, "let me ask you this: if a man falters in his relationship, who does he turn to?"

We all looked at Tamer with blank stares, understanding the question but a little unsure of where he might go with this. When nobody answered, Tamer singled one of us out.

"Who does he turn to, Darren?" Tamer demanded.

"His beer," Darren replied, holding up his glass, and everyone laughed.

"You're wrong," Tamer continued, shaking his head. "I'll give you a hint. It's the only thing a man can truly count on."

All of us sat there waiting for Tamer to fill in the blank.

"It's his friends, isn't it? Isn't it, gentlemen?"

The guys all nodded and murmured in agreement.

"Not that I want to diminish the importance of the life cycle and all the joys and accomplishments that come with family, but neither do I want any one of us to lose sight of the fact that friendship takes a backseat to nothing."

Tamer paused to let this sink in as well.

"To nothing, gentlemen!" Tamer said with fire, driving the point home.

He then addressed me directly. "So, old man, I'm going to say it: I hope your marriage is long and happy, but don't you dare forget that it's the friends—you hear me, the friends—that makes us capable of embracing our future with the edge that comes from having . . . just a little bit of certainty."

Tamer then raised his glass. "So my toast is to friendship, gentlemen. May Grant—may every one of us here—never, ever take it for granted!"

"To friendship," we all echoed with enthusiasm, and then we thrust our glasses together in a spray of beer and downed our drinks to the very last drop.

After this motivational speech, Brad-to-the-Bone stood up and trudged to the head of the table. He dug deep in his pocket and pulled out a wrinkled piece of old foolscap with messy writing on it.

Very deliberately, he seemed to examine everyone slowly before clearing his throat and saying, "I wrote this poem to commemorate Grant's relationship with Emily. It's called 'Homegrown Mystery,' and I hope the old man truly appreciates the sentiment behind it and how much I admire him."

Brad then held the page up, and began to read in a slow, narrative voice:

She's homegrown. A beauty. A marvel . . .
She lights my path for me.
She's not from Paris, and she's not from Asia.
She's homegrown. A beauty. A marvel . . .
She fills my heart with joy.
She's not from Venus, and she's not from Mercury.
She's homegrown. A beauty. A marvel. A mystery . . .

By the time Brad's poem was finished, which was almost the moment he began reciting it, tears could be seen forming in his eyes as he was quite moved by his own words and perhaps affected by the amount of alcohol he had consumed. Everyone remained quiet, most likely not sure what to make of the spectacle. He then handed the crumpled paper to me as a memento of this occasion and awkwardly lumbered back to his seat.

"Happiest man in the world!" Tamer cried out, breaking the silence and leading everyone in applause as the bearded giant stood wiping his eyes in front of his chair.

Once these two jackasses got their sentimental feelings out of the way, it was truly time for Tamer to shine. He had warned me that he'd made arrangements for a stripper to come out and give me a lap dance. Even if she ended up being knock dead gorgeous, I told Tamer beforehand that I wasn't at all interested. So when he brought out a woman that kind of resembled an old gargoyle, everyone laughed and enjoyed the little routine she put together. When she was done, many of the guys complained to Tamer that it was anathema to insult convention. So he brought out an even uglier stripper. This wad of dough flopped around for a while everyone watched her with a combination of horror and curiosity on their half-smiling faces. Finally, after everybody's hope for some skin had all but evaporated, Tamer brought out a stunning dancer that resembled a woman he might have dated at one point. This obviously satisfied the guys, but I held my ground and insisted that this little exhibition had more to do with the tradition and less with my wishes. Tamer, always a stickler, made sure that I at least participated vicariously, and so our French friend, Jean-Marc, volunteered to endure a lap dance in my place.

"Believe it or not, they all cost the same," Tamer explained. "There's this agency with a girl for almost any fetish imaginable: fat, tall, skinny, old . . ."

After the girls had departed, Cooper went back to playing the guitar. Milano, Sweet Johnny, Darren, Shawn and Clue teamed up to try to make our poor server Brian come to terms with his latent affection for men. They sat him down at our table and tried to explain to him that it was ok to come clean about his orientation. Brian insisted he had a girlfriend; if we wanted, a simple phone call could produce an appearance from her to end the debate once and for all. There's no reason to feel too sorry for Brian, though. He defended himself quite well for a skinny, socially inept kid. And besides, so much cash was being thrown his way that the other servers were trying to hone in on his action, abuse and all. But we would have nothing to do with them. Brian, our little effeminate elf, was our adopted server for the night and he was paid exorbitant amounts of cash to entertain us in ridiculous fashion.

It was about an hour later that the night took a different turn. Justin Fancy, of all people, walked into the pub and stumbled over to our table, drunk to the gills. He sat down next to me and ended up putting his arm around my shoulders. Tamer watched with noticeable interest as Justin began to pour out his heart to those of us who remained at the table.

"Grant was once my best friend," Justin slurred.

"Please don't start," I begged, feeling the full weight of his arm across my back.

"We were inseparable," Justin continued, oblivious. "I even got him to go to seminary with me."

"I know the story," I muttered.

"But I screwed up. I screwed up. And it's never been the same since."

I disentangled myself from the drunken mess and looked at him. For some reason, I felt a surge of compassion when I saw him tormented and drunk.

"I realize I should have invited you tonight," I said.

"Really?" Fancy asked.

"You know, I'm glad you're here," I told him. "I don't know what's different between us, but it feels right, doesn't it Tamer?"

"Sure, old man," Tamer agreed, but without enthusiasm.

"No, I'm serious," I said. "Justin has paid his dues."

"I feel like I've ruined everything," Fancy said in a melancholy voice, his gaze to the floor.

"When you think about it," I began, perhaps a little inebriated myself, "perhaps it was your encounter with Emily that ended up pushing us together. It's almost like you had a hand in all this, 'cause in the end you made us more compatible with each other."

Fancy looked into my eyes and I saw misery and confusion. "I still feel like I've ruined everything . . . no matter what you say . . . My God, it's the one act that won't go away . . . it haunts me . . . I can't apologize my way out of it . . . That's why I resigned from the church today . . ."

"You what?"

"You heard me. I resigned. The disparity between my ideals and actions is too wide. It's swallowed me whole and I can't climb out."

"Justin, I can't believe it's come to this," I said, my stomach sinking.

"It's time I take responsibility. It's the only way."

"Well, I'm trying to forgive you, if you'll let me," I said.

I looked at Tamer, who was listening quietly, and shrugged at him in confusion. Tamer's face was expressionless.

But this confession did not alleviate Fancy's suffering. "There is no forgiveness for this type of atrocity. Don't you understand? You can't help me."

"Then I'm asking you to forgive yourself. In a roundabout way, you've helped me immeasurably—I'm not lying."

Fancy examined me with bloodshot eyes, and then said softly, "I know you're determined to be with Emily . . . but when she begged me to marry her in your place I realized that hell truly is for all eternity."

I felt like I had been smashed over the head with a crowbar.

"What are you talking about?" I asked, incredulous. I then turned to Tamer, who was unmoved by this information.

"But you're still marrying her," Fancy continued, "because it's become your obsession to see to it that you experience Emily the same way I have. And there's nothing I can say to convince you otherwise."

"You're telling me that Emily tried to convince you to marry her instead of me?" I struggled to remain calm enough to get some clarification.

Justin's tortured eyes met my own. "She said that we belonged together."

"You're lying," I said, feeling my heart sink. "Admit that you're making a last-ditch effort to keep us apart, and I'll call you a cab."

Justin looked me straight in the eyes. "I can't, Grant—"

"Admit that you're lying, you slobbering mess!" I shouted, jumping to my feet.

Brad and Tamer closed around me to intervene, grabbing me and pulling me away from the table before my rage could boil over, but I wanted to strangle Justin for coming in and destroying my night when I was so close to a new beginning.

"I'll tear him to pieces," I snarled, my anger gaining momentum.

Justin held his hands up in surrender. "I didn't ask for any of this, Grant, I swear."

With all the commotion, the guys were gathered around us now. Cooper had stopped playing and now Gizzer, Johnny, Darren, Jean-Marc, Clue, Shawn, Milano and even Brian were standing there in awkward silence.

"He's a liar," I sputtered, trying to convince everyone around me that Emily's reputation was being dragged through the mud by this despicable pastor.

"You're acting surprised," Fancy defended, clearly confused. "But you made it clear that you'd discussed this with Emily and that her explanation satisfied you."

"Just leave!" I yelled in disgust, fully aware that I had ignored his warning. It didn't matter to me at this point. "I better not see your face at the wedding tomorrow!"

Tamer then took control, putting his hand on my shoulder and dragging me to the corner of the pub so I could simmer down and get my bearings back.

After he had my attention, he said with great discomfort, I could see it in his eyes, "Grant, there's something you need to know."

I just kept glaring at Fancy, who was being helped to his feet by Brad.

"Did you hear me? I have to get this into the open."

"What could you possibly say in the wake of this disaster?" I demanded.

I was still so distressed that I was trembling inside, like my soul was a caged lion. With the old wounds of betrayal bleeding profusely again, rage was my only coagulant.

"Calm down," Tamer ordered.

"How do you expect me to do that?" I snapped.

"Perhaps you should sit for this," Tamer instructed, pulling out a chair for me.

"I don't want to sit."

"Sit down!" he commanded before thrusting me onto the seat.

"What do you want, Dan?"

"I should have told you this already," Tamer began.

I was hardly listening to him, still thinking about how much I wanted to punish Fancy.

"I didn't know how to go about it," Tamer continued. "I was confused about the right thing to do."

"I'm getting out of here," I said impatiently, trying to rise from the chair.

Tamer restrained me and kept me sitting. "Do you know Jimmy B?"

"Yes, but we've never spoken," I growled. "What does it matter?"

"Justin's probably not lying." Tamer exhaled heavily. "I ran into Jimmy right after the rehearsal. When I told him that I was the best man and that you and Emily were getting married, he thought it was crazy because he's had an open relationship with her for years. He said he could have had her yesterday if he wanted."

My good friend definitely had my attention now. It was like I'd had the wind knocked out of me, and almost instantly I felt like throwing up. Instead, I went totally limp and pretty well slid onto the floor. It was the knockout blow. After the initial experience of frozen horror had melted away, I immediately felt this rush of embarrassment—I had been such a fool all along. It was as if this whole night of celebration had been contrived, a lie, and everybody in the universe but me had known the actual truth while I went on like the best thing to ever happen to me was about to transpire. This whole thing between Emily and I was imaginary, a dream, and it had been from the moment I met her.

Tamer got me back in the chair.

"Jimmy caught me so off guard, I didn't know how to bring it up . . . I promise you, Grant, I was going to, though."

I looked over to see all of my friends watching us with concern. It was mortifying. It was a nightmare.

"Do you have a cigarette?" I asked.

"Sure," Tamer replied, pulling out his pack and digging in his pocket for a lighter. He even lit it for me while I had it in my mouth.

I took a few drags.

"I wonder how many other men Emily throws herself at," I said cynically.

Tamer gave a wincing smile, then became serious. "You realize you have to talk to her. You have no choice but to end this now."

"I know," I agreed, trying to come to terms with my emotion. The cigarette at least created a little buzz to calm me down.

"I'll call us a cab, Grant. I should have told you. But I promise you, I'll stand by your side as your witness when you confront her about this. I won't make you do this alone."

I continued sitting there in shock for a few minutes. Tamer pulled up a chair and sat next to me. Everyone else kept their distance. Fancy, wisely, had slunk out of the pub by this point.

"What am I going to tell my parents?" I asked, my voice cracking. "I've never been more disgraced." I looked right in his eyes. "Dan, what am I going to do?"

"We're going to end this thing and then I'm going to start making the necessary calls to inform everyone that a wedding will not be taking place. I'll take care of it. You don't have to do anything."

"Then what?"

"And then we're going to make up for it with plenty of tennis this year, old man."

"Tennis?"

"Believe me, with time you're going to be just fine," Tamer said with forced confidence. "You realize you've dodged a bullet. I mean, you know she's a bitch now, right?"

"Yeah, how fortunate I am," I said bitterly.

Tamer smiled. "Old man, the situations you find yourself in . . . I tell you . . ."

And then Tamer let out a little chuckle. Even I had to crack a smile of disbelief, despite my world crashing down around me.

Who else in the world would have poured so much time and energy into a woman who would rather marry anybody else but him?

*****

The concept of being chosen is hard to grasp. To be chosen is beyond your control, and the terrifying part is that people on the outside might have a clearer perspective of your fate by the very fact that they lie outside the circle of involvement. The moment that Tamer corroborated Fancy's story I knew that fate, once again, had intervened in my life. The question became, was this all for my betterment? On the one hand, I was treading dangerously close to denial and so I needed something earth shattering to change my mindset. On the other hand, it would have been so much easier for me if Emily had been the woman I'd imagined her to be.

But this wasn't what I was thinking about as Tamer and I taxied back to my place. I was thinking about myself as a child and how I'd had no clue as to the types of experiences I was destined for and how many lessons awaited me. Part of me felt responsible to that young little guy and I totally separated myself from the child I had been and all the dreams he'd had. I thought about how as a child I was most sensitive to nature, how awestruck I was by the grandeur of the world around me. And then this seemed to be replaced by activities more aggressive and intellectual as I followed my education. It was through meeting Emily that I retained that childhood sense of awe; and it was this understanding that made me so confident that we were going to walk hand-in-hand with each other into the unknown. At the very least, I knew our future included landscape and wildflowers and lots of happy dogs.

I also thought about the little girl in Emily. She never asked to grow up confused. She never asked to have such emotional struggles. She had been chosen for a different fate when she was blessed with kindness and goodness and yet cursed with an inability to remain true to any single object of her affection. It's like she was born to sabotage herself, and fate had decided it was time I came to the realization that this was never going to change, whether I liked it or not. It was destined in the stars that the moment Emily was to be mine she'd launch into a full retreat, and that if we had married the cycle would have continued on indefinitely. Emily, for all her values and principles and goodness, would never allow herself to be possessed in any relationship. The thought of it triggered a response in her to seek out someone else, anybody else but the one she so desperately desired.

When we arrived at the house, my stomach felt nervous, I had a difficult time swallowing, my mouth was dry, and I found myself trembling. Tamer paid the taxi driver and then accompanied me to the house while I took those agonizing steps toward the end of a dream and the beginning of reality.

At the door I hesitated, but Tamer nodded at me and gave me no time to reconsider. He opened the door and pushed me across the threshold.

There was music playing. The women had been making margaritas using the blender and were dancing with each other. Emily was in the middle of it all, holding a margarita glass and looking like she was having a wonderful time. When she saw me, she broke into a smile and danced on over. Tamer and I stood there like idiots when she came over swaying her hips and tried to draw me into dancing with her.

"You couldn't stay away from me even for a night, could you honey?" she cried, clearly a bit drunk.

"I need to talk to you, Emily," I said, trying to take her by the hand.

She pulled away. "Don't ruin all the fun. Come dance with us." She then turned to her friend. "Come on, Brandy, the men are here. I get the good-looking one."

Then Emily tilted her head back and began giggling.

"We need to talk upstairs," I said sternly, grabbing her hand again.

"What's this about?" she asked, cluing in that I was serious.

"Upstairs," I repeated.

"Fine," she pouted.

I then led her up the stairs and into our bedroom. I told Tamer that although appreciated, I didn't need his support.

When we got to the bedroom, Emily clung to me and tried to pull me onto the bed. She was laughing and pulling at my clothes. I was able to extricate myself, finally, and convince her to sit on the bed.

"I need to talk to you about something," I explained, sitting beside her.

"About what?" she replied, her happiness turning to irritation. "I don't like you treating me like a little girl."

"Justin showed up at the bachelor party tonight and got a little something off his chest."

"I don't see how this concerns me," Emily said.

"Is it true that you'd prefer to marry him in my place?"

"Is that what he said?" she asked, sounding surprised.

"He said you pleaded with him to marry you."

Emily started laughing. "Yeah, so. If I want to rub it in a bit, it's my prerogative."

"Rub it in?" I repeated. "He said you begged him."

"Oh, Grant," Emily began like it was all a big misunderstanding, "Justin came into the restaurant when I was tending bar one night and I was showing off my engagement ring. I was blinding everyone with the bling of my diamond. I was joking to all of the men that I could be theirs—if they could provide me with a better bling. I was joking and carrying on and having fun . . ."

"That doesn't explain your ongoing relationship with Jimmy."

"Jimmy?" Emily echoed in disbelief, her eyes momentarily flashing angry. "Are you kidding me?"

"Do I look like I'm joking? This is our life together that we're talking about."

"What kind of character do you think I have?" Emily demanded.

"I don't know," I replied. "You tell me. It seems that everyone else in the world knows what's going on but me."

"Well, I know about as much as you do, Grant."

"I don't believe that," I told her straight up. "Just tell me how long you've been messing around with him. I'm going to find out one way or another."

Emily considered this for a second. "Ok, I'll tell you. But I just thought you were better off not knowing."

"Tell me."

"While you were dating other people I was seeing Jimmy. But that ended."

I started shaking my head in disbelief.

"What, it's ok for you, but not for me?" she cried.

"I just don't understand why you didn't tell me about him before."

"He's not worth mentioning. So please, before we get married, do you have any other concerns? Or do you just not trust me?"

"This afternoon Jimmy said that you two still have an open relationship."

"Yeah, he wishes," Emily said sarcastically.

"What do you mean by that?"

"I can't help it if he comes and flirts with me while I'm bartending. He's a customer, and if I still make him feel special it's because it's my job."

I couldn't say anything for a second. I knew I didn't believe her.

"It's the truth," Emily insisted, leaning in closer to make eye contact.

Unwilling to dance around the issue anymore, not buying her excuses, and completely fed up, I told her my decision. "Emily, no matter what you say, this wedding isn't going to happen. I'd have to be crazy to go through with this now—an absolute lunatic."

"Don't talk like that," Emily replied. "I love you. I want to share my life with you."

"Then why did you make such a fool out of me?"

"I didn't—"

"We're through, Emily. I'm not going to change my mind."

Emily sat there for a second, showing no emotion, like it was dawning on her that I was actually serious. But rather than give in, she took the offensive. "Who was it that kept pushing for this relationship? Was it me?"

"Not exactly," I said. "However—"

"In fact, didn't I try to warn you that things get complicated for men who get close to me?" Her eyes blazed.

"Yes, but—"

"So let me get this straight. You convince me that you're prepared to love me unconditionally, and now you're ending our relationship based on hearsay? Does that pretty well sum it up?"

"What my best friend tells me is a lot more than hearsay," I said.

My resolve seemed to invite a soberness that washed over her entire expression.

"So what does this mean, that we don't get married and we continue on like we did in the past?" she asked softly.

"It means that we totally separate," I said.

"I can't believe this is happening," Emily said, rubbing her forehead.

"Neither can I. But I don't have a choice. You've given me no choice."

"Let me ask you this—when you got fired at the shelter, who supported you?" Emily asked, becoming combative again.

"Yes, you never got angry over me losing my job," I admitted.

"I was completely understanding."

"You were."

"Then why can't you extend me the same forgiveness?" she pleaded, taking my hand into her own and stroking it gently.

"Are you admitting to something then?" I asked.

"No, because I didn't do anything wrong," she insisted, thrusting my hand away vindictively.

I stood up. "Well, at least you'll have the rest of your life to consider how lucky you were to avoid marrying the man who unjustly accused you."

"Are you leaving then?" she asked, almost like she was surprised. "Is there nothing else to say?"

"Tamer's calling everybody up in the morning to let them know that there will be no wedding. I'm sorry. I wish it didn't have to be this way."

"Fine then. No wedding. See if I care," she pouted.

"Goodnight Emily."

As I turned to leave, I was calm. My emotions still had not caught up with the significance and finality of this encounter. I didn't make it two steps before Emily threw herself at my feet and began pleading with me.

"Oh, Grant, you can't leave me!" she sobbed, clutching at my legs.

I looked down at her and felt such overwhelming sympathy and tenderness that I wanted to take her in my arms and reassure her that everything was going to be ok and that I was never going to leave her. My instinct was to protect her and even go so far as to delude myself and give her the benefit of the doubt. After all we had been through together, it seemed unfair to either of us to suddenly quit now.

With both arms wrapped around my legs, she looked up at me with pleading, tear-filled eyes. "Please don't go. I can't stand to be without you!"

Somehow, though, I remained determined to see myself through to the other side, heartless as it may seem.

"I have to leave, Emily," I said calmly and with compassion in voice. "You have to let me go, honey. I can't be part of a marriage that is fundamentally flawed."

But Emily would have nothing to do with it, tightening her grip around my legs. "Don't leave, Grant, I don't know what I'll do without you. Please, please, please reconsider. I love you. I love you so much. I would do anything for you!"

Emily was now streaming tears and shaking all over. When I tried to free myself, I lost my footing and tripped right into the nightstand with a huge crash that resounded throughout the house.

Now that she had me on the ground, Emily crawled on top of me and began weeping on my chest. "Please don't leave me, Grant. I love you. I'll do anything, anything if you just give me the chance to show how truly devoted I am to you."

At this point, the music downstairs had stopped and soon after everyone had joined us upstairs to investigate the crash. Tamer, all the girls, they all walked into the room to find Emily sobbing on top of me like an injured little girl desperately in need of comforting.

Everyone stared at us with their jaws dropped, unable to make sense of the spectacle before them.

In front of this audience, I slowly peeled Emily off me and managed to get to my feet. Then, very deliberately and with purpose, I walked across the room with the cold indifference of a sociopath while everyone except Tamer stared at me as though I was a monster. After I made my way through the crowd of angry-eyed women to the door, Tamer put a hand on my shoulder and started to lead me out of the room. One last glance back revealed Emily still curled up on the floor—a defeated, sobbing mess. The last sound I remember was choking and weeping. I then followed Tamer down the stairs and into the night air.

It was then that sickness hit me—my emotions had suddenly caught up with my actions as reality derailed my dream.

Tamer stuck a cigarette in my mouth while we waited for our cab, but at this point my world was spinning out of control and my feelings were a whirl of contradictions. Shortly after, the contents of my stomach were on the grass, but I certainly didn't feel better. I was what you call inconsolable.

POSTSCRIPT

When Emily was still in my life, she found it annoying that I reminded her every day how beautiful she was to me. I found her response confusing, for how could she expect me to keep such moments of adoration to myself? Sometimes I experienced such joy in her presence that poetry would form on my lips, as if words could convey the overwhelming gratitude I felt in my heart. It was clear to me that she mistook my praise for flattery, but deep down I knew the truth: by voicing my attraction I was able to keep my astonishment in check. How, indeed, could this mysterious, radiant creature choose to share her life with me?

It's almost like each time I reminded Emily of her beauty, I was pinching myself to be sure it was all real—that she yearned for my affection and was equally smitten. And yet as powerful as my devotion became, in the end it was a force of nature that had to be conquered in order to carry through with the separation. My part in the whole mess seemed completely counter-intuitive. Everything within me screamed to protect and provide, to please her, to try to understand her, and to ultimately see to it that I was meeting her relationship needs to the best of my ability. Outside of her faithfulness, all I had hoped for in return was the knowledge that I was doing a good job and that I was appreciated and admired for my efforts.

Leaving Emily was the most difficult thing I've ever had to do. Yet there was no choice to be made, for quite clearly the choice was taken out of my hands.

An old adage in life is that if you wish to be loved, you have to first love yourself. When you think about it, this means that loving someone and being loved is something within your control as long as you're living the right way. After parting ways with Emily, I came to understand that love's really out of your hands, and I wondered how I could have been so idealistic to begin with. No doubt, living in the aftermath of our separation was a brutal transition. Once Emily moved out, I was left with an empty house that constantly reminded me of her. Even the dogs made me recall all we had been through together. In the months that followed, I lived in a state of shock, where the past's serrated edge seemed to cut the present off from any hope for a meaningful future. Emily's spirit haunted both the physical property and my dreams at night. From my friends' point of view, I basically disappeared into my own world and managed my pain in seclusion. And it's true, I spent almost all my time alone, struggling with this relentless guilt that wouldn't go away despite constant affirmations by those around me that I was justified in walking away from the woman I thought had been destined to become my wife.

While I was working through these issues, I still managed to make good decisions in an attempt to begin a fresh chapter and move forward. I accepted my father's offer and began working with him at his shop. To make ends meet, I also allowed Tamer to convince me to be his assistant manager at the pizza place. But little did they know that they were employing a zombie—a corpse of a man that no longer had any context. The world had ceased to make sense to me and no analogy I created could resurrect an emotional connection to the circumstances I now found myself in. With no other place to turn, I began sifting through all my journal entries over the last several months for scraps of insight—anything that could help explain how everything unraveled so quickly. When I found nothing of value in their singularity, I decided to use them to create an account of my last months with Emily.

I figured that somewhere in the writing process a healing and understanding could take place that would lead to a sense of closure.

Besides attempting to write my way back into a new sense of identity, I made a concerted effort to bring some normalcy back to my everyday routine as well. As in past years, I stood on the sidewalk and observed the collection of floats as they made their way down Main Street in White Sands' yearly Winterama parade. I also attended the local maple syrup festival a few towns over. I thought that participating in our community's events might make my world seem normal more quickly, but these experiences just weren't the same without Emily forcing me to go with her in the first place.

Other developments took place all around me. Gizzer and Megan announced their engagement in late February. Brad kept me updated on the small dent he'd made in transferring his sci-fi collection from video to DVD. Cooper finished his album and was working on a record deal. Darren moved to the city to put some distance between him and his wife. Fancy went back to school to work on his PhD. And Tamer began discussions with me about the idea of buying a house together and doing a property management business. As for myself, I was able to find homes for most of the remaining dogs in the shelter out back, including Tory and Lady. With so much time to myself, I also made great strides in the book I had been working on and had even drawn interest from a publisher. All these instances of progress forced me to realize that at some point in the near future I would have to get back in the game.

The biggest surprise was when Sweet Johnny moved back from BC with a girl he had met in his travels. With no forewarning, he appeared one afternoon and introduced me to his own new fiancé, Linda. Once he got himself situated in town again, he came over for a beer on the back porch and explained that he had considered the matter thoroughly. He thought it was simple. All I needed was to get back to the basics by fishing with him on a regular basis. By "basics" Johnny meant getting out the hip waders and trekking through farmers' fields and sliding down treacherous, wooded slopes to reach our spot on the Sturgeon River. Although I appreciated the sentiment, the physical challenge proved to be nothing more than a distraction. And not even the fresh rainbow trout I ended up catching as the result of Johnny's prodding was enough to inspire my imagination and bring me back to the land of the living.

Tamer, however, was done with my moping and sulking around. So he dragged me to play tennis with him one sunny afternoon in late May. We liked to play in a private tennis court owned by a local yacht club that overlooked the water. Tamer was so put-off by my attitude that he likened our match to the duel to the death between Hector and Achilles. With weapons drawn, we sparred under the hot sun for a torturous two hours. No punches were spared, and energy-wise we left nothing on the table. As built up as it had become, the results were almost tragic. After Tamer had psyched himself up all winter, I prevailed without much of a challenge. It was as though I channeled all of my anger and frustration into each swing of the racket and for the first time in a dog's age I felt truly satisfied—right about the same time exhaustion hit my body.

After we gorged ourselves with water, Tamer insisted that I join him for a cigarette in the shade of a leafy apple tree beside the parking lot. We sat on the lawn and smoked together in calm silence, the only disturbance being the occasional shrill protest of a seagull coming from the docks. The slight wind carried the odor of rotting fish and seaweed, which, believe it or not, was pleasant to me. There were extravagant sailboats all around us, but my gaze was fixed on Magazine Island, the small island that every boy from White Sands had swum to at one point in his life. Beyond the island and on the other side of the bay, you could see hills garbed in a strange embroidery of hardwood and evergreen forests. The sky was clear and blue, making the water appear a deep navy, while the sunshine added a golden quality to everything it brightened.

It was at this point that Tamer confronted me.

"You've got to get over it, old man," he said. "You have to realize it's not your fault."

"It's not a matter of choice," I replied, taking a deep drag. "The world doesn't seem the same to me anymore . . ."

"Unacceptable," Tamer pronounced.

"What do you mean?"

"It's unacceptable that a man's so dependent on a woman that months later he's still a hermit."

"But—"

"No buts," Tamer said with authority. "Get your ass back on the court."

"I'm exhausted," I complained, laughing.

To Tamer, it wasn't a game. He was completely serious.

"You think the suffering you're experiencing over a woman is painful, Grant? Well, it's about time you experienced some suffering over a friend."

"Get real, Dan . . ."

But there was no discouraging him. We crushed our cigarettes into the ground and dragged ourselves back on the court. It was decided that we would play until either one of us won the set or submitted to the other. With the sun baking down on us, we began to rally for serve. Given the circumstances, both of us were afraid of surrendering any advantage. This tentativeness resulted in an endless string of harmless volleys that zapped most of our energy before a single point was scored. Finally, I got a little too aggressive and missed long while trying to finesse a shot just inside the right sideline, allowing Tamer to capture first serve.

Tamer took his position behind the baseline and well to his right of the center mark. I prepared myself for a violent serve as I watched him toss the ball up high in the air, but to my surprise he caught the ball instead.

"Love serving love!" he shouted. "Appropriate way to begin, isn't it?"

"Quit stalling," I said.

Tamer smiled. "I know what your problem is, old man."

Then he tossed the ball in the air and served up a rocket that landed just outside the service box. The carom sizzled by my right ear.

On his second serve, Tamer managed to loop the ball over the net and I returned it to his back hand with the hope of forcing a mistake. Instead, he ripped it down the right sideline for an easy point.

"Fifteen serving love," he said, wiping the sweat from his face.

"So what's my problem?" I asked, walking to the net.

"You don't believe Emily can be replaced," Tamer said.

Without waiting for my response, Tamer began to set his feet as a polite indication that I was to get back into position quickly. This time he made his first serve count. I barely managed to get enough of my racket on the ball to flutter it back over the net. Once again, we found ourselves locked in a cautious exchange that deprived us of energy and left us more parched. The rally probably would have gone on for an eternity if Tamer hadn't allowed himself to lose concentration and wander a few feet inside the service line. This left me with an opening to deliver a well-placed lob that made him scamper to the back of the court and beyond the baseline. Without having the space to generate any power, he gave a half-assed flail at the ball that resulted in a weak shot that fluttered like a wounded pigeon and softly hit the net.

"Fifteen serving fifteen," Tamer said.

Between deep breaths and panting, I said, "You're wrong, Dan. That's not what I'm worried about."

Tamer was doubled over, looking exhausted.

"Oh yeah, then why is your world so different?" he gasped.

"Because I don't trust myself anymore," I explained.

Tamer wiped the sweat from his eyes using a handful of his already soaked shirt, tossed up the ball, and delivered a first serve change-up that caught me off guard. In fact, it was a struggle just to muscle it back over the net on his forehand side. Tamer sliced at the ball and I had to get my racket down quickly or the shot would have skipped past me. Once again, we were volleying with smooth, easy strokes. Tamer was a great technician, but he couldn't match my consistency. In order to challenge me, he knew he had to take chances. And when he did, I almost always made him pay. So when Tamer hit the ball deep and to my backhand—close to the corner where the sideline and baseline intersect—he decided to accelerate the outcome by charging the net. Unfortunately, his set-up shot had too much air under it. This provided me with the perfect opportunity to launch a gentle lob over his head that he was powerless to defend.

My chest hurt and my eyes stung. I was lightheaded. My feet were uncomfortably hot and I sensed that the moisture was causing blisters. I was so thirsty I might have sold my soul for a drop of cool water on my tongue. But I had no intention of giving up.

Tamer walked to the back court like he was on stilts.

"It's not you, old man, it's them," he said. "How many times have we gone over this?"

"I take responsibility for my life," I pointed out.

"Nonsense," Tamer scoffed, still breath heavily. "Fifteen serving thirty."

"Wait," I said.

"Grant, everything you value can vanish overnight. That's the world we live in."

Tamer then tore off his shirt and wiped his face with it before attempting to mop up some of the sweat from his hair. Then he tossed the ball up in the air. This time he absolutely crushed it. The tennis ball streaked past me as I stood there defenselessly.

"Ace!" Tamer cried out in excitement. He rubbed it in by playing some air guitar with his racket before throwing himself repeatedly into the caging.

It was a calculated point that I surrendered. I needed a few more seconds of oxygen and took the opportunity to drop to one knee. At this point, there was no breeze on the court and the sun continued to beat down on us. Heat could be seen rising from the surface of the court, forming miniature mirages. It was like playing tennis in the desert.

"We're all in the same boat," Tamer said, taking his position. "Why do you take everything so personally?"

"It's part of my process. When I mourn my losses, it's so I can treasure them down the road," I managed to reply, still struggling to catch my breath.

"Are you ok, buddy?" Tamer asked, looking concerned.

"I'm so hot I can't breathe, Dan," I complained, panting and fanning myself with my racket. "I need a breeze to come through."

"You surrendering?"

"Of course not," I said defensively, far from buckling.

"Hey Grant," Tamer said with a weary smile.

"What?"

"Why not just live a comfortable life? We have our friends, our tennis. If we could cut our work week down to, say, three days, we'd be all set."

"It's not that simple," I said.

"Thirty serving thirty!" Tamer shouted in response.

Tamer's next serve probably was more vicious than his last, but I now had the energy and focus to stretch out my racket and muscle a laser down the line. Tamer had anticipated my strategy, though. His next shot made me drift well beyond the baseline on my backhand side. Tamer seized the opportunity to charge the net again, putting himself in the ideal position to smash my weak return. His mistake was that he sizzled the ball right at me. I was able to get enough racket on the ball to back him to mid-court and we resumed a long series of ground strokes. I was tiring quickly, though, and Tamer sensed it. He began to move me around more and more, coaxing me to become more aggressive. I had such a bad cramp in my side that it felt like a knife. Although I showed signs of weakening, the longer the rally went the more determined I was to prevail. Finally, Tamer placed a strong shot inside the right sideline using his growing mastery of the topspin, but because I was leaning to that side already I was able to find a sharp angle for myself. My return barely cleared the net and clipped the right sideline just beyond the service line with no chance of a counterstrike. Another point was mine.

I dropped to my knees, gasping for breath. My eyes continued to sting, the pain in my side was relentless, and my feet were on fire. Tamer sat on his butt with his back up against the cage.

"There's a big difference between us," I said between breaths. "I'm more interested in developing myself than leading a comfortable life."

"Bah," Tamer said, standing up slowly and stumbling back to the line. "Look how miserable you are. You're coming to terms with giving up. You're in your death throes."

I rose to my feet and took my place on the court. Every time I breathed the knife went in and out.

"Well, I'm the one with a breakpoint," I said.

"Thirty serving forty!" Tamer shouted, tossing the ball up high in the air.

This time his first serve was weak by design and perfectly placed. I easily returned it to him, but with no advantage. With an energy that came out of nowhere, Tamer ripped the ball right back at me—only it hit the tape and fell on my side of the net. I lunged and only got enough of the ball to manage an unintentional drop shot myself, leaving Tamer in the predicament of having to cover the entire court to keep serve. He was successful in reaching the ball, but any edge he possessed in terms of energy was now expended.

Now that I was comfortably positioned in my court, I started to work him: backhand, backhand, backhand, forehand, forehand, backhand, forehand, forehand, backhand, backhand. In a way, I lulled him into a defensive posture where I dictated the rhythm while creeping closer and closer to the net. Three more forehands in a row was all it took to convince him to slightly favor his right side. This was the moment I was waiting for. Now I had the angle to put the ball deep and to his backhand to set up the killer blow. My shot was perfectly placed. His only option was run along the baseline and stretch as far as he could.

For a second, everything seemed to slow down. The ball launched off Tamer's racket and went high in the air, leaving him at my mercy. In the meantime, I was at the net waiting like the wolf. When the ball descended on my side of the court, the anticipation was too powerful to let it bounce first. Instead, I delivered an overhand smash that contained such torque that the ball could be seen stuck in the caging afterwards. Game one was mine.

I collapsed to the court.

"So you surrender?" Tamer shouted sarcastically from his knees, doubled over again and trying to catch his breath.

"No," I replied weakly, suffering greatly myself.

"Then pull yourself together and serve me your best shot, buddy. I'm feeling spirited."

I tried to get up, but was very dizzy. Sensing my weakness, Tamer capitalized on this moment to claim his victory.

"Are you done feeling sorry for yourself?" he asked.

"I am," I gasped. "I'm totally spent."

"Then to hell with it!" Tamer shouted, dropping fully to the ground. He rolled onto his back and lay there, breathing heavily.

"I hope you've learned your lesson, old man . . ." he choked. "Don't make me doubt you again."

I dragged myself to the far corner of the court and took a seat with my back to the cage. At this point, I had stopped sweating and I found it hard to breathe. The knife in my side wouldn't go away. I took off my shoes and socks. The air felt cool on my feet.

A few minutes later Tamer managed to stumble his way off the court to fill the water bottle at the fountain. Good friend that he is, he wouldn't permit himself to take a single sip before offering me the bottle instead. I tried to refuse the courtesy, but he wouldn't hear of it. I'm not sure I've ever been thirstier and I imagine he felt the same way. Once I'd had a few gulps, he finished the remaining water and went for a refill. Since the sun had shifted, a bit of shade from an old oak tree had crept into my corner of the court, so we sat there propped up against the caging while we tried to recover. Tamer lit a cigarette.

Tamer looked at me with his red, sweaty face and shook his head.

"You still hold out hope, old man. After being so despondent for months, I was sure you were walking into the same bleak outlook as me and Brad."

"Never," I said with absolute certainty.

"How in the world can you still have hope for a good relationship?"

"I'll never let an isolated experience ruin things on the whole," I said.

"What if you take our combined experience?" Tamer asked with a grin.

"Don't be stupid," I said.

"So what do you do now?"

"I have to weigh my experience," I explained. "With Emily, I had her love and never her affection; and with Megan, I had her affection and never her love."

"Maybe the two of them together made a pretty healthy relationship," Tamer offered.

"Or maybe each one of them only got one side of me."

"Don't worry it about it, old man," Tamer comforted. "Think of Brad-to-the-Bone, the happiest man in the world. He has no aspirations, he has no need for introspection and self-improvement—or ambition, for that matter. He just needs his simple pleasures to carry him along."

"I told you, I'm not so easily satisfied."

"Well, there are plenty of women who like you. Misty, the young waitress at the restaurant, goes on and on about you . . ."

"I'm not interested in finding a new girlfriend right now."

"I'm just saying . . ."

"Dan, I happen to know that you're now dating the girl from the pub," I blurted, stopping him in his tracks.

Tamer almost looked stymied when I said this.

"Who told you?" he asked.

"Gizzer filled me in, but it doesn't matter. I just can't believe you'd keep this a secret from me—especially after all I've shared with you. I mean, the hurt really runs deep this time."

Tamer considered his words for a second.

"Well, buddy, given your mental state, I didn't think this was the right time to tell you. It just didn't seem fair to you and all."

I had to smile when he said this. He was always so considerate of me that he'd shelter me from the truth if he thought it was for my own good.

"And things are going well with this girl?" I asked.

Tamer nodded his head.

"To be honest, after flirting with her for a few weeks she declared one day that I was going to be her boyfriend. The choice was out of my hands. Can you believe a woman finally claimed me?"

"I'm in shock," I said honestly. "I hope you reward her confidence in you."

"I will."

"Is there a chance it might work out this time?"

"More than a chance," Tamer replied with conviction.

"Why is that?"

"Because old man . . . and don't you dare repeat this to anyone . . . and don't get the impression that my opinion of women has changed in the least . . . but I'm experiencing feelings for this girl that I never knew existed."

"What kind of feelings?"

"Damn you, Grant," Tamer spat, "don't you get it?"

I shrugged.

"I love her!" Tamer exclaimed. "There, I said it, are you satisfied now?"

I sat there in disbelief, almost wondering whether what I'd heard was the voice of the wind, the squawk of the gulls, anything but the man I considered to be one of my closest friends. I just couldn't believe my ears.

Then Tamer flicked his cigarette with almost a sense of finality behind it and jumped up with a sudden burst of energy, extended his hand, and helped me to my feet. He gathered his gear together and began to make his way home, trusting that I'd follow. As I watched him depart the cage without so much as a glance back over his shoulder, I was struck with the thought that there's a lot to be said about friendship . . . but even more to be said about someone capable of speaking his mind to you like Dan Tamer . . . someone who's willing to do anything or say whatever it takes to see you through to the other side.

* * * * *

In the early part of June, Sweet Johnny convinced me that it was time to take a short canoe trip into the wild Canadian north with him. While we escaped White Sands, Gizzer agreed to take care of the dogs because it gave him the opportunity to share house-sitting responsibilities with my former girlfriend, his new fiancée.

I told him I thought this arrangement sounded a bit bizarre, but he didn't care, nor did Megan object to staying with him at the house.

Our adventure began in the choppy waters of Georgian Bay. Sticking as close to the shore as possible, we paddled by Beausoleil Island and eventually into the peaceful seclusion of McCrae Lake. We set up camp on a big rock and cooked steaks, burgers, and freshly caught fish over an open fire while drinking wine or beer. In the evening, Johnny would strum his guitar before we'd retire to our own tents to the sound of loons calling out into the night air. Even though the water was still rather cold, we swam and cliff jumped. We even took the occasional hike. But most of our time was spent scouring McCrae's black water and weedy shorelines for northern pike and largemouth bass. When our supplies ran out, we made our way back along a different route. We canoed across the park and into the Gibson River, which took us into the Musquash, and by late Friday afternoon paddled into Honey Harbor where a vehicle was waiting for us. Although we were exhausted, we arrived at home with a renewed appetite for the amenities of civilization that would probably last us until Labor Day. I'm sure many people would agree that there is nothing better than returning from a camping trip to a hot shower and a good meal cooked on a stove, away from the torment of mosquitoes, black flies, cold, and rain.

Once home I was greeted by a joyful group of dogs. Crystal seemed especially excited to see me and couldn't stop whining and washing my face with kisses. After a long, steaming shower, I walked into the kitchen to make myself some dinner and noticed that Gizzer had left a note on the counter. It said that Emily was planning on picking up the last of her belongings on Saturday. I have to say, this news made me nervous and excited at the same time. Since the wedding had been canceled, we hadn't spoken a word to each other and I couldn't help but wonder how it would feel to be in her presence again. My agitation over this discovery pretty much negated any advantage in exchanging a sleeping bag for a comfortable bed that night. Instead, I tossed and turned from the moment I hit the pillow.

The next morning I was in the bathroom. I had just finished shaving and brushing my teeth. I definitely felt hung over from the lack of sleep and was trying to pull myself together. Then, seemingly out of thin air, Emily appeared in the doorway. I hadn't heard her come in and Crystal and the other dogs had been so indifferent that they didn't bother barking.

"You startled me," I said.

"I'm here to get the rest of my stuff," she explained.

"It's in a small pile by the door downstairs"

Emily nodded. "Yeah, I saw it. I wanted to say goodbye, though."

"You look great," I said, noticing that her hair was shorter and that her eyes were just as beautiful as ever.

"You need a haircut and you look a little skinny," Emily observed.

"It's been a treacherous few months, hasn't it?"

She avoided the question. "I've been living in Toronto. There hasn't been much time for anything. I'm trying to get on with my life, starting with going back to school."

"Really? What do you plan on studying?"

"I was accepted into a science program. I'm going to pursue my interest in flowers."

"I didn't know you can make a career of such a thing."

"It takes a long time, but you can. Looking for flowers is about the only respectable diversion I've ever known."

"Your one escape."

"Exactly."

"I'm thinking about selling the house," I confessed. "Since you moved out it feels too big for one person."

"I'll always think of it fondly," Emily said. "But this house has become a symbol of failure."

"I don't see it the same way. But with things not working out between us, I've come to take responsibility for my part."

Emily looked at me dubiously.

"It's true. I always thought you understood me like no other person. But I've realized I never made the same commitment to understanding you."

"It's hard to understand someone who doesn't understand herself," Emily replied. "But I've accepted the fact that I am where God wants me to be."

"Just know that I want you to be happy. I do miss you, you know. More than you could ever imagine . . ."

Emily moved in close, placed her hands on my hips, and gazed into my eyes as though searching for a truth beyond me. I braced myself for an emotional outburst. But slowly, using her hand, Emily drew my face to her own so that she could kiss me. As this kiss grew more passionate, I found myself being dragged forcefully to the bedroom. Soon after, with clothes being torn off and everything a blur, it was actually happening between us: finally, I mean finally, we were physically experiencing the desire we had built up in those long years together.

There are times in life when you know you're just as blessed in that exact moment as any other person in existence, regardless of their status, achievement, income, or celebrity. For me, this was every bit one of those moments. It was surreal, to say the least, but what made the encounter so special was the knowledge that what was happening between us could never be taken away.

Afterwards, Emily looked deep into my eyes and we shared an unspoken understanding. I smiled at her. I found I couldn't stop smiling.

In Emily, though, I was sure I detected the immediate onset of regret. Her demeanor betrayed a certain resentfulness when she recognized the happiness she had been able to inspire—as if she was incapable of being a participant herself. Rather than allowing herself to be held, she got out of the bed and methodically began to put her clothes back on, almost like she was depressed. Then she started to walk across the room, without so much as an explanation.

"Where you going?" I asked.

Emily stopped halfway out the door. "We can never be together, Grant."

"I know," I replied, understanding that I was forfeiting my opportunity to object.

"But you still slept with me as though I was your wife."

"That's true," I admitted.

"So you really are no different from any other man?"

I stared back at her, unable to defend myself.

"You should have trusted me, you know."

Emily then walked away without even a glance back over her shoulder, her footsteps growing fainter as she descended the stairs. There was nothing left between us to salvage.

Now some men would have felt properly ashamed of themselves. But you know what? Without realizing it, Emily provided me with exactly what I needed to move on. To be honest, I felt validated, like the past couple of years had not been a waste. She had opened her inner door. Make no mistake, she gave me my confidence back and authenticated the experiences we'd shared together. Knowing this allowed relief to set in, and deep down I felt that I was truly ready to begin a new chapter.

Sunlight filled the bedroom and it resonated well with my soul. I yearned for a cup of coffee on the back porch so that I could sit and enjoy the sound of the brook while being warmed by the sun. I wanted nothing more than the chance to ponder and reflect and savor the satisfaction that filled me from our recent encounter.

Over the next few days, I came to love myself again. With my dogs at my side, my family, my friends—but mostly a sense of spiritual renewal—I now felt the urge to explore the possibility of ministry again. There was a super-jail in the community that housed people much like the dogs in the shelter. The possibility of becoming a prison chaplain had always appealed to me and it now seemed that I had the energy and motivation to go forward.

At this point, I was ready to make peace with Justin Fancy and allow him to become a regular part of my life again. In fact, I was even considering co-authoring his book. We both were equally intrigued by the idea of "passion," particularly the thesis that a powerful gravitation towards self-destruction may actually be a person's passion to experience their own redemption.

But the biggest impact was on my view of relationship itself. Never again would I allow myself to be so captivated by a woman that I would feel inclined to pinch myself in order to believe it—to trust it. Instead, I realized that I much preferred the security of knowing that the woman I would end up marrying would be there for me no matter what. And with Emily gone, I now felt this was not only possible, but imminent.

As for Emily, her essence was in her mystery, and her mystery was her shelter. Therefore, during this surge of vitality and opportunity, it seemed almost appropriate to me that Emily exited my life under the same conditions she had entered: as a woman belonging in dream . . .

Made in the USA
Charleston, SC
21 August 2011